THE
AMERICAN
CRUSADE

THE
AMERICAN
CRUSADE

A POLITICAL THRILLER

MARK SPIVAK

TCK PUBLISHING.COM

ISBN: 978-1-63161-070-7

Published by TCK Publishing
www.TCKpublishing.com

Get discounts and special deals on books at
www.TCKpublishing.com/bookdeals

Sign up for Mark Spivak's newsletter at
www.markspivakbooks.com/free

For those who left us too early:

Harry Fishman

Lee Romaine

Sherman Robbins

Barry Alberts

David Albertson

Linda Tagliaferro

EDITOR'S NOTE

The novel you are about to read includes excerpts from the thirteenth-century eyewitness account *On the Conquest of Constantinople*, written by historian and crusader Geoffrey de Villehardouin (1160–1213). The chronicle is the oldest surviving example of French prose, and one of the most important sources on the Fourth Crusade. The passages selected for inclusion have been translated from the original French.

Jacob Steven Mohr, Editor

To President George Cane, the assembled group represented "the full force and moral authority of the United States of America."

To the Reverend Sanford J. Bayer, head of the White House Office of Faith and Reconciliation (known internally as the Woofers), they symbolized "the lawful arm of God's righteous Kingdom ... preparing to strike at the heart of our enemy."

To Salman al-Akbar, leader of the worldwide terrorist organization Husam al-Din and the reason the dignitaries were gathered at this press conference, they were "the cancerous core of modern civilization, bleeding like an ulcer that must be removed."

They included the heads of both houses of Congress, the Joint Chiefs of Staff, the directors of the FBI and CIA, most of the cabinet, and the chief justice of the United States.

To the vice president, who had assembled this improbable group, they were the usual suspects.

CHAPTER 1

S COTT LEVENTHAL, CHIEF OF STAFF to the vice president, poked his head into his boss's office without knocking. "The Speaker of the House is on the phone, sir."

"Jesus."

Robert Hornsby looked up from his paperwork and narrowed his eyes at Leventhal. Hornsby was an imposing man, bordering on huge, with a polished bald head and a perpetual glower that made him appear as if he were constantly squinting into the sun. But on rare occasions such as this, his stern expression melted slowly into a look of sarcastic good humor.

"Let me guess," said the vice president, leaning back in his chair. "He's concerned about his placement at the press conference."

Leventhal grinned. "How'd you know, sir?"

"Well, I assume he hasn't grown since I last saw him."

The Speaker was five-two and slender, seemingly half the size of the vice president, and choreographing his public appearances was a perpetual challenge. To avoid embarrassment, he was usually placed in the front row on a riser, yet behind the podium so the news cameras couldn't show him receiving such a boost.

The vice president picked up the phone.

"Andy, how are you? Putting on your Sunday suit, I hope?"

Leventhal settled into a chair facing his boss, wearing a look of barely repressed amusement.

"Of course, of course. Absolutely. You know we take every precaution … hell, you never see the TV crew shining a light on my bald head, do you … ? Don't worry about a thing. It's our show, Andy, leave it to me."

The vice president hung up the phone, removed his steel-rimmed glasses, and rubbed his eyes.

"Do me a favor, Scott?"

"Sir?"

"Kick the riser out from underneath the son of a bitch, will you? There's no point in letting al-Akbar have all the fun."

"I'd love to."

"Well, are we ready?"

"Like clockwork, sir. Everyone will arrive at quarter-past. The president's limo will pick you up outside. The two of you will enter together, and we'll start on the dot at one-thirty."

"Coverage?"

"Anybody who's anybody, sir. Networks, all the major cable stations, NPR, the White House press corps. They're killing each other to get in."

"Good. I want to you make sure al-Jazeera is in the front row."

"Done, sir."

"What about Reverend Woofer?"

"He's totally under control. The invocation has been cleared by our team."

"I hope so. We don't want him going off the deep end and pissing off a billion Muslims."

"He's muzzled, sir. No worries."

"All right, then."

"Everything is set. All you have to do is look tough."

"Kiss my ass, Scott."

The vice president rose and cleaned his glasses with a pocket handkerchief. Early in his political career, they had been a source of controversy among his staff, who wanted him to get contact lenses and soften his image. "If I wanted to soften my image," Hornsby had snorted, "I'd start visiting orphanages."

He looked at his chief of staff. "How's Citizen Cane doing?"

"Just fine, sir. They have him completely prepped. They tell me he could recite his speech in his sleep."

"Good."

"Hopefully he won't fuck up, sir."

"Scott, Scott, Scott." The vice president walked around the desk and put his hand on the younger man's shoulder. "Don't worry about a thing. He'll be magnificent."

"I hope so. There's a lot at stake."

"Trust me, he'll be fine. He gets to play the president on TV. He loves that."

"Yes, sir."

Hornsby grinned. "Hopefully, he stayed in a Holiday Inn Express last night."

"Would you like me to answer that, sir?"

"Lighten up." The vice president thumped his chief of staff on the back. "Let's go declare war on evil."

CHAPTER 2

IVE DAYS EARLIER, ON MAY 1, a hijacked 757 jet airliner crashed into the Mall of America.

Members of an organization called Husam al-Din had seized control of the jet shortly after takeoff in Minneapolis. The plane was packed with fuel and headed for Los Angeles. They forced their way into the cockpit and slit the throats of the pilot and copilot with box cutters. The men then turned the plane around, headed south toward Bloomington, and smashed into the side of the mall. They missed the Victoria's Secret on the second floor by less than one hundred yards.

"Sons of bitches almost hit the Panty Depot head on!" the vice president had muttered later that evening as he reviewed the situation reports. "They used the plane like a goddamn smart bomb. How many of *our* pilots could do that?"

The Mall of America, which Hornsby assumed had been chosen for its symbolic significance, erupted in a fireball that could be seen for nearly twenty miles in all directions. Fire trucks roared in from all over the state, but they were slow to respond due to the distance of rural communities from the mall. Before the day was over, nearly two thousand innocent shoppers were dead. Many had been trampled to death.

Later that day, suicide bombers walked into selected targets around the country and blew themselves up. The venues included an elementary school in Virginia, a synagogue in New Jersey, a post office in New Mexico, and a high school football practice in Texas. By midnight, the death toll was over three thousand.

The terrorists also hijacked a second airliner, but this attempt proved to be the one redeeming moment of the day. The Husam al-Din agents who commandeered the plane placed it on a direct course for Washington, but in an act of spectacular heroism, the passengers of United 54 overcame the terrorists and took control of the aircraft, which crashed in a field south of Wilmington, Delaware.

The public was horrified, of course, and traumatized. But to seasoned warriors like Hornsby, a former CIA director, the frightening thing wasn't the loss of life or wanton destruction—it was the sheer *precision* of the operation. In addition to hijacking two planes, the terrorists had set off six suicide bombs within fifteen minutes of each other. This meant dozens of sleeper cells, hidden factories across the nation manufacturing suicide belts, and an expert military commander supervising the entire affair. And it had all happened under their noses, making the American defense team seem like a team of bumbling half-wits by comparison.

When the plane hit the Mall, President Cane had been officiating at a state fair in Kansas, preparing to award the best-in-show ribbon to the Future Farmers of America dairy competition winner. According to reporters on the scene, the president did not react immediately, although it was impossible to pinpoint the moment he knew about the attack. The Mall had been burning for twenty minutes before he left the fair and headed for the airport. On Vice President Hornsby's orders, the president was flown to Cheyenne Mountain in Wyoming, where he would be safe for the duration. By the time Cane took off, Hornsby was already in the Situation Room—and in total control of the government.

The vice president remembered Scott Leventhal approaching him in the middle of that endless afternoon. "Sir? I have the captain of Air Force One on the phone. He wants an estimate on how long the president will be there."

"Tell them to seal up the fucking mountain," said Hornsby through his teeth, "and give him a year's supply of canned tuna."

As far as the public knew, President Cane had directed the response efforts from his command post in Cheyenne Mountain. At the very least, he had been given minute-by-minute updates by his security team and monitored the dispatch of the National Guard to Minnesota. When he returned to the White House that evening, his youthful face was stern and lined with stress.

"Our nation has suffered an attack on an unprecedented scale," he intoned on the South Lawn. "Not since Pearl Harbor have we seen such a display of villainy by a vicious enemy. Unlike the events of Pearl Harbor, however, this was not an attack on our brave men and women in uniform. This act of terrorism was aimed at innocent civilians—schoolchildren, shoppers, citizens pursuing their right to worship as they choose. Nearly three thousand of our people were ambushed by agents of a foreign ideology. Our hearts go out to these innocent folks, as well as their bereaved families. As your commander in chief, I give you my word that this act of cowardice will not stand. In the weeks to come, we will hunt down the perpetrators of these unspeakable acts and bring them to justice—so help me God. Now, please join me in a moment of silent prayer for all the innocent souls we have lost today."

After the prayer ended, the president retreated into the bowels of the White House, where lights were seen burning throughout the night. Hornsby slept in improvised quarters in the West Wing, where he would remain for several weeks before returning to his official residence at Number One Observatory Circle. No matter what his doctor might say about his age and heart condition, he was not about to let George Cane out of his sight—not with this much on the line.

CHAPTER 3

ERY FEW PEOPLE OUTSIDE THE inner circle understood exactly how close the government came to unraveling that day.

The situation in Minnesota was a Chinese fire drill. It started with Minneapolis air traffic control, who tracked the plane going off course. But since the controllers had no direct channels of communication with the federal government, the incident was unknown to Washington almost until the exact moment the aircraft nosedived into the Mall. A loop of videotape replayed endlessly on the evening news showed mothers carrying small children with their clothes on fire, swatting them in a desperate attempt to put out the flames. There was no coordination among the local police and fire and rescue teams, no links between Bloomington law enforcement and the Feds. The rugged, rural Minnesota landscape made it impossible for enough fire trucks to reach the scene on time, and the local TV station had their hands full—it was the Hindenburg on steroids.

Sitting in the White House Situation Room that day, Vice President Hornsby thought he was witnessing the perfect storm. *All those years we thought it would end with a nuclear launch from the Soviets*, he thought bitterly. *Now I have to watch a bunch of jokers in turbans destroy the world.*

FBI Director Edward Gambelli entered the room and approached the head of the table. "Most of the planes are out of the sky, sir. The airspace is almost secure."

"What do you mean, *almost?* For shit's sake." The vice president gestured toward the electronic map on the wall, where aircraft were represented by red dots. "That's a lot of dots up there, Eddie."

"They're mostly private planes, sir. Joyriders out for a spin. We're contacting the ones that have radar. The fighters will intercept the others and escort them down."

"What about the other plane?"

"It's still heading for Washington, sir. Just passed Wilmington."

"How long before it gets into rural airspace?"

"Five minutes, sir. Ten at the most."

"What's happening on board?"

"We've received radio and cell phone communications. The passengers are still fighting. They've overcome two of the hijackers, and they're trying to get into the cockpit."

Hornsby glanced to his right, to the chair occupied by his protégé, CIA Director Admiral Mike McCardle. McCardle nodded.

"When it gets over unoccupied land," Hornsby said, "I want you to shoot it down."

"Sir?"

"Eddie, we have the tapes, correct?"

"Yes, but—"

"These people are dead already. None of them can fly the plane. It's the least we can do to bring comfort to their loved ones. The public will eat it up. The passengers will be heroes."

"But—"

"Eddie, that's an *order*. Shoot it down once it gets over unoccupied land. I've got your back."

"Yes, sir."

Hornsby was filled with disgust beyond expression. At that moment, he could not say whom he hated more: George Cane, who had offered him the job; *Herbert* Cane, George's uncle and ex-president, who had talked him into taking it; or William Hampton, Cane's womanizing and worthless predecessor in the Oval Office, who let the towelheads to grow into a threat. *If I could get them all in here with me*, he thought, *I'd force them to make a decision. For once in their lives. Then I'd strangle them all, one by one.*

McCardle picked up the phone, listened for a moment, and turned to the vice president.

"The head of the president's Secret Service detail, sir. He wants to speak to you."

"Yes," Hornsby said wearily, putting the phone to his ear. "No, I wouldn't say things are under control, but I think it's as good as it's likely to get … Yes, he can come back … Tell him I'll set up the photo op on the South Lawn, and he can make a speech when he gets back … Tell him to call me."

He hung up the phone and looked at McCardle.

"Well, Mike? Nothing like having the war gift wrapped and dropped on your goddamn doorstep."

"You can say that again, sir."

Gambelli entered the room and walked up to the vice president. His face was as white as his shirt.

"Well?"

"Done, sir."

"Good job." Hornsby rose and shook hands with the FBI director. "You have the tapes?"

"Yes, sir."

"Edit out anything suspicious. We can release them in a few days, when the public needs a shot in the arm."

"All right, sir. I'll get them ready."

"Nice work, Eddie." He patted him on the back. "You've just created the heroes of United 54. History will thank you."

Gambelli left the room, and the vice president slumped down in his chair. *Sixty-four years old. Too old for this shit.* In the days to come, the public would begin to piece together the broad outlines of the radical Muslim conspiracy bent on destroying the United States. What they would not know, at that point, was that there had been advance warning of the May Day attacks—that the administration, Hornsby included, had known about Husam al-Din all along.

CHAPTER 4

T
HE ARCH-CONSERVATIVE STANDARD BEARER," SAID *The Washington Post* on
their editorial page.

"The most dangerous man in America," observed *The New York Times*,
ignoring everyone sitting on death row at that moment.

"The power behind the throne," said CNN, spotlighting his time at the CIA.

"The spy who refused to come in from the cold," quipped *The New Yorker*,
filled with loathing but still unable to ignore him.

These were only a few of the descriptions applied to Robert Barton
Hornsby during his years of public life. "He would have been one of the great
lightning rods in American politics," conservative guru William F. Buckley, Jr.,
had once remarked, "save for his refusal to attract lightning."

"You gotta understand, this guy is a creature of Washington." On another
occasion, a Republican strategist spoke on deep background to a reporter in
the lobby lounge of the Willard Intercontinental over cognac and cigars. "Over
time, he was smart enough to learn the lesson that the real source of power is
not running for office himself."

Hornsby was born in Montana in 1938, the youngest son of two frontier
shopkeepers who had survived the Depression by their wits alone. He was a
large, unremarkable boy who excelled in sports and sang in the church choir. By

the time he earned a full football scholarship to the University of Wisconsin, his parents assumed he was heading to the fledgling National Football League and a career as an underpaid jock.

Hornsby earned his scholarship at Wisconsin, becoming the leading rusher in the school's history. To the surprise of many, he was also a straight-A student who could hold his own with intellectuals in a low-key, unassuming way. In his senior year, he married Alice Porter, a farm-bred Wisconsin girl with a stubborn streak and a penchant for apple-pie common sense. Throughout the decades of their marriage, she was never once quoted in the press—nor did she ever miss an opportunity to tell her husband, behind closed doors, what she thought of his positions.

Hornsby took a close look at the NFL of the early 1960s and opted for law school instead. He was accepted at Georgetown, and the couple scraped by on Alice's salary as a low-level congressional aide. They socialized on the Hill in their few moments of spare time, and the Republicans who looked at Hornsby liked what they saw. After he passed the bar, they encouraged him to return to Montana and enter politics. He was elected to Congress in 1970, at the age of 32.

His freshman term in the House coincided with one of the most turbulent periods of American history: Cities were burning, college campuses had become breeding grounds for angry and violent Vietnam protests, and Nixon was rooting out his enemies in the name of national security. Hornsby steered steady through the madness. He denounced welfare and was a hawk on Vietnam, yet he refused to support the president when he was impeached, believing that the Republican party would only recover if its next generation of leaders didn't spend their formative years looking up to a crook.

By the time Reagan was elected, Hornsby was in the Senate. He became chairman of the Select Committee on Intelligence after the Reagan landslide of 1980, and toiled patiently to rebuild the intelligence community from the rubble of the 1970s. Congressional committees had blown the whistle on domestic spying by the CIA during a series of public hearings in 1975, and covert operations had become a dirty word in the post-Watergate era. By the early 1980s, however, Reagan had revived the Cold War and spycraft seemed more important than ever. Hornsby steadily increased appropriations for the agency, and pushed hard to make them less accountable for how they spent the money. In one of his most famous exchanges, a left-leaning Democratic colleague was questioning him vigorously on funding for a supplemental request.

"I just want to know for the record, Mr. Chairman, if my friend from Montana really wants to see a return to the covert, black-bag operations of the past, to an era where the CIA is free to do as they please with absolutely no public accountability."

"Not at all, Senator," replied Hornsby jovially. "I just believe that every time a KGB agent sneezes, his CIA counterpart should be standing next to him holding a handkerchief."

When Herbert Cane was elected president in 1988, Hornsby was offered the post of director of the Central Intelligence Agency. He took it. His four-year tenure was marked by a return to good old-fashioned spycraft where the ends justified the means—and the means were invisible to the naked eye. Langley was compartmentalized, and the political appointees frequently had no knowledge of what the career officials were doing. During his time at the CIA, Hornsby's visits to the Hill became eagerly awaited media events, with network anchormen chortling over his cheerful evasiveness.

But his most significant achievement, the one kept completely hidden from the public, was the creation of the Patriot Detail.

The Detail was actually the brainchild of Admiral Mike McCardle, a career agency man who was Hornsby's confidant and right hand. It began as a small, elite group of supremely loyal agents who consistently volunteered for the tough assignments. As Hornsby and McCardle developed the concept, the Detail matured into a miniature CIA, a shadow agency divided into distinct fiefdoms—surveillance, electronics, misinformation, wet work, and station management. Its members became a palace guard of sorts, ideologically motivated and fiercely committed to the wills of their bosses.

Hornsby liked McCardle. In fact, he believed the admiral was everything a hero should be: Naval Academy graduate, family man, former Vietnam prisoner of war—someone who would unhesitatingly give his life for what he believed in. He also appreciated McCardle's loyalty and sense of teamwork, qualities he had learned to value on the football field. As a teenager, Hornsby had been fascinated by the first successful ascent of Mount Everest in 1953. What intrigued him wasn't just the heroic image of Edmund Hillary, but the realization that the mountaineer would never have made it to the summit without his Sherpa. He knew there were moments in life when you needed someone standing next to you, holding an oxygen tank.

One of those moments occurred during the 1992 campaign, when it appeared to a horrified Hornsby that William Hampton might actually be elected president. He quickly appointed McCardle deputy director; if Hornsby returned to private life, the admiral would at least counterbalance whatever idiot Billy Bob might appoint as the next CIA chief.

His worst fears came to pass. William Hampton, a grinning and enigmatic Southern governor, became the forty-second president of the United States. He appointed an ideologue from a leftist California think tank to head the CIA, promising "a new era of transparency in our intelligence community," as Hornsby prepared to assume the chairmanship of one of America's largest defense contractors.

"Shit, boss," said McCardle dejectedly, as he watched Hornsby clean out his office before the inauguration. "What am I supposed to do?"

"Mike, cheer up. You're going to steer the boat, that's what. I don't have to tell you that."

"What about the new guy?"

"He'll never know what hit him."

"I can handle him. I just feel like I'm disappearing behind the dark side of the moon."

"Don't you worry. I'll be back, and we'll have some fun. In the meantime, keep the Detail together. That's job one. Not to mention the only way you'll save the country from these clowns."

During Hornsby's eight-year exile, the two men spoke every few days. McCardle gave his former boss intricate and completely illegal briefings on intelligence matters, and kept him informed about daily issues at the agency. Robert Barton Hornsby took a great deal of pleasure in knowing that every major intelligence operation that occurred during the Billy Bob administration was planned by him and executed by McCardle. The Hampton team never had a clue.

One day in the fall of 1999, Hornsby received a call from Herbert Cane. The ex-president was sailing in Nantucket, and he sounded as upbeat and cheerful as ever.

"How are you, Mr. President?"

"Super, Bob, just super. I'd prefer 'Herbert' these days, but I guess that's not going to happen."

"Not with me, sir."

"Just as I thought. So, tell me—are you keeping up with the news, or are you too busy trying to become a billionaire?"

"I see that your nephew is considering a run for president, sir, if that's what you mean."

"Let's cut right to the chase. The boy is going to need a lot of help, Bob. He's very personable, you know, but he's not exactly the sharpest tack in the box."

"Very forthcoming of you to say so, sir."

"How about signing on as a foreign policy advisor? Give him the rules of the road?"

"I'm awfully busy, sir."

"Too busy to help me out? That's not the Hornsby I know."

"What exactly do you want me to do?"

"Show him the goddamn map." Cane chuckled. "Explain the difference between Kabulistan and New Jersey. Somebody has to do it."

"How long is this going to last?"

"Who knows?" said the ex-president. "With any luck, you'll be running the government in eighteen months, so stop complaining."

"Jesus. I don't believe this."

"Bob, can I assume you're not interested in making a run for it yourself?"

"That's correct, sir."

"Then here you go. This is the next best thing. I appreciate it, Bob, I really do. I knew I could count on you."

"Did I say yes?"

"I can't pay you, obviously, 'cause you can probably buy and sell me at this point. But you'll have my gratitude."

"I'll settle for the thanks of a grateful nation."

After Hornsby hung up, he sat in his office staring at a framed portrait of Winston Churchill. He had always admired the British leader, even going so far as to endorse his controversial decision—arrived at with Roosevelt and Stalin—to carve up the Middle East at the end of world War II into the superstates of Kabulistan, Sumeristan, and Persepostan. While human rights activists still complained bitterly about ethnic minorities suffering loss of identity, Hornsby was sanguine. "Fewer state actors," he had maintained, "means fewer power centers to balance and negotiate with—always a good thing."

In the past decade of his exile from power, Hornsby had come to identify more closely than ever with his idol. He now understood the importance of holding steadfast to principle in the face of political opposition and public apathy. As he contemplated the possibility of returning to the fray, he realized he would have to filter his policies through the young and inexperienced George Cane.

He could deal with that. Without puppets, a puppet-master was out of business.

CHAPTER 5

A S THE SUN SET IN Washington on May Day, Hornsby and McCardle
sat in the Situation Room with General Bayard Stevenson, the
secretary of defense. Stevenson had finally landed at Andrews Air
Force Base one hour earlier. When news of the attack broke, he had
been returning from a NATO meeting in Germany. On Hornsby's orders,
Stevenson's plane had circled the Northeast for several hours, and the general
was furious.

"Do we know who this was?" he asked as the vice president concluded
his briefing.

"Husam al-Din, General," said Hornsby. "There's very little doubt."

"They've taken responsibility?" McCardle nodded. "Then how do we
know it's over?"

"Frankly, we don't." Hornsby removed his glasses and rubbed his eyes.
"But for the moment, the airspace is clear. The National Guard has moved into
the top fifteen metro areas. We have the bureau and the agency watching all
known Islamic threats."

"What about the second plane?"

"A heroic story." Hornsby smiled. "The only bright spot of the day. The
passengers revolted, took control of the aircraft, and brought it down rather
than let the Arabs fly it into Washington."

"Is that right?" Stevenson glared at Hornsby across the conference table.

"That's correct, General," said the vice president evenly. "We have the tapes, and we'll release them to the public in a few days."

"Speaking of the public: When do they get to find out what the hell's going on? Or are we going to let CNN handle that?"

"When the president returns to Washington this evening, he'll have a statement. I imagine it will take a few days to piece everything together, and then we can give them a full report."

"I'll bet you won't keep *his* plane circling for three hours, will you?"

"He's expected to address the nation at nine."

"After you let him come back from Timbuktu, or wherever you have him stashed?"

"General?" said McCardle gently.

"Yes, Mike?"

"It's been a very difficult day, sir. For you, for us, for everyone. It's important that we all keep our heads."

"Mike, your plane wasn't stacked up over Philadelphia while you had no idea what was happening. I'm the secretary of defense, dammit."

Could have been worse, thought Hornsby. *You might have been the secretary of state. She'd still be circling.*

"We acted out of an abundance of caution," said the vice president.

"I'd say so."

Hornsby stared at Stevenson. *America's soldier,* he thought. *The first black general in the U.S. Army. The hero of Panama. The chairman of the Joint Chiefs of Staff, who saved Herbert Cane's ass once upon a time. Now you're pissed off because you're out of the loop. If you were such a detail man, you should have run for president yourself, instead of wasting time handing out sneakers to ghetto kids. No guts, no glory.*

"I can assure you," said McCardle, "that the vice president has had to make some very tough decisions. At every step of the way, he had everyone's safety in mind—yours, the president's, and the public's."

"Damn," muttered Stevenson. "You should run for office yourself—you already sound like a politician."

"What would you want me to do, General?" demanded Hornsby. "Let you fly into potentially hostile airspace and get shot at?"

"Wouldn't be the first time, sir."

"I'm sure that's so. In the meanwhile, I stand by my decisions."

"I imagine it was difficult." Stevenson stood up, six foot two and perfectly erect in posture. He was an imposing man, almost as formidable as Hornsby.

"As we go forward, can you assure me that the rights of law-abiding Muslims in this country will be protected?"

"If they're innocent, yes," said Hornsby. "Remember, we had six suicide missions. That means dozens of sleeper cells. *Somebody* had to put the explosives together, and *somebody* had to supervise the operation. Somebody had to finance it—people here were complicit. I intend to root them out."

"As well we should. I just want to make sure we're not looking at a replay of FDR rounding up the Japanese."

We interrupt the apocalypse, thought Hornsby, *for a brief lecture on the rights of our oppressed minorities.*

"I can assure you, General, that we'll take every precaution. Persecuting innocent people won't make any of us safer."

"Agreed."

"And when we find the real villains here, we'll be relying on you to put together a military response that will blow them to Kingdom Come."

"I look forward to that, Mr. Vice President."

McCardle waited until Stevenson had left the room before turning to Hornsby.

"Do you want me to put him under the microscope, boss?" he asked, using the internal code for wiretap surveillance.

"No need to go that far," said the vice president. "Just monitor his communications with the undersecretaries and field commanders. We want to make sure he sticks to the plan."

"What plan?"

"Whatever plan develops. We can't have our warrior chief going off the reservation."

CHAPTER 6

A T THE PRESS CONFERENCE, THE entrance of the president and the vice president was ceremonial and solemn. One by one, they shook hands with the dignitaries on the podium. When Hornsby reached the Reverend Sanford J. Bayer, he leaned forward and whispered in his ear.

"Short and sweet, Bubba. No surprises."

"Your people cleared my speech," said Bayer, aiming a beatified look at the camera.

"I don't want you receiving any last-minute divine inspirations."

"Bad enough your staff is constantly looking up my rear end. Now you have to push me around?"

"They're just public servants, Reverend. Probably looking for pieces of Noah's Ark, just in case there's another flood."

The two men took their places on either side of the Presidential Seal. The vice president cleared his throat and nodded to George Cane, who approached the microphone. Hornsby was relieved to see that the president's youthful face was cloaked in an expression of studied severity. Early in the campaign, the grinning Cane had become a target of liberal media outlets, who had gleefully compared his face to Alfred E. Neumann. In fact, there had been a definite resemblance—particularly when his mouth was open and teeth were exposed.

"Smile if you want to," the consultants had said, "but keep your mouth closed. And don't smile when you don't know what else to do."

The president began to speak. "Ladies and gentlemen of the press corps, distinguished guests, my fellow Americans. I want to thank everyone for coming on short notice. At this time, I would like to call upon the Reverend Sanford J. Bayer, director of the White House Office of Faith and Reconciliation, to give the invocation."

Reverend Bayer stepped forward and shook hands with the president. He wore a purple robe, which offset his white collar and wavy blond hair. Hornsby glanced at McCardle. *Nice outfit,* he thought. *Probably got it at a goddamn costume store. I guess he can't let himself be outdone by the chief justice.*

"Heavenly Father," said Bayer in his melodious Southern accent. "We gather here today at a trying time in our nation's history. With deep sorrow, we recall those among us who perished in the recent May Day attacks. We extend our prayers to their loved ones, and hope that time will offer them a measure of peace. During this challenging period in our history, we place our faith in our leaders. We ask you to grant them the courage to take the necessary steps to lead us as a nation toward both victory and healing. With your help, heavenly Father, they cannot possibly fail. Amen."

The president shook hands with Bayer a second time, and solemnly approached the microphone once again.

"My fellow Americans, I speak to you today in a time of sorrow. Five days ago, three thousand of our fellow citizens were slaughtered in an act of cowardice perpetrated by forces who hate the United States of America and everything we stand for. We extend our deepest sympathies to the victims and their families.

"Yet this is also a time of hope, a time to confront the challenges we face and steer a steadfast course. I ask you today for your support, and I know in my heart that when Americans are united, they can truly accomplish anything.

"It is easy to condemn those who attacked us as cowardly believers in an evil ideology. To defeat them, however, we must first understand who they are and what motivates them. Only then can we implement a strategy that will lead to the inevitable triumph of freedom and the American ideal."

Keep that goddamn grin off your face, thought the vice president as he stared dutifully at George Cane, as if he could beam his thoughts into the younger man's brain. The speech had been carefully crafted over the past five days, with attention paid to every phrase. *Tolerance toward our allies and peace through strength for our enemies—don't screw it up now.*

"The name of this organization is Husam al-Din, or 'Sword of the Faith.' It is a loosely knit, worldwide group of Muslim terrorists who are committed to defeating the United States in our never-ending quest to spread freedom around the world. They are not a traditional military, wearing uniforms and appearing on the battlefield in the light of day. To the contrary, they are organized into secret cells that operate undetected in dozens of the world's nations. Rather than engage the military might of the United States, which would surely defeat them, they commit cowardly acts such as the attack they perpetrated five days ago. By doing so, they hope to weaken our morale and cause us to doubt our principles. But this is not the time for doubt.

"When I describe these folks as Muslim terrorists, it's important to understand that their beliefs are a mutation of the religion of Islam. The Muslim faith is one of the world's great religions, practiced peacefully by over one billion people. In our communities, we know many Muslims who live among us. They are our friends and neighbors, and they mean us no harm."

Hornsby scanned the crowd, examining their expressions of rapt interest. He paid particular attention to the TV cameras, making sure they were focused solely on the president and not panning to provide a view of the room. Every few sentences, he shifted his attention to the al-Jazeera reporters in the front row.

"Unfortunately, a handful of evildoers have taken this great religion and distorted it. They use it to motivate their followers to harm the United States, in the belief that they will cause us to doubt ourselves and our mission. While we bear no ill will toward the peaceful followers of Islam, we will not tolerate the aims of a group of radicals bent on our destruction. We must rise to meet this challenge, knowing in our hearts that there is no greater goal in the modern world than the preservation and spread of liberty.

"In the days to come, I will ask our military commanders to prepare a campaign against Husam al-Din outposts in the country of Kabulistan. At the same time, we will use diplomacy to assemble a coalition of freedom-loving peoples to wipe out this scourge in the name of our children's safety. We hope to enlist the aid of the Dua Khamail, the current rulers of Kabulistan, to help us isolate and wipe out the terrorist cells and training camps of Husam al-Din. The extent of the Dua Khamail's allegiance to the leaders of Husam al-Din is not totally known at this time, but we expect their full and complete cooperation to eradicate the evildoers in their midst. Should they resist, we will not hesitate to defeat them, reinstate Selim Hanjuk and the true government of Kabulistan, and then go after the followers of Husam al-Din with all the resources at our command. When our plan of action is ready, and when it meets the approval of our commanders in the field, I will address you once again."

So far so good, thought Hornsby. *He sounds like he actually knows what he's talking about, rather than someone who memorized the names overnight.* Early on, when the vice president had been serving as a national security advisor to George Cane at his uncle's request, he had discovered that while the young man did know the difference between Kabulistan and New Jersey, his knowledge didn't go much deeper than that.

"This will be a first step, but only a first step. To prepare an attack of this magnitude and commit the atrocities we witnessed five days ago, the agents of Husam al-Din required a great many sympathizers within the United States. We must identify these traitors in our midst—not only the ones who helped plan and carry out the cowardly May Day attacks, but also all those who were complicit through financial help and strategic cooperation. In carrying out this mission, we must be careful not to confuse the true followers of Islam with our worst enemies. We intend to take every precaution to ensure that the civil liberties of innocent citizens will be protected.

"Even so, our course of action is clear. As your president and commander in chief, I give you my word that we will hunt down every single one of these evildoers, capture them, and bring them to justice. The full resources of our government will be committed to making certain that an attack such as this will never happen again. We have the resources to do this, we most certainly have the will, and we most assuredly will not falter. As we begin this modern-day crusade against the forces of evil in our midst, I ask for God's help and yours. With your steadfast support, we will pass along a better and safer world to our children. With God's help, we cannot possibly fail.

"I thank you for your time and attention today. God bless you, and God bless the United States of America."

Hornsby paid careful attention to the press as the president uttered the word "crusade." When he saw the print reporters scribble in their notebooks, he smiled and nodded approvingly.

CHAPTER 7

KNOW THAT, *1197 YEARS AFTER the incarnation of Our Lord Jesus Christ, in the reign of the Roman Pope Innocent, of King Phillip of France, and King Richard of England, there was a holy man in France whose name was Fulk of Neuilly ... and this Fulk of whom I speak began to preach God's word in France and in other neighboring lands, and Our Lord performed many miracles through him. Know that this holy man's renown spread so far that it reached Pope Innocent, who sent word to France and instructed him to preach the cross with papal authority. Later he sent one of his cardinals who had taken the cross, Master Peter Capuano, and through him offered the indulgence I describe here: All those who would take the cross and serve God for a year in the army would be free from all the sins they had committed and confessed. People's hearts were greatly moved because the indulgence was so generous, and many of them took the cross because of this.*

Then the barons held a conference at Soissons to discuss when they should leave and in which direction they should go. At that time they could not come to any agreement since it seemed to them that not nearly enough people had taken the cross so far. Less than two months later in that same year all the counts and barons who had taken the cross gathered for a meeting at Compiègne. Many opinions were given and taken, as a result of which it was determined that they would send out the best envoys they could find and give them full authority, equivalent to that of their lords, to attend to all of their affairs ... They provided these six envoys with charters, to which their seals were attached, declaring that they would be strictly bound by whatever agreements they made in the seaports and towns they visited.

The envoys ... conferred together and agreed that they could be confident of finding a greater supply of ships at Venice than at any other port. They rode on, day after day, until they arrived there in the first week of Lent in the year of our Lord 1201.

The Doge of Venice was a most wise and most venerable man whose name was Enrico Dandolo. He and the other people of Venice treated the envoys most honorably and were very pleased to welcome them. When the envoys presented the letters from their lords, the Venetians were very curious about what business had brought them to their country ...

On the appointed day, they went inside the Doge's palace, which was very grand and beautiful. They found the Doge and his council in a chamber and delivered their message thus: "Sire, we come to thee on the part of the high barons of France, who have taken the sign of the cross to avenge the shame done to Jesus Christ, and to reconquer Jerusalem, if so be that God will suffer it. And because they know that no people have such great power to help them as you and your people, therefore we pray you by God that you take pity on the land overseas and the shame of Christ, and use diligence that our lords have ships for transport and battle."

"How would the barons wish to acquire them?" asked the Doge.

"In whatever way that you urge or advise them," replied the envoys, "in so far as what you propose may be within our means."

"This is certainly a substantial request they make of us," said the Doge, "and it seems they are planning an ambitious expedition. We will give you our answer eight days from today. And marvel not if the term is long, for it is meet that so great a matter be fully pondered."

—*Geoffrey de Villehardouin (1160–1213)*
Memoirs, or Chronicle of the Fourth Crusade and the Conquest of Constantinople

CHAPTER 8

THE DAY AFTER THE MAY Day attacks, Hornsby sat in the Oval Office with the president. Most of the morning had been absorbed by briefings from McCardle and Gambelli. The CIA gave the president their best and latest information on Salman al-Akbar and Husam al-Din, while the FBI provided details on domestic terrorist cells currently under investigation. This was followed by lunch with the cabinet and the legislative leadership. Now the two men sat on a couch, distracted by the flat-screen TVs mounted on the wall above them. The networks played and replayed the video of the airplane crashing into the mall, interspersed with footage of al-Akbar hiking in the mountains of Kabulistan. Most of the press believed that he lived in a series of caves hidden in the country's tribal areas. The anchors seemed to revel in the man's Bedouin dress and turban, in the deep-set, mournful expression of his eyes, and most of all, in his sudden and unexpected aggression toward the West.

"How long are they going to make people *watch* this crap?" asked the president. "No wonder everybody's depressed."

"They don't have anything else, sir," said Hornsby. "At least for right now. We're almost at the end of the news cycle. By this evening, they'll have the video of us meeting with the cabinet and the legislature. It'll look like we're doing something."

"What's next on the agenda?"

"A visit from a delegation of Muslim leaders. It'll give us a chance to show how open-minded we are."

"What's the bottom line on this guy, Bob? What's his problem?"

"Salman al-Akbar?"

"Yes."

"As you know, he's distantly related to the Saudi royal family." Decades of experience had schooled Hornsby in the best way to educate high-ranking politicians. "His family made a fortune in the construction business. As far as we can tell, he was outraged by the presence of our troops on Saudi soil during the 1991 war."

"My uncle has been dealing with the Saudis for decades. He never mentioned this lunatic to me."

"Al-Akbar has no influence with the royal family. Zero. But apparently, he was infuriated that the United States was deploying troops to the country and using it as a staging ground for the war."

"We saved his ass, for God's sake. Without us, Saudi Arabia might be a colony of Sumeristan."

"True enough, sir. But to him, we're infidels with no business on Saudi soil. As we both know, he doesn't speak for anyone's official position."

"All right," said the president, rubbing his eyes with both hands. "How are we coming along on the domestic security thing? Is Admiral Baldwin ready to go?"

"He's all set, sir."

"And you vouch for him?"

"There was no finer man in the service than Chester Baldwin, sir. He was in for three decades, fought in four wars. More to the point—if you give him a job, he'll do it."

"Sounds good."

A buzzer sounded on the president's desk. Cane walked over and picked up the phone.

"Yes? What channel? All right, we'll take a look."

The president fiddled with the remote control, and Oprah flashed onto the screen. Sitting to her right was the Reverend Sanford J. Bayer, decked out in his purple pastoral regalia.

"Isn't that nice?" Hornsby grinned. "Oprah finally got religion."

"Did someone authorize this?" said the president, squinting up at the TV.

"I believe he was told he could be out and about, as long as he kept it low-key."

"Reverend Bayer," said Oprah, leaning forward toward the camera. "What would you say to Americans listening today with regard to their Muslim neighbors? What advice would you give them about how to interact with those followers of Islam who are law-abiding, whose children go to our schools, and play dodgeball with our kids on the playground?"

Cane looked at Hornsby.

"Muslims play dodgeball?" asked the president. "That's news to me."

"It's a metaphor, sir," said Hornsby patiently.

"I would counsel them to follow the teachings of Scripture and love their neighbors as themselves," said Bayer smoothly. "I think you hit the nail on the head, Oprah, when you referred to them as our neighbors. It's important for us to remember that the people who perpetrated these horrible attacks have hijacked one of the world's great religions for their own evil ends. They are not to be confused with the folks we see at PTA meetings and soccer practice. Patriotic Muslims are part of our communities and our fabric of life, and the actions of an irresponsible few cannot be allowed to alienate them from us—"

Cane raised the remote and turned off the TV.

"What the hell," he said. "If they can come here and get their picture taken with me the day after they killed three thousand of our citizens, I guess they can play dodgeball with our kids."

"He's making a good point, sir."

Inwardly, Hornsby was surprised at Reverend Bayer's conciliatory tone. He had pressed for the same sense of balance in George Cane's public remarks, yet he had also lobbied to include the word "crusade" in the text of the president's speech at his press conference, knowing that it would infuriate the rulers of hostile Arab nations.

"I suppose," said Cane. "I know you're not a fan of his."

"He can get a bit hysterical," said Hornsby. "But I think we have him under control."

"Like him or not, he's one of the godfathers of the evangelical movement in this country. And without the evangelicals, I wouldn't be sitting here today."

You wouldn't be sitting there, thought Hornsby, *if your uncle hadn't called me. Not because some nancy preacher in a purple robe visits homeless shelters on your behalf.*

The buzzer sounded on the president's desk, and he picked up the phone again wearily.

"Yes? She is? So what do you want me to do? All right, hold on for a moment." He covered the speaker with his hand. "It's the secretary of state," he told Hornsby. "She's about to land at Andrews. What now?"

"Have her come here immediately," said Hornsby firmly. "She'll have a high-level meeting with you to discuss the diplomatic strategy of the situation. Film at eleven."

"Please tell the secretary that I want to see her immediately," said Cane into the phone. "Have her come to the White House at once after she lands."

He hung up and looked at Hornsby.

"I want you here for this, Bob," said the president. "You know how uncomfortable she makes me."

"Absolutely, sir."

Jennifer Caldwell, the secretary of state, was a holdover from the Hampton Administration. After years as a top diplomat, she had been appointed ambassador to the United Nations by William Hampton, and became secretary of state in the final two years of Billy Bob's term. She was a large, physically hideous woman, and Hornsby had always assumed she had been promoted to demonstrate that you didn't need to sleep with Hampton to succeed in his cabinet.

After the contentious election of his nephew, Herbert Cane thought it would be wise to retain at least one cabinet member from the previous administration. This idea created a great deal of controversy among the incoming team. Hornsby spent Thanksgiving of 2000 with the elder Cane, and he remembered their discussion on the subject. Sipping bourbon on the porch of Cane's Cape Cod house, Hornsby had voiced his objections to allowing an outsider to penetrate the inner sanctum of the new administration.

"Lighten up, Bob," said Herbert Cane cheerfully, playing with one of his spaniels. "It'll be seen as a ... a magnanimous gesture of bipartisan support. You can't possibly see this woman as a threat."

"She doesn't threaten me, sir. But I can't be everywhere at once. Sooner or later, somebody will tell her something that she shouldn't know."

"So box her out," said Cane. "Keep her out of the loop. You think she'll care? She just needs to put in two years with you before she can write her memoirs."

"I thought my main goal was to box out Bayard Stevenson."

"You can take care of them both." The ex-president grinned. "Shit. You were director of the CIA, for Chrissakes. Unlike Bayard, she probably won't even figure it out."

And now, sitting with Cane's nephew in the Oval Office, he heard the buzzer again.

"Yes? All right, I'll be with them in a minute. Tell them I'm concluding a conference on national security with the vice president."

He put down the phone and looked at Hornsby.

"The Arabs are here."

"Muslims, sir. Some may be Arabs, some not."

"Whatever. You carry the ball on this."

"Absolutely. Just remember, lots of close-up shots. Earnest discussions, empathetic looks."

"Will do." The president patted Hornsby on the shoulder. "And thanks for looking out for me yesterday."

"Sir?"

"I know you had my back, and I appreciate it. Thanks for getting me to safety. No matter how bad things get, it's important for folks to know that their leaders are safe, and that they're in charge of the situation."

"No problem, sir. That's what I'm here for."

CHAPTER 9

ESPITE ROBERT HORNSBY'S CONNECTION TO the Cane family, he had come very close to refusing a spot on George Cane's ticket.

The sticking point: Courtney Cane, the Governor's twenty-five-year-old daughter, who had come out as a lesbian four years earlier. Hornsby had no personal objections to the homosexual lifestyle, but he believed that it was bad politics, particularly for a Republican candidate. The situation festered for months and finally surfaced during a meeting at Cane's Texas ranch.

"My uncle tells me you're on the fence." George Cane sat back in a rocking chair on the porch, gazing out at the expanse of scorched brush that opened out into the horizon. "What's that about, Bob?"

"I think we might have some problems with the base." Hornsby sipped his lemonade and tried to think of ways to be diplomatic. "If we do this, we need to have a clear shot to go all the way. I'm not totally convinced we have that now."

Cane squinted at him. "This is because of my daughter?"

"I don't make judgments." Hornsby shifted in his chair. "I like Courtney, always have. This is a political calculation, George. I don't know how to finesse this. We've got the evangelicals to deal with—they're a huge force, both in the primaries and in the general. I just don't know how to package this in a way that's acceptable to them."

"We're talking about my daughter. If her lifestyle is acceptable to me, it should be fine with everyone else."

"That's state politics, George. We're talking national. Out in the Midwest, in the Louisiana canebrake, they won't be so tolerant."

"The hell with them, then. They'd rather have a president getting blow jobs in the Oval Office than one whose daughter is pursuing an ... alternate lifestyle?"

"Not so simple."

"Don't get me wrong. I'd be happier if she was playing shortstop for the Kansas City Royals, but she's still my daughter."

"I understand. Tell me, how much influence do you have over her?"

"We're close."

"She takes your advice?"

"I'd like to think so. She listens, anyway."

"Then please stress to her that she needs to be careful about her associations. Her *relationships*."

"I'm not sure I follow."

"No unsavory characters." Hornsby took a breath and exhaled slowly. "You know what I mean. No muscles, tattoos, cigarettes dangling from their lips. No one who looks like a truck driver or the bearded lady at the county fair. No offense."

"None taken." Cane chuckled. "But in that world, Bob, the available suitors don't exactly look like the finalists at the Miss America pageant."

"Someone who looks like the girl next door, with a few minor differences."

"This was never an issue for my uncle."

"With all due respect, Courtney hadn't even hit puberty back then. Besides that, the evangelicals call the tune now. You can't even get the nomination without them, much less win the general."

"Give me a break, Bob. They've been a major force ever since Dick Viguery organized them back in the early eighties. When I was screwing around in college, he was putting them into databases, for God's sake. Nobody even had an idea of what a database was back then. For that matter, I don't even know what it is now."

"This is different," said Hornsby patiently. "This isn't 1982. Back then, they only dreamed of having the power they have now. Let's be realistic, George—you're going to be a presidential candidate with a lesbian daughter. It's a potential time bomb, unless we handle it right now."

"So what do you suggest?"

"Okay." Hornsby leaned forward and hunched toward Cane conspiratorially. "I think you have to strike some chord with them that they can relate to. A chord of Christian compassion."

"You mean, hate the sin but not the sinner?"

"No, no. No mention of sin. You need to be pure as the driven snow. There's no sin within a thousand miles of your house. It has to be something like this: You're empathetic, you understand, you're a real human being like everyone else."

"Not sure I get this."

"Everybody who goes into the voting booth to pull the lever has a fucked-up kid. Mind you, I'm not saying that Courtney is fucked up—simply that because of issues within your own family, you can relate to the problems of the average person. You've been there, you know how they feel. Talk about *feelings*. Look at how well that worked for the Democrats. You empathize with them. You extend empathy to their children, just as they try to."

"I like it."

"Excellent." Hornsby was warming up now. "You talk about how the major parties have missed the boat on so many issues because of their extreme views. Scratch that. *Don't* talk about major parties. You say that certain elements in our society have blown things out of proportion, driven people to extremes. It's either black or white to them, and that's not how real life is. You see a different way. *A third way.* You see how to treat people as human beings, without all these destructive labels."

"Damn," muttered George Cane. "You're good."

"Not my first rodeo, George."

"Even so."

"And while you're at it, every once in a while, make some reference to your faith. Nothing too blatant—you don't want to sound like a holy roller and scare the moderates. Remind them that you're a man of faith. Quote from the Bible occasionally, but don't call it the Bible. Refer to it as 'Scripture.'"

"What's the difference?"

"It sounds more reassuring to certain constituencies. And remember: You are the candidate of reconciliation. You represent the third way."

"What else are we reconciling?"

"We'll make that up as we go along."

"Okay." George Cane leaned back in his chair and grinned. "Can I count on you, then?"

"You tell me." Hornsby allowed himself a smile. "Can I count on you to stay on message?"

"If it gets me elected, sure."

George Cane's first major interview—and the one that would set the tone for the campaign—was an exclusive with Barbara Walters that took place three weeks after he won the nomination, on the eve of the Democrat convention. "It has to be Wah-Wah," said Hornsby when his running mate objected to the arrangements. "She's the queen of the softballs." Cane was serious but relaxed as he sat in an armchair, wrapped in a cardigan, answering her questions thoughtfully.

"Governor," she said toward the end of the half-hour, "we have a few minutes remaining. Do you mind if I get personal?"

"Ask me anything, Barbara."

"Your daughter Courtney made headlines four years ago when she came out publicly as a lesbian. As you know, there are many people in your party, people of deep faith, who have serious objections to the homosexual lifestyle. Some trace their objections back to the Bible, and regard homosexuality as a sin. At the same time, you're going to need the support of those evangelical voters. How do you plan on handling this issue?"

"I'm glad you asked, Barbara. And no, the question isn't too personal. When you run for president, after all, your life is an open book." Cane smiled, but remembered to keep his mouth closed.

"One of the reasons I'm running is to try and heal some of the divisions in this country, divisions that have become far worse over the past eight years. One of those divisions is certainly over the homosexual lifestyle. Along with many other things, we've watched the issue become increasingly politicized, with debates over gay marriage and gay people in the military.

"At the same time, sexual orientation is a matter of personal choice. I learned this four years ago when Courtney chose to share her lifestyle with me and with the world. I have great respect for people of faith, and as you know, I'm a person of faith myself, but some things are simply matters between the individual and God."

He looked directly into the camera.

"I reject the polarization that has been forced on us over the past eight years. I don't believe that life is made up of extremes. I believe in a third way—a path of empathy and reconciliation."

"Does this mean that you've softened your position on gay marriage as a result of your experience with your daughter?"

"Not at all, Barbara. I still believe that marriage is the union of one man and one woman. It means is that I've become a more understanding and compassionate person as a result of this experience. And I know that I'm not alone, because a great many folks out there have had conflicts in their own families, and they've gone through things with their own children that have been difficult. I'm in a better position now to understand how those folks feel, and to respect the choices of others."

"Governor, that is truly touching. I appreciate your candor, and I'm afraid we have to close on that note."

The headline in the following day's *New York Times* was the best outcome the campaign could have hoped for: "Cane proposes 'third way' on gay rights," with the subhead "Calls for new political era of compassion and understanding."

CHAPTER 10

LANTERN LIGHT FLICKERED AGAINST THE walls of the cave. It was nearing midnight on May 1 in the tribal areas of Kabulistan, a mountainous and impenetrable region near the Persepostan border. Salman al-Akbar sat on a cushion, surrounded by his inner circle. Fazil Ahmadi, his director of operations, had just finished briefing him on the aftermath of the Mall of America attack and the subsequent suicide missions around the United States.

"Allah be praised!" Al-Akbar's normally sad eyes were bright and jubilant in the lantern-light. "We have succeeded beyond our wildest expectations, beyond the reach of our dreams. Allah is most with us."

"This is so," said Fazil Ahmadi. "Had we dreamed it, it could not have gone better."

"What time is it now in Washington?"

"Four-thirty in the afternoon, sir."

"And where is the young American president now?"

"We have no knowledge of his whereabouts, sir. He is in hiding."

"*Hiding?*" Al-Akbar's eyebrows arched toward the ceiling of the cave, and his normally expressionless face was close to registering hilarity. "From whom is he hiding? Robert Hornsby?"

"He has been removed from sight, sir. We suspect they took him to one of their nuclear installations."

"Do they actually think we are in possession of nuclear weapons?"

"We believe it is a precaution on their part, sir."

"Allah be praised!" Al-Akbar clapped his hands in glee.

"They will most certainly retaliate, sir."

"Against whom?" asked al-Akbar with contempt. "Our forces are safe. The loyalty of the warlords is secure. They will not betray us."

"We believe their most likely target will be the Dua Khamail. They will wage war against them and will surely defeat them. Then, they will restore Selim Hanjuk to power."

"Let them have the Dua Khamail," al-Akbar shrugged. "To us, it matters not who is the ruler of Kabulistan. Any war they wage against the innocent population can only help us. It will bring more recruits to our side."

"This is true."

"One thing I will guarantee you. They may topple the government of Kabulistan, or all of the governments of the earth, but they will never be at peace again. As they fall off to sleep, they will see our faces in their nightmares."

"Yes, sir. Our position is strong, and the Americans will find invading Kabulistan like wading through quicksand. They will never find us, much less defeat us."

"Their memories are short," mused al-Akbar. "They forget that the Russians tried and failed. It was their Vietnam. And the Americans are far weaker than the Russians. They do not have the will for prolonged conflict."

"Let us not underestimate their military strength, sir."

"These infidels are like the Crusaders of old." Al-Akbar's fingers worked prayer beads in the darkness of the cave. "They have many troops, they have excellent weapons, and they have knowledge of warfare. But they lack the fire of belief, as well as the support of their people. And they do not have Allah on their side." He smiled approvingly at his lieutenant. "You have done well today. And soon we will do better still. Today is the beginning of the great jihad. Nearly eight hundred years ago the East was ruled by Saladin, and the true believers were victorious. That day will come again."

CHAPTER 11

WITH LIGHTS FLASHING AND SIRENS screaming, the motorcade headed across the Maryland countryside toward the District of Columbia. It was eight o'clock in the evening. Secretary of State Jennifer Caldwell sat in the back of the limo with Mandy Parisi, her personal assistant and chief of staff. They ran a succession of red lights as they moved steadily toward the city.

"What's the point of all this, ma'am?"

"Theatrics," said the secretary. She smiled at her protégé. "This'll all be on the eleven o'clock news. They will be seen as active and vigorous. The president is strong, on top of things, in command. To prove this, he summons me to the White House at the very instant I return."

"Who did you mean by 'they'?"

"The whole cabal: Cane, Hornsby, Stevenson. Whoever."

"Do you think they're actually considering a diplomatic response to this?"

"Of course not," said Caldwell. "They're going to bomb a bunch of innocent slobs back to the Stone Age. But they need diplomatic cover. By the day after tomorrow, I'll bet we'll be heading over to Kabulistan to see if we can reason with the Dua Khamail."

"If you know it's a sham, why put up with it?"

"It's better than teaching at Berkeley." The secretary rested her head on the soft leather. "And as long as you're in the game, you have a chance of being a player."

Nearly sixty years later, mused Caldwell, *and we're still cleaning up after Roosevelt and Churchill.* She thought of the weak and dying president, meeting for his last summit with Churchill and Stalin in the Pacific in 1945. Against his better judgment, and perhaps because he was too tired to fight it, FDR gave in to Churchill's half-assed plan to carve the bulk of the Middle East into three massive superstates: Kabulistan, Sumeristan, and Persepostan. There had been nothing but trouble since. *The English screwed it up after World War I, and he let them do it again. We would have been much better off with two dozen petty fiefdoms. Then we could have sat back, popped popcorn, and watched them kill each other off.*

The motorcade entered the South Gate of the White House and came to rest beneath the portico. A uniformed Marine escorted Caldwell and Parisi to the door of the Oval Office.

"Jennifer!" George Cane bounded energetically toward her and gave her a peck on the cheek. "How the hell are you?"

"I'm fine, Mr. President. You've had quite a time, I suspect."

"All in a day's work."

"Mr. Vice President, I hope you're well."

"Madame Secretary." Hornsby shook her hand. "How was the Ivory Coast?"

"It's a mess, quite frankly: runaway inflation, political instability, plus an AIDS infection rate of nearly forty percent."

"Too bad," said Hornsby, gesturing toward the couches. "Shall we get down to business?"

Caldwell and Parisi settled on a sofa, wearing looks of solemn interest.

"Do we know who was behind this, sir?" asked the secretary.

"Husam al-Din has taken responsibility," said Cane.

"We know they have training camps in the tribal areas, as well as a network of command posts," said Hornsby. "What we're unsure of is the nature of the relationship between Husam al-Din and the Dua Khamail."

"Obviously they're complicit," said Caldwell.

"They have parallel relationships with the warlords," said the vice president. "This much is obvious. Otherwise, the Dua Khamail couldn't keep the lid on the country, and Husam al-Din wouldn't have a place to hide out and train recruits. But we need to know how the two forces intersect. Is the Dua Khamail retaining their hold on the fundamentalist faction with the help of Husam al-Din? Is al-Akbar receiving aid and comfort from the government?"

"We'd like you to go to Kabulistan tomorrow," said the president. "Meet with the Dua Khamail, see what you can find out."

"Mr. President, you know very well that they're not about to tell me if they're collaborating with Husam al-Din."

"Of course not," said Hornsby. "But see if you can pick up any clues. At the very least, stall for time until the agency can come up with something."

"With all due respect," said Caldwell, "this is not the type of situation where undercover operatives can infiltrate easily. Intelligence is going to be limited."

"We'll see about that," said Hornsby.

"Jennifer," the president cut in, "I'm committed to finding a diplomatic solution somewhere in this mess. That's why I'm asking you to go. It's not just about showing the world that we're using diplomacy. We need to find the best possible approach."

"Very well," said the secretary. "We will conduct high-level talks with the leaders of the Dua Khamail. I will convey to them the seriousness of the situation, the need for their cooperation, and our government's desire to find a diplomatic way forward."

"Excellent," said the president. "Now, there's one more thing."

"Sir?"

"In the unlikely event that a diplomatic solution fails, we need to have a backup ready. This has been a very traumatic event for the country, and folks are expecting swift action one way or the other. I want you to start sounding out possible coalition partners in case we have to take military action against the evildoers."

Caldwell stared at him. "The evildoers," she said finally.

"Damn right," snapped Hornsby. "The bastards who killed three thousand innocent citizens yesterday."

"Did you have any thoughts on possible coalition partners, sir?"

"Well, the usual folks to start," said the president.

"You mean England and Australia?"

"We assume they'll come aboard if and when the time comes. But we'd need a broader assortment of partners. When my uncle invaded Sumeristan in 1991, he had a coalition of thirty-two countries. Of course, some of those nations only contributed a few hundred forces, and some didn't send any combat troops at all. I'd say we'd be shooting for half of that, maybe fifteen nations. It would be nice if we had a bunch of Arab nations in there, just like my uncle did."

"If the time comes," said Caldwell.

"That's right," said the president amiably. "As they say in my part of the country, good Lord willin' and the creek don't rise. Now why don't the two of you get some sleep? You've had a long day, and you'll have a longer flight tomorrow."

"Thank you, Mr. President," said Caldwell. "Good night, and be well."

They watched the ladies walk to the portico and disappear into their limousine.

"Diplomatic solution, my ass," said Hornsby when Caldwell and Parisi had left the room.

"You've got that right," replied George Cane. "The public wants blood, and we damn well better give it to 'em."

CHAPTER 12

ON THE OUTSKIRTS OF BAGHDAD, the rows of low-slung cinderblock apartments were cold in the winter and hot in the summer. Although trees had been planted near the flat rented by Abdul Alghafari's parents, it would be many years before they would provide shade. Often young Abdul lay awake for hours past his bedtime, waiting for the air to cool enough so he could sleep.

His mother would look back on a night when she gently opened the door to check on him. It was the moment when it all started, at least for her. He was eight years old.

"Yes, Mama?"

"It is past ten," she said as sternly as possible. "You need to sleep, so you can be alert at school tomorrow."

"It is too hot to sleep."

"Why don't you try? If you try long enough, you will succeed."

"Mama, can I ask you something?"

She came over and sat down next to him on the bed.

"What is it, Abdul?"

"Do you think that someday we can go to America?"

"America!" She laughed in spite of herself. "What makes you ask such a thing?"

"I was hearing about it in school. All the buildings are air conditioned there. Everyone has a television and many cars. And you could have a washing machine."

"Abdul, I do not believe that you were learning such things about America in school."

"Not in class, no. But a friend of mine was talking about it during recess. His uncle went to America a few years ago. There is much opportunity there."

"Abdul, there is opportunity here as well. Look at your father—he started his own business as a spice merchant, and he is doing very well. We have electricity and running water. When I was growing up, these things were unheard of. They were only for the rich."

"It's not just the air conditioning, Mama. America is a free country. You can say whatever you want, and the people vote for their leaders. Here, everyone is afraid of Hussein Ghazi."

"Hush!" His mother put her finger to his lips. "You must never speak like that."

"But I'm only talking to you, Mama."

"I know, I know. But here is the problem: When you speak like that in private, someday you may say something in public. It may become so familiar that it seems normal. And then you will be in danger, and we will be as well."

"That's exactly what I mean, Mama. Why should we be afraid of words? We should be free to say what we want."

"Abdul," she said, taking his hands, "we have a good life. We are all happy together. This is our home—our family has been here for generations. You must promise me that you will not go around saying such things."

"But Mama—"

"There are more important things in life than being able to say what you want. Tomorrow, when you see that boy at recess, I want you to avoid him. Go to another part of the playground and play with someone else."

"That isn't fair."

"Sometimes things are not fair. You must learn this. Regardless of how you feel, you must not speak like this."

"Yes, Mama."

"Now try to go to sleep." She kissed his forehead. "Soon it will be morning, and you will not want to get out of bed."

"Mama?"

"Yes?" She paused at the door.

"If we do go to America, I will buy you a washing machine."

CHAPTER 13

SHORTLY BEFORE SEVEN IN THE morning, Hornsby unlocked the door to his inner sanctum in the Executive Office Building, breaking the tamper-proof seal. He gathered the daily pile of classified folders and reports, and settled down at his desk to read the overnight intelligence briefings. The tamper-proof seal was placed in the door shortly before dawn each morning by a member of the Patriot Detail, signifying that the premises had been swept and were certified clean. The vice president's caution dated to his first week in office, when he had arrived early one morning to find an "electrician" doing repairs in his suite. He had asked for identification, and soon discovered that the man didn't even have a security clearance. The electrician protested that his company had done contract work for the Hampton Administration, which might have been true, but Hornsby was furious all the same. He called McCardle and demanded a full sweep of the premises each and every morning by a trusted member of the Detail.

At exactly seven-fifteen, the red phone rang. McCardle was on his way over to the White House for the daily presidential security briefing. Since taking office, it had been Hornsby's practice to clear the briefing with McCardle before it went to the president. He wanted to make certain that George Cane received intelligence that was concise, understandable, and responsive to the administration's agenda. "How are you, Mike?"

"Good, sir. Everything seems quiet."

"I just finished reading the overnights. It sounds like you don't have much."

"Not yet, sir."

"I would omit or reshape item number eight: 'Motivations of Dua Khamail unclear, possibly linked to political instability within Kabulistan as much as fundamentalist ideology.' Until we have all the facts, I don't want to plant the idea in the president's head that these folks are just well-meaning politicians trying to survive."

"We'll omit it, sir. It doesn't contain much in the way of information."

"Good. How are we coming along with putting someone on the inside?"

"It's a bitch, sir. This isn't Berlin. We don't have that many native speakers, and Kabulistan is a closed society."

"Well, keep trying."

"Absolutely, sir."

Hornsby hung up. Ten days had passed since the May Day attacks. They would have to come up with something soon. The Democrats were sniping at them, complaining that an administration with a former CIA director as vice president should be able to get to the bottom of what had happened. The implication, of course, was that the nation was at risk and something had to be done before another attack ensued. Even worse, some Southern members of the Republican congressional caucus were starting to make noise. He would have to meet with them on the Hill shortly, as soon as he figured out what the hell to tell them.

"Good morning, sir." Scott Leventhal poked his head into Hornsby's office.

"Morning, Scott. Come in."

Leventhal settled into a chair opposite his boss and unpacked the contents of a Dunkin' Donuts bag. He passed the vice president a large coffee and a chocolate-covered cruller. Given Hornsby's heart condition, his wife was in charge of his diet; any opportunity to indulge had to come away from home.

"Thanks, Scott. How are you?"

"Never better, sir. Ready to do battle for truth, justice, and the American way."

"Excellent." Hornsby grinned. "Have any gossip for me?"

"Nothing we can use today, sir."

"Damn. No naked pictures of Mandy Parisi and the ambassador of Sumeristan?"

"Afraid not."

Hornsby liked Scott Leventhal and trusted him absolutely. This was highly unusual, given that Leventhal wasn't an agency man and had no links to the intelligence community. They had met at a cocktail party midway through Hornsby's eight years of exile, and the two had immediately formed an ideological bond. At the time, Leventhal was a brilliant operative at the capital's leading Republican think tank, and neoconservative to the bone. During their conversation, Hornsby realized that Leventhal believed in the primacy of U.S. military force, the absolute imperative to confront Islamic radicalism, and the necessity for supporting Israel as the last bulwark against anti-American forces in the Middle East. Even better, he was Jewish, had converted to evangelical Christianity, and had gradually drifted toward the neocon position during his years at Yale. Now, as Hornsby looked at his chief of staff, he saw the irrepressible glimmer of something triumphant winking at him behind his Styrofoam coffee cup.

"All right." Hornsby smiled. "I know you've got something. What is it?"

"Can't tell you, sir. Saving it for a rainy day."

"Dammit, Scott. Why should you have all the fun? Let's have it."

Leventhal placed his cup on the desk and looked at the vice president.

"It appears, sir, that David Burnham may be gay."

Hornsby whistled. "You've got to be kidding. Don't tell me you have pictures?"

"No such luck. But we're working on getting a statement from a former staffer."

Burnham was administrative assistant to Congressman Andrew Neponski of Michigan, the Speaker of the House. He had enthusiastically supported Neponski's lukewarm position on gay marriage. On more than one occasion, Burnham had told reporters that although he believed that true marriage was the union of one man and one woman, it might be possible at some future date to consider civil unions for gays.

"This is huge."

"Potentially, yes. I'll continue to pursue it until I get something. But mum's the word, sir."

"Absolutely. But you understand we have to be very careful about this."

"I know, I know. The president's daughter."

"Different situation," said Hornsby thoughtfully. "Courtney Cane practically hired a skywriter to tell the world she was a lesbian, but Burnham's in the closet."

"So he can be blackmailed."

"I wouldn't call it that, Scott. I'd say that his situation could potentially make him a very valuable ally. If it turns out to be true, this is a gift. Let's not overplay our hand—this isn't the McCarthy era."

"Understood."

"In the meantime, let's lock down that staffer."

"Priority one, sir."

"So what's on the docket for this morning?"

"Bayard Stevenson at 9:30, I'm afraid."

"Jesus," Hornsby groaned. "What have I done to deserve this?"

"You were elected, sir."

The vice president was still digesting his chocolate-covered cruller when Stevenson arrived at nine-twenty with military punctuality and was ushered into Hornsby's office. The vice president looked at Leventhal.

"Any housekeeping notes, Scott?"

"We have the briefing with the president tomorrow evening, in the residence," said Leventhal. "He wants to go over the military options before Thursday's meeting with the Joint Chiefs."

"Very well. Anything else?"

"No, sir. I'll let the two of you talk in private."

"Bayard," said Hornsby as the door closed. "What have you got for me? What's our best plan of attack?"

"It hardly matters, sir. The Dua Khamail don't really offer a formidable challenge. Support for them within the army is dubious. On top of that, Kabulistan has no air force and very little in the way of sophisticated weaponry."

"Excellent."

"The real issue will be logistical. We can deploy carrier fleets, but someone has to let us stage our troops. You can forget about Syria, Jordan, Lebanon, or any of those countries. Turkey is the most obvious choice, but we have to be careful not to burn them out. We may well need them later on."

"Those bases belong to us, if I recall."

"True enough, sir. But we can't be constantly putting them in a position of aiding us in attacking their Muslim neighbors. Their own political situation isn't that strong."

"Let us worry about the politics of it. What about the Husam al-Din strongholds in the tribal areas?"

"There's no way you're going to identify them. The only option is to bomb everything in sight and hope for the best, and that won't work—it'll make us look like Lyndon Johnson. After the government is toppled and Hanjuk is back in power, it might be possible to buy off the warlords, but you're talking about a huge sum. It would be very difficult to get it appropriated."

"We'll see about that."

"Shouldn't we be discussing this with the president, sir?"

"Of course, and we will. I want to get some clarity on our options before we present them to him tomorrow night."

"Do we have proof of the collaboration between the Dua Khamail and Husam al-Din?"

"We're working on that," said Hornsby. "Obviously, we know that the Dua Khamail have been one of the most repressive Islamic regimes in history. Women can't even go out in public without being stoned, and Kabulistani Christians have been put to death. I don't think there's much doubt that we'll be greeted as liberators."

"And how does this make us safer, sir?"

Hornsby stared at Stevenson. Getting the general on board had been an enormous coup for George Cane's presidential campaign, and the presence of both men at Cane's side had gone very far toward reassuring the public that the young and somewhat goofy governor might be a serious candidate after all. Stevenson was a hero, the man who had permanently erased the legacy of Vietnam in the minds of the public. Therefore, at moments such as these, Hornsby counted to ten before he answered.

"We can't even begin to move against the Husam al-Din strongholds in Kabulistan until the Dua Khamail are toppled and Selim Hanjuk is back in power. When that happens, we can begin to work with the warlords and try to eliminate threats to our security. It's only a first step, and it must be handled correctly. That's why I'm grateful we have you at the helm."

"General Carmichael is very capable, sir."

"I don't argue that. But at the end of the day, we want you calling the shots."

"I'll do my best, sir."

"I know you will."

CHAPTER 14

LIKE ANY COURTSHIP, THE RELATIONSHIP between Cane and Hornsby had rough spots at the start. Glitches. Occasional flare-ups of temper went unaddressed, and were buried as the pair realized they were inextricably stuck with each other.

"I gather I'm going to hear bad news," Cane said as the two met shortly after the election.

"Why would you think that, sir?"

"Because we're sitting on the porch." The president-elect shifted in his chair. "Seems like every time we talk out here, I hear something unpleasant."

"Not all," said Hornsby. "Just a few loose ends." He motioned to the head of the Secret Service detail. "Fellas, give us some privacy for a few minutes, would you? Step back a hundred yards or so."

The agent looked unhappy, but Hornsby cut him off before he could respond.

"That's an order. Just out of earshot. Keep a sharp eye out for gophers."

"I've never seen a gopher here," said Cane as the detail retreated.

"They don't know that. Let them think they're earning their skinny black ties."

"All right. What is it?"

"Just a few suggestions about the Office of Faith and Reconciliation, sir."

"Why are you calling me 'sir,' by the way? All of a sudden?"

"Because you were elected. So you're now referred to as 'Mr. President' or 'sir.' If I call you George in private, I might slip and do it when the cameras are rolling."

"Don't tell me you object to the Office of Faith and Reconciliation."

"Not at all."

"Faith has played a huge role in my life. I wouldn't be sitting here if I hadn't accepted Christ."

"I know that."

"On top of that, Bob, it dovetails with our agenda against big government. Faith-based groups can play a huge role in societal change. When we were growing up, if we had a problem, we went to our pastor. We didn't go running to some government agency for a bureaucratic solution."

"That all sounds great. But for starters, we need to make sure it's a non-denominational organization."

"It will be. Every Christian denomination will be represented."

"That's what I mean, sir. It has to be interfaith. Jews and Muslims need to be in the mix, so it doesn't look like we're making an end run around the separation of church and state."

"I see." Cane sipped his lemonade thoughtfully. "Well, we can make that happen. What else?"

"The next point is a bit delicate, sir."

"I was waiting for the kicker."

"I understand you're considering Reverend Bayer to head the group."

"Absolutely."

"You might want to reconsider."

"Bob, Sanford Bayer was Carlton Post's handpicked successor. Post was the spiritual advisor to seven presidents, including my uncle."

"I realize that."

"He's a great man in the eyes of many. I'm sure you remember Journey for Jesus."

"I do."

"He converted millions of Africans or Haitians, whatever they were, to Christianity."

"They were Africans."

"Carlton Post is a great man."

"Sir, Sanford Bayer isn't Carlton Post."

"What's wrong with him?"

"Honestly, doesn't he strike you as a bit ... effeminate?" Hornsby cleared his throat. "As you would say, he's not exactly playing shortstop for the Kansas City Royals."

"So you actually think he's gay?"

"Certainly looks that way, sir. Wherever he goes, he's surrounded by a half-dozen lisping acolytes. They never get any older, either. Because they're constantly being replaced. If he were a Catholic priest, I'm sure he'd be exiled to the North Pole by now."

"I don't believe this." Cane shook his head. "Do you have any proof?"

"Not exactly proof, no. But everything seems to add up. Would you like to read his file?"

"I most certainly would not. That's your bailiwick."

"We have to be careful with this." He paused. "I don't want to offend you."

"Go ahead." Cane grinned. "Nobody can hear you except the gophers."

"We need to be mindful of your daughter's situation. We were able to sidestep the issue neatly during the campaign. But she's still your daughter. People understand how powerful that bond can be, and the last thing we want voters to think is that you're using your office to legitimize the gay agenda in any way. We have to think about your reelection."

"I was just elected less than a month ago, for God's sake."

"We're thinking about the base, remember. To those folks, everything adds up."

"Let me get this straight." Cane rubbed his eyes wearily. "Because my daughter is a lesbian and Sanford Bayer seems a little effeminate to you, people are going to think I'm being manipulated by some gay conspiracy?"

"Just a word of caution, sir. You're the boss, and you'll get Sanford Bayer if you want him. But I suggest we watch him carefully. Keep him on a short leash."

"Sure." Cane grinned again. "I have no doubt that's exactly what you'll do."

CHAPTER 15

I T WAS DUSK IN PARIS, and Selim Hanjuk sat in the study of his apartment on the Avenue Foch and waited for *Meet the Press* to begin. As Tim Russert's face appeared on the screen, the chestnut trees outside Hanjuk's window were bathed in soothing yellow light.

"Our guest this morning is Robert Barton Hornsby, the vice president of the United States. Mr. Vice President, welcome back."

"It's a pleasure to be here, Tim."

The camera flashed to Hornsby, who was wearing a dark blue suit with an American flag pin in the left lapel. He leaned forward, head tilted slightly to one side, with his customary scowl replaced by a patient smile—an expression of benevolence reserved for journalists he felt he could manipulate.

"Sir, Washington was buzzing this week as the nation waited for President Cane to announce his military response to the May Day attacks. A great deal of speculation has centered on Kabulistan and the government of the Dua Khamail, which is rumored to be in league with Husam al-Din. What can you tell us about the plans going forward?"

Hanjuk's secretary and personal assistant, Ali Jebuti, entered the room and sat down in an armchair next to the deposed ruler.

"Well, Tim, obviously I can't reveal any of the preparations for a military response to the attack, although President Cane may choose to address the

American people on that subject very soon—possibly this week, in fact. What I can tell you, Tim, is that a number of courses of action are being considered in consultation with General Stevenson, and everything is on the table."

"At the grass roots level,' said Russert, "many Americans have expressed impatience that our government hasn't countered with an immediate military response."

"I understand the frustration of patriotic Americans everywhere, but obviously our response has to be carefully considered and measured. We need time to weigh the intelligence and time to consider our military options. Then, too, we wanted to wait until Secretary Caldwell had the opportunity to meet with the Dua Khamail and hear their side of the story."

"When Secretary Caldwell returned from Kabulistan, she indicated that the Dua Khamail had denied any connection with Husam al-Din, and they also resisted any suggestion that they had been involved in the May Day attack."

"Of course they deny it, Tim. But we have intelligence—classified intelligence that unfortunately I can't share with you—that the government of the Dua Khamail has been plotting with Husam al-Din since the beginning of their reign in Kabulistan."

"Sounds like we should start packing," said Ali Jebuti. "In a sense, it is a shame. I have truly enjoyed our time here."

"As I have."

"Although President Cane might still decide on a more reasonable course of action."

"I'm afraid not," said Selim Hanjuk. "When this man speaks, the government acts."

"When Secretary Caldwell met with us on her way back from Kabulistan," said Hanjuk, "she seemed to indicate that the Dua Khamail had a narrow scope. She said they were focused on maintaining internal order, not attacking the West."

"So she said," muttered Seljuk. "But it hardly matters now."

"How can defeating the Dua Khamail reassure Americans that they will be safer," asked Russert as the camera cut to him, "and prevent another attack on our soil?"

Hornsby replaced his smile with an earnest expression, modulating his voice carefully. "Tim, we can't begin to move against Husam al-Din strongholds in Kabulistan until the Dua Khamail, who have been complicit with them and possibly funded them, are removed. At that point, we can begin to forge alliances with warlords in the tribal areas who may be protecting Husam al-Din headquarters and training camps."

"I see."

"There are also humanitarian considerations here. People have to understand that this has been one of the most brutal and repressive regimes of modern times. They have persecuted Christians, laid down absolute Islamic law, and basically tortured or executed everyone who disagreed with them. By restoring the rightful government of Kabulistan, we will be fulfilling the moral function of a great democracy."

"Now they are concerned," observed Hanjuk. "When the Dua Khamail drove us out of the country and slaughtered thousands of our followers, they couldn't be bothered."

"At that point," said Jebuti, "it had not yet affected them."

"Do you have any intelligence to indicate that Husam al-Din may have infiltrated into nearby Sumeristan and Persepostan?" asked Russert.

"Obviously, Tim, I can't reveal any classified information." The vice president's tone was soothing but authoritative, as if he were addressing a child or a dog. "But I can tell you that this is a conspiracy with many more tentacles than we have been able to count. What Americans have to understand, and what the president will stress to them the next time he addresses the nation, is that this is a struggle that will not be over in a month, a year, or even a decade. We will be involved in this battle with the forces of evil for a long, long time."

"It looks like we're going home, sir," said Ali Jebuti. "With the help of the Americans."

"Yes," said Hanjuk bitterly. "The cemeteries of the East are littered with the graves of those they have helped."

Speaker Andrew Neponski sat in his Capitol office drinking a Crown Royal on the rocks. It was shortly before nine in the evening. David Burnham, his administrative assistant, relaxed in an armchair next to him.

"It's almost time, sir," said Burnham. "Which channel?"

"Doesn't matter," muttered Neponski. "It'll be the same bullshit, regardless."

"Sir, you don't have to watch this. They'll send over the text."

"I want to see his body language. Since we're being deprived of watching him strut into the House chamber like the champion of the rodeo, at least I want to see his face."

"Can I refill your drink?"

"Damn straight."

Burnham switched on the TV, and they saw George Cane sitting in the East Room, surrounded by drapes embroidered with the Presidential Seal. His face was solemn as he looked directly into the camera.

"My fellow Americans, I speak to you tonight at a defining moment for our nation. As we mourn the deaths of three thousand innocent citizens and struggle to absorb the terrible lessons of May Day, we are aware that this is not the first time in our history that crisis has been thrust upon us. From the battlefields of Concord and Lexington to the smoke and ruins of Pearl Harbor, each and every generation has been called upon to defend America and redefine the unique nature of our freedom."

The president clutched a sheaf of papers as he looked into the camera. They were a prop, of course—he was reading off the teleprompter—but his tight grip on them heralded his nervousness as surely as a trumpet blaring inside the East Room.

"The situation confronting us tonight is equally challenging. The United States has been attacked by a band of terrorists who hate everything we stand for. The name of this terrorist group is Husam al-Din. They wear no uniforms, nor do they come out and fight bravely in the light of day. Instead, they operate in the shadows, using covert and cowardly means to harm our citizens and to attempt to create fear among us. They engage in these shameful tactics because they know that if they engaged us fairly on the battlefield, they would surely be defeated. The leader of this worldwide group is Salman al-Akbar, a man who has attempted to attack us unsuccessfully in the past. He presides over a vast network of secret operatives, working silently for his cause in many nations of the world—including this one."

"He looks like a teenager who got his girlfriend pregnant," said Neponski, "and they just told him she's decided to have the baby."

"You may ask yourself, why do these folks hate us? For one thing, they resent our material prosperity, as well as the talent and hard work that have enabled us to become the greatest superpower in the world. They mistrust our open and accountable system of government, exemplified by the men and women who work hard every day to represent the people of America. Above all, they cannot understand the freedom and liberty of a nation that allows its citizens to think for themselves and to worship as they choose.

"Since the 1991 war with Sumeristan, Husam al-Din has established its headquarters in the tribal areas of Kabulistan. This region is mountainous and inaccessible, ruled by feudal warlords who bear little allegiance to the government of Kabulistan itself. Salman al-Akbar and his key lieutenants operate from caves, equipped with modern technology but hidden from the reach of civilization. Husam al-Din has also established dozens of training camps in this remote area, where recruits are transformed into killers capable of carrying out operations such as the May Day attacks."

Cane stumbled slightly on the pronunciation of Husam al-Din. At this point, his face looked like he had been sucking on a lemon since the beginning of the speech.

"Over the past several weeks, our intelligence services have unearthed information that links Husam al-Din to the Dua Khamail, the radical Islamic sect that overthrew the government of Selim Hanjuk four years ago. The Dua Khamail has provided both support and sanctuary for Husam al-Din, allowing them to operate, to expand, and to flourish. In exchange for a few pieces of silver, they have allowed the enemies of the United States to prosper."

"What's with the biblical allusions?" asked Burnham.

"That would be Hornsby's doing," said Neponski. "He wants to reassure folks in the heartland that God is on our side."

"In addition to giving aid and comfort to our enemies, the Dua Khamail have presided over one of the most vicious and repressive regimes on the planet. They have imposed strict Islamic law on their population, persecuted Christians and other nonbelievers, and executed anyone who stood in their way. If our national security did not demand the removal of this government, our consciences surely would.

"As your commander in chief, I have asked General Bayard Stevenson to devise a plan of battle that will allow us to engage the Dua Khamail, to defeat them, and to restore the rightful government of Kabulistan. In the months to come, we will position our forces to carry out General Stevenson's plan, and then defeat the enemy at a time and place of our choosing. After Selim Hanjuk, our friend and ally, is once more in charge of Kabulistan, we will work with him as well as with the tribal warlords to isolate and crush the Husam al-Din."

"Sounds like a declaration of war to me," said Neponski. "The way I read the Constitution, he's supposed to be asking for the approval of Congress."

"They think they have the public on their side, sir."

"I hope Hornsby knows what he's doing. You ask me, this kid looks scared to death."

"You know, sir, all the hijackers on the two planes were Saudi. So were most of the suicide bombers. I think we'd be better off invading Saudi Arabia."

"Don't hold your breath waiting for this bunch to invade Saudi Arabia." He stirred his drink. "The House of Saud and the House of Cane are thick as thieves."

"My fellow citizens," said the president, "this battle to come will only be a small part of our struggle against the forces of evil. For the May Day attacks to be successful, it was necessary for Husam al-Din to establish dozens of cells of his supporters across America. These agents helped plan and execute the attack, while hundreds or thousands of others were complicit in providing funds for the massacre. While proceeding with sensitivity to the rights of all Americans, it is imperative that we flush out the traitors in our midst and bring them to justice.

"Accordingly, I have asked retired Admiral Chester Baldwin to coordinate the effort of reinforcing our internal security. Admiral Baldwin is a distinguished military hero who has served his country over three decades and in four different wars. I have complete confidence that he will protect our security in a way that also respects the liberties we are fighting to preserve. He will occupy a cabinet-level position, and he will also have my complete support."

Cane's mood seemed to lift as the end of the speech approached, and his face grew less contorted.

"To our Muslim friends and allies around the world, I once again want to stress that our upcoming struggle is not a battle with Islam. We have the utmost respect for the faith of Mohammed, and we know that this small band of terrorists have hijacked your great religion for their own evil ends. As we begin this conflict against our true enemies, we extend a hand of brotherhood toward our Muslim neighbors."

"A hand of brotherhood," said Neponski. "That's rich."

"Well I guess he's in a tough position," said Burnham. "These guys did kill thousands of people on our soil."

"Sure. But they've been looking for the hand of brotherhood from us for a couple of hundred years."

"Unlike wars of the past, this coming conflict is not likely to end in a few months or even a few years. It may not be over in our lifetimes. Even so, it is the great calling of our time: a modern-day crusade against the agents and forces of evil. If we succeed in our mission, as I know we will, it will be the final crusade. We ask for the help of all Americans in this struggle, with the knowledge that once the American people put their hearts and minds into a cause, they cannot possibly fail.

"God bless you, and God bless the United States of America."

"God help us, every one," said Andrew Neponski.

CHAPTER 16

T THE END OF THE *time set by the Doge the envoys returned to the palace*
... this was the Doge's final word:
"My lords," he said, "we will tell you what we have decided, subject to
the approval of our Great Council and the people of Venice, and you may
consider whether you have the will and the means to go ahead.

"We will build horse transports to carry forty-five hundred horses and nine
thousand squires, with forty-five hundred knights and twenty thousand foot sergeants
traveling in ships. And we will agree to provide food for all these horses and people
for nine months. This is the minimum we would provide in return for four marks
per horse and two marks per man. All the terms we are offering you would be valid
for one year from the day of our departure from the port of Venice to do service to God
and Christendom, wherever that might take us. The total cost of what just has been
outlined would amount to 94,000 marks. And we will provide, for the love of God,
fifty armed galleys, on the condition that for as long as our association lasts we shall
have one half of whatever we capture on land or at sea, and you will have the other."

The envoys left, saying they would confer together and give their response the
next day ... The following day they came before the Doge and said, "Sir, we are ready
to confirm this arrangement." And the Doge said he would discuss the matter with
his people and tell the envoys what transpired.

On the morning of the third day, the Doge, who was very wise and valiant, assembled his Great Council, comprised of forty men who were also among the wisest in the land. And the Doge, by his clear wisdom and wit, brought them to agreement and approval ... Then he assembled ten thousand of the people in the Church of St. Mark, the most beautiful in the land, and bade them hear a Mass of the Holy Ghost, and pray to God for counsel on the requests and messages that had been addressed to them. And the people did so right willingly.

When the mass had been said, the Doge desired the envoys to humbly ask the people to assent to the proposed covenant. The envoys came into the church ... [and] Geoffrey of Villehardouin, the Marshal of Champagne, acted as spokesman and said unto them:

"Lords, the most high barons of France have sent us to you; and they cry for mercy, that you take pity on Jerusalem, which is in bondage to the Turks, and that for the sake of God you help to avenge the shame of Christ Jesus. And for this end they have elected to come to you, for they know full well that there is no other people having so great power on the seas as you and your people. And they commanded us to fall at your feet, and not to rise until you consent to take pity on the Holy Land which is beyond the seas."

Then the six envoys knelt at the feet of the people, weeping many tears. And the Doge and all the others burst into tears of pity and compassion, and cried with one voice, and lifted up their hands, saying: "We consent, we consent!"

All the good and beautiful words that the Doge then spoke, I cannot repeat to you. But the end of the matter was, that the covenants were to be made on the following day, and made they were, and devised accordingly. When they were concluded, it was notified to the council that we should go to Babylon (Cairo), because the Turks could be better destroyed in Babylon than in any other land; but to the folk at large it was only told that we were bound to go overseas. We were then in Lent 1201, and in the following year the barons and pilgrims were to be in Venice, and the ships readied for their coming.

When the treaties were duly indited [sic] and sealed, they were brought to the Doge in the grand palace, where had been assembled the great and the little council. And when the Doge delivered the treaties to the envoys, he knelt greatly weeping, and swore on holy relics faithfully to observe the conditions thereof, and so did all his council, which numbered fifty-six persons. And the envoys, on their side, swore to observe the treaties, and in all good faith to maintain their oaths and the oaths of their lords; and be it known to you that for great pity many a tear was there shed. And forthwith were messengers sent to Rome, to the Pope Innocent, that he might confirm this covenant—which he did right willingly.

Then did the envoys borrow five thousand marks of silver, and gave them to the Doge so the building of the ships might begin. And taking leave to return to their own land, they journeyed day by day until they came to Placentia in Lombardy. There they parted.

CHAPTER 17

TWILIGHT WAS DESCENDING AROUND THE vice president's residence at Number One Observatory Circle. Hornsby was wrapping up his briefing with Admiral Mike McCardle, who at Hornsby's insistence had been appointed CIA director at the beginning of the Cane Administration. The two men spoke daily, partly to keep Hornsby in the intelligence loop and partly to allow him to monitor what was being fed to George Cane at the president's morning security briefings.

Lately, these conversations took place over the phone on a secure line, with personal meetings limited to once or twice a week ever since a *Washington Post* reporter somehow got his hands on the visitor's log and discovered that McCardle was dropping in every day. The ensuing *Post* story used their meetings as further evidence of some vast, unspecified right-wing conspiracy.

"Okay, Mike." Hornsby leaned back in his chair. "What else you have for me?"

"We're almost done."

"I know there's something else, and I also know you're saving it to the end, so it's probably not good."

"Well, sir." McCardle hesitated. "Ever hear of Marilyn Monrovian?"

"Mike, what the hell are you talking about?"

"What about the Lavender Menace?"

"Weren't they the group that protested in front of the Supreme Court a few years back? Raised a ruckus, got themselves arrested?"

"That's them. They're a radical group dedicated to lesbian rights. The name comes from something Betty Friedan said at the beginning of the feminist movement. She called lesbians the lavender menace. She was afraid that being linked with them would endanger the feminist cause, prevent them from being taken seriously."

"I thought a number of feminists were lesbians, and vice versa."

"We won't go there, sir. The point is that lesbians feel they've always been treated as second-class citizens in the struggle for women's rights. After Friedan's comment, a group called the Lavender Menace was formed to protest the exclusion of lesbians from the women's movement. Rita Mae Brown, people like that."

"I think I remember that." He squinted at McCardle. "So what's this about Marilyn Monrovian?"

"She's a leader of the local chapter—they see themselves as the inheritors of the original group's cause. Real nasty piece of work. She has a police record longer than Bill Hampton's dick. Her real name is Carla Stennings."

"Should I ask why she doesn't go by Carla Stennings?"

"She would say that's the name given to her by the system of male oppression. Stennings is her father's name—she's not married, of course. So she took the name Marilyn Monrovian. All the leaders of this group have taken on names that they feel symbolize male exploitation of women."

"Hell." Hornsby grinned. "If they want to protest the exploitation of Marilyn Monroe, why don't they go picket the Kennedy compound?"

"You won't be laughing in a moment, sir."

"Then tell me."

"We think she might be having an affair with Courtney Cane."

"Jesus." Hornsby rubbed his bald head vigorously. "What did I do to deserve this."

McCardle was silent.

"What do you mean, you *think* she's having an affair?"

"We're not totally sure. They haven't been together in public, but Courtney's been seen leaving Stennings's apartment several times. It could be innocent enough—maybe dropping off some papers, attending a meeting, something like that."

"Mike. If the president's daughter is associating with felons, that's not innocent in the eyes of the public."

"True."

"How long does she stay when she visits?"

"We don't know. That is, we can't be precise."

"You don't know much, do you?"

"Sir, you didn't want a 24/7 tail on her. You said you didn't want it to be obvious. Those were your orders."

"Okay, you're right." Courtney Cane had been under surveillance since the beginning of the campaign, but Hornsby had insisted on keeping it low-key. *The last thing we need is the goddamn New York Times running a piece saying we're spying on the president's daughter,* he had told McCardle. "I think it's time that we stepped it up a notch or two. Just be careful."

"You mean, track her?"

"Not during the day. No one cares about that. But we need to know if she's spending the night."

"Got it."

"And Mike, I want *professionals* on this. Career people who know what they're doing. Not any idiot who just mustered out of the Marines and is looking for work."

"Right, boss. Understood."

"Just be careful," said Hornsby. "The president and I have to run for reelection someday, remember."

CHAPTER 18

THE TALL, GAUNT MAN THREADED his way across the parched and barren landscape. Although he used a walking stick for support, he had no physical infirmity. The stick was insurance against falling into the crevices of the rocks strewn across the mountain path. His face was solemn, almost mournful, and he was followed by an entourage of young men in loose-fitting white robes. He might have been mistaken for a pilgrim, except that in this isolated border region between Persepostan and Kabulistan there was really nowhere to go.

He turned toward the sounds of steps on the path and saw Fazil Ahmadi, his trusted chief of operations, running toward him. Salman al-Akbar smiled.

"I remember when I was young enough to run like that. Still, you should use caution—the path is treacherous."

"Sir, I have remarkable news!" Ahmadi panted. "I wanted to waste no time in telling you."

"I am anxious to hear your news."

"The young American president has decided to invade Sumeristan rather than Kabulistan."

"Is this so?" Al-Akbar stroked his long, wispy beard as he tried to absorb this information. "I'm not sure I understand."

"No one seems to understand yet, sir."

"How do we know this?"

"He will go on television tonight and make another speech. The news channels are full of speculation, but no one appears to know the reasoning for sure."

"Tell me more."

"Apparently, he has decided that Hussein Ghazi is the immediate threat, the one who must be dealt with first. He wants to remove Ghazi from power and replace him."

"Why is this?"

"According to CNN, the American government believes that Ghazi has large stockpiles of chemical weapons, and that he might even be working on a nuclear bomb."

"Weapons," al-Akbar laughed. "Everyone has weapons. As to the nuclear bomb, we know this is not true."

"The network that opposes him, MSNBC, is saying that this is a personal matter, that he wants to make up for his uncle's failure to get rid of Ghazi."

"Perhaps." Al-Akbar shook his head. "Even so, it makes no sense. It would be an act of incredible stupidity, and they are not stupid. Do you think this is a ruse to lure us out into the open, where we can be attacked?"

"No, sir. The news channels are talking of nothing else. The president is scheduled to go on the air in a few hours."

"How will he convince the Americans that Ghazi is the true villain, since we are the ones who attacked him?"

"We believe that CNN is only reporting what the government has leaked to them. They are saying that Ghazi has links to the attackers, and that he has given large amounts of support to Husam al-Din."

"And we also know this is not so." Al-Akbar stroked his beard again. "We have no more than one or two cells in each city, perhaps four in Bagdad. This is very curious."

"We will not be able to see the speech, of course, but the newspapers will carry the text. We will have them delivered by courier tomorrow."

"Allah be praised!" Al-Akbar raised his eyes and arms to the sky. "Our luck continues."

"The Americans have a saying, sir," said Ahmadi, who had attended college in Boston. "They say it is better to be lucky rather than good."

"Well …" His mentor smiled. "It seems we are both."

CHAPTER 19

BY THE TIME ABDUL TURNED fourteen, the Alghafaris were prospering. The family had moved into a small house with a modest garden, several miles from their old apartment, so the children could have their own rooms. There was no air conditioning, but the home was cooled by the shade of a half-dozen date palms.

Abdul's father was becoming more successful in the spice trade, but at a price. The hours were long, and he had less and less time for his family. Frequently he was not home for dinner, and sometimes did not return until the children were in bed. He tried to compensate on the weekends by spending time with Abdul and his eleven-year-old sister, but the gesture was usually unappreciated; the children had their own circles of friends, and didn't care to have their free time monopolized by their parents.

Abdul in particular was becoming a problem. He was argumentative and headstrong; he stayed out too late on weekends, and paid little attention in school. His grades had always been excellent, but now he was barely passing. His mother was frequently called to school to discuss his antisocial behavior, whether he was talking back to teachers or fighting with classmates.

There were other problems as well. Abdul had purchased a transistor radio with an earpiece, and he listened to it late into the night when he was supposed to be sleeping. He no longer spoke of going to America. This was not surprising, of course. After the 1991 invasion of Sumeristan, the United States had become the country's most hated enemy. Abdul's criticism of America would have been looked upon favorably by the Ghazi regime, and it might even have qualified him for a government job if his grades ever improved, but there were other things that greatly troubled his mother. He spent his evenings listening to radio stations run by radical Arab nationalists in the region, and although not particularly religious, he increasingly made vague references to the inevitable rise of Islam.

Like most parents of teenaged boys in Iraq, Abdul's mother was haunted by the memory of what had occurred at al-Mansour High School slightly less than a decade earlier.

Located three miles from the center of Baghdad, the Mansour neighborhood had always been upscale and expensive. It tended to attract mid-level government officials, families affluent enough to afford homes with security gates, servants, and even bodyguards. Their children attended the elite high school with the understanding that they, too, would someday be officials of importance within the regime.

After the 1991 U.S. invasion and the collapse of the Sumeri Army, cracks began to appear in the facade of Hussein Ghazi's absolute rule. Murmurs of dissent were heard for the first time, and some of those even found their way into the receptions and dinner parties of Mansour. For a dictator who postured himself as infallible, the total battlefield defeat had been humiliating. Ghazi loyalists in Mansour whispered doubts about the regime to their neighbors for the first time.

In the fall of 1991, the first graffiti appeared on the walls of the school. Initially they were mild: "Freedom for Sumeristan," or "First Persepostan, now us," referring to the desires of many radical Muslims to replace Ghazi's secular dictatorship with an Islamic state. Despite warnings from the principal and continual lectures by classroom teachers, the messages appeared most mornings throughout the school year, although they were erased almost immediately by nervous janitorial staff.

The graffiti appeared again with the start of the 1992 school year, but two things were different. The messages had grown more strident, proclaiming "Down with Hussein Ghazi" or "Death to the regime." More importantly, the school now had a new principal, a fierce Ghazi loyalist who was determined to wipe out any traces of dissent. Like his predecessor, he issued several general bans on student graffiti. When these proved ineffective, he called in representatives of Hussein Ghazi's dreaded security force.

The agents carefully went through the students' files. They interviewed teachers and encouraged them to pass along the names of young dissidents.

They also bribed students to turn in their classmates, offering the incentives of good grades and government jobs.

In the winter of 1992–1993, over forty students were rounded up and arrested. Some were children from modest backgrounds who commuted from other parts of the city, but a number came from the privileged households of Mansour. Those homes were ransacked as security personnel went through the families' possessions, searching for evidence of disloyalty.

The students were transported to Abu Ghraib prison, where all but two were tortured and hanged. Their families never saw them again or received any word of their fate, but their households were systematically persecuted for the rest of Hussein Ghazi's rule. Fathers who were government officials lost their jobs, and agents from the security services raided their homes several times each year, usually in the middle of the night, to terrorize the residents.

"We had no idea how far any of it would go," said one of the survivors, interviewed in exile in Persepostan. "We were just being kids. At most we thought we would get a slap on the wrist—certainly no one thought they'd be executed." It was not until much later, after Hussein Ghazi's overthrow, that the death certificates surfaced and the parents had their worst suspicions confirmed.

After a month in which she was called to school three times about Abdul fighting with other boys on the playground, his mother made an appointment with Kasim Hamdani. When the day arrived, she took the bus across town to see him.

"I am grateful for your time, Dr. Hamdani," she said as she sat down in his office. "I know you are busy, and I thank you."

Although his face was expressionless, his lips were pursed tightly together. "I have been looking through Abdul's school records," he said. Then, to her surprise, he smiled at her. "He seems quite rambunctious."

"I'm afraid so."

"Perhaps not much different from many fourteen-year-old boys, in my experience."

"We are very worried, sir. He has bought himself a transistor radio. It has an earpiece, but we are aware he listens to it late into the night. As far as we can tell, he is tuning in to some radical stations, some of which are in Persepostan."

"Hmm." His lips came back together, and he regarded her sympathetically. "That is dangerous."

"We understand how dangerous it is, sir. So far none of it has surfaced, but we are afraid he will say the wrong things to the wrong people." Tears formed in her eyes. "He is our only son, and it would break our hearts to lose him."

"And how do you think I can help you?"

"We want him to transfer here, to your school, to be under your direction."

Abdul's mother was not sitting in Hamdani's office by accident. The principal was known officially as a staunch defender of the regime, the leader of an academy that had produced many diplomats and civil servants. But in the neighborhoods of Baghdad, he had another reputation: that of a double agent. Under Hussein Ghazi, no one was free to voice their dissent for fear of the consequences. In the privacy of many families, Dr. Kasim Hamdani was known as someone who could teach your child to accommodate the government and prosper from it, until the day finally arrived when the regime could be changed.

"You realize that his grades are not good enough to allow for such a transfer."

"Recently, yes, you are correct."

"In fact, I hope I won't insult you when I say they are terrible."

"But that is only the last year or so. If you look back, you will see that Abdul has always been an excellent student."

"This is true."

"He needs guidance, Dr. Hamdani. He needs *your* guiding hand. Without it, I am afraid he will perish."

"I know you are concerned, but I believe you are exaggerating somewhat."

"What if he comes to believe the things he hears—that someday a religious state will rise here, as it did in Persepostan? He will join some radical groups, and eventually the regime will arrest him." She began to cry. "He is just a child, sir. Please help us."

As the tears flooded down Mrs. Alghafari's cheeks, the principal pushed a box of tissues toward the distraught mother. "Here is what I will do. He may come here for the first semester, on probation. We will set an academic threshold for him to attain in order to continue. He will have to stay after school at least three days each week, to attend a remedial program. And he must enroll in a special program conducted by me, a type of patriotic watchdog group. It meets once each week on Wednesdays, following class."

"Thank you, sir. Thank you."

"We'll see if we can get some of this radical nonsense out of his head. If so, we can transform him into a useful member of society."

"Thank you a thousand times. May Allah shower blessings on you."

"Do not worry." He patted her hand. "We will not fail."

CHAPTER 20

MAYBE IT WON'T BE THAT bad, ma'am."

"Trust me—it will be worse than you can possibly imagine." Jennifer Caldwell was notoriously mercurial. Just as she was unable to repress her delight when happy, she was equally incapable of concealing the disgust on her face now. "You don't know what this crew is capable of."

Mandy Parisi sat in the secretary's office at Foggy Bottom, trying unsuccessfully to cheer up her boss as they watched George Cane deliver another national address from the Oval Office. Cane had just announced the startling discovery that Hussein Ghazi's government in Sumeristan was a far greater threat to the country than the Dua Khamail, Husam al-Din, and the boogeyman put together.

"Since I last spoke to you from this office," Cane said in a grave voice, "I have reviewed intelligence that reveals the extent of the war preparations made by Hussein Ghazi in Sumeristan. Some of this data is shocking, and all of it is disturbing. For the past five or six years, stretching back into the administration of President Hampton, the government of Sumeristan has been producing chemical and biological weapons on an unprecedented scale.

"These are weapons of exceptional savagery and brutality. They are almost always fatal, and they cause irreversible damage even when they're not. For this reason, nearly two hundred countries, representing ninety-eight percent of the world's population, have signed on to the 1993 Chemical Weapons Convention. Hussein Ghazi has used these weapons before in warfare, and we have no doubt that he would do so again.

"In addition to the military threat posed by the current government of Sumeristan, there are humanitarian concerns. Hussein Ghazi has enforced one of the most brutal regimes in the region. He has systematically persecuted, tortured, and killed anyone who disagrees with him. His citizens live in a state of fear. There is no freedom of the press, of religion or assembly—none of the freedoms we hold so dear. In removing Hussein Ghazi from power, we would be performing an act of humanitarian kindness as well as well as eliminating a threat to our safety and security. Rather than be the epitome of a totalitarian state, Sumeristan could eventually become a beacon of democracy in the Middle East."

"Great," snorted Caldwell. "We're going to turn Baghdad into a replica of Omaha, Nebraska—an Arabic Epcot, where everybody eats hot dogs and goes to 4-H meetings."

"As your president," said Cane, "I feel it is imperative to stop Hussein Ghazi's chemical weapons program before can deliver them from airplanes or on the heads of missiles. We will immediately launch an all-out diplomatic effort to make him account for his stockpile of chemical agents and allow inspectors into the facilities to observe the extent of their development.

"When I first spoke to you after the horrific events of May first, I told you that the battle against the forces of evil would be a long and difficult one. Unfortunately, my assessment has not changed. We must be ready to respond to threats as they arise, but fighting on multiple fronts for a prolonged period of time will not be easy for the brave men and women of our armed forces. We need to be alert enough to prioritize threats as we see them, and it may well turn out that Hussein Ghazi's Sumeristan is a greater long-term threat to our safety and security than the Dua Khamail and Husam al-Din combined."

"What's his problem?" Parisi asked. "Why does he have such a bug up his ass about Hussein Ghazi?"

"It goes back to his uncle." Caldwell reclined on a sofa, sipping a Diet Coke. "Everybody at the time thought he should have gone all the way to Baghdad and removed Ghazi from office."

"And you don't agree?"

"Of course I don't agree," snapped Caldwell. "What the hell would we have done with Sumeristan after we captured it? It would have been a horrendous mistake. I don't think George Cane sees it that way, though, I believe he views it as unfinished business."

"So where's the pressure coming from?"

"From Hornsby, of course. From all the holdovers from the first Cane Administration. From the neocons. From the right-wing think tanks, the Heritage Foundation—all those geeks who want to make decisions they don't have to take responsibility for."

"Ma'am," said Parisi, "why don't you reach out to Bethany Hampton? You have a good relationship with her. She could give you a sense of what people are thinking in the Senate."

"I *had* a good relationship with her. That was before I agreed to stay on as secretary of state and enable these clowns. Anyway, we both know she'll be running for president next time around, so I'm sure she doesn't want to tip her hand—on this subject or any other."

"Well, do you think they have the intelligence?"

"God knows what they have. If they don't have it, they'll make it up."

"Ma'am, they can't do that."

"Don't think so? Did you ever read the Pentagon Papers?"

"Not all of it."

"Well, most of that was made up."

"Not by the same people, certainly."

"Not the same people, no, but by people very similar to them." Caldwell leaned her head back on the sofa and closed her eyes. "I swear, with every passing day this reminds me more and more of the Fourth Crusade."

"I'm not following you."

"I gather you didn't study history?"

"I majored in political science."

"Primatology." She laughed. "The study of the baboons in charge. Well, the Fourth Crusade was launched by the Pope around the year 1200. The original idea was for the expeditionary force to march across Egypt and take Jerusalem back from the Muslims. The crusaders went to Venice first, which was the richest trading nation in Europe at the time, and cut a deal with them for half of the profits of the Crusade in exchange for bankrolling them. At the last minute, though, they changed their plans and diverted to Constantinople. It was a tragic mistake."

"Why did they divert to Constantinople?"

"It turned out they couldn't afford to pay the Venetians the sum they agreed upon. The prince of the Byzantine Empire offered them financial backing if they would restore his deposed father to the throne as emperor."

"What's this got to do with Cane and Hornsby?"

"The emperor was murdered shortly after he was returned to the throne, and the Crusaders weren't paid. They decided to sack the city of Constantinople, which turned out to be a major diversion and distraction. Only a small percentage of them ever made it to the Holy Land."

"Well, you know the saying: Those that don't learn from history are doomed to repeat it."

"Mandy, please. If I wanted to watch Masterpiece Theater, I'd turn on PBS." She sat up and yawned. "The only piece of vaguely positive news here is that no one will blame me for it. They'll make Bayard Stevenson take the heat."

"You think so?"

"I know so. He's the only one who's believable. I'm a Democrat, so they can't trust me. And even the most naïve citizen is aware that these clowns have an agenda. I'm afraid this will be the crowning achievement of Bayard's career: tap-dancing for the public while George Cane plays war."

"Maybe they won't invade Sumeristan in the end."

"They'll invade," said Caldwell. "You can bet your degree on it."

At the apartment on Avenue Foch in Paris, the mood was somber as Selim Hanjuk and Ali Jebuti watched President Cane's second Oval Office address to the nation.

"And so, my fellow Americans, I ask for your support in the struggle to make America a safer place and rid the world of evil, wherever we may find it—in Hussein Ghazi's Sumeristan, in the tribal areas of Kabulistan, or right here at home among those who take freedom for granted. In the coming days, my administration will introduce a resolution to Congress authorizing me to use military force to combat the evildoers wherever I may find them.

"We will also ask for the establishment of a new government agency designed to ensure that those who sympathize with the cause of evil will not be able to operate freely within the boundaries of the United States. This new agency will have cabinet-level rank and be headed by Admiral Chester Baldwin, a career officer with a distinguished service record.

"I expect that Congress will debate both proposals vigorously, as is their responsibility. But I also expect swift passage of both laws, which will allow us to protect the freedoms all of us hold so dear.

"In closing, I want to assure you that while the fight for freedom and domestic tranquility may be ongoing, it is a fight we can and will win, with your support and God's help. God bless you, and God bless the United States of America."

"I suppose this means we're not going home soon," said Jebuti.

"Yes," replied Hanjuk.

"What will happen?"

"This young president will invade Sumeristan, to vindicate his uncle. Things will go well at first, but soon the Americans will find themselves in quicksand. It will be Vietnam all over again."

"How long will they be there?"

"Who knows? Perhaps a decade, perhaps longer. Until they declare victory and pull out."

"This is a sad development, sir."

"It is," said Hanjuk with a bitter smile. "Enjoy your chestnuts and your crepes, your sunsets and your evening strolls. We are not going anywhere."

CHAPTER 21

I
T TURNS OUT MY MOTHER was right," said Andrew Neponski. "Watching
TV really can rot your brain."

The Speaker sat in his spacious Capitol Hill office with his administrative
assistant and chief advisor, David Burnham, while George Cane addressed
the nation once again from the Oval Office. As the president outlined the case
for invading Sumeristan, Neponski grew more and more disgusted.

"You don't have to watch it, sir," said Burnham. "We can review the text
later and draft your response."

"I've told you before. I want to see his body language."

"And what does that tell you this time?"

"He's one confused cowboy. He's a bull rider at the rodeo, and he can't
figure out which of the animals is the least dangerous. At the last minute, he
chooses the one his uncle told him was safer."

"We need to be alert enough to prioritize threats as we see them," intoned
the president, "and it may well turn out that Hussein Ghazi's Sumeristan is a
greater long-term threat to our safety and security than the Dua Khamail and
Husam al-Din combined."

"You know what this reminds me of?" asked Neponski.

"What, sir?"

"*1984*. You remember the book?"

"Vaguely. I think I read it in high school."

"The government of the superstate, Oceania, was constantly changing their policies, as all governments do. But each time they did an about-face, they had to go back and rewrite all the history up to that point, just to prove they were right. They were at war with Eurasia, but suddenly they were at war with Eastasia. And thus they had *always* been at war with Eastasia."

"I don't follow …"

"America is at war with Sumeristan, not Kabulistan," Neponski explained, swirling the ice cubes in his Crown Royal. "America has always been at war with Sumeristan."

"Do you think this is Hornsby's doing?"

"Not him specifically, but the whole bunch—the entire conservative mafia. All the guys left over from Herbert Cane's administration. They've been waiting for their moment of vindication ever since. George Cane is just their front man. He's the face guy. We knew that from the start."

"We'll need a response, sir."

"Go ahead and draft it. We find the president's speech to be interesting and somewhat surprising, as we imagine many Americans do. We eagerly await the evidence to support his assertion that Sumeristan is the true threat, and we look forward to supporting him after we've received it and have time to review it. Show it to me before you send it out."

"Yes, sir." Burnham shifted in his chair. "You know, the resolution will be coming down the pike very shortly."

"I imagine so."

"What's your thinking?"

"It depends on what he comes up with. If the intelligence actually exists, and it proves what he says, we're in a bind."

"A bind, yes." Burnham hesitated. "You might want to prepare yourself for the possibility that you'll actually have to support him this time."

"Give me a fucking break, David. I'm the Speaker of the House, and the de facto leader of my party. I can't support his maniacal scheme unless he can stick a Geiger counter up Hussein Ghazi's ass and have it come out radioactive."

Burnham had received the first phone call a few days earlier. The caller identified himself as a member of the Log Cabin Republicans, a gay group devoted to working for change within the framework of the GOP.

"Well," Burnham laughed, "I'm a Democrat. In fact, I'm Andrew Neponski's AA."

"I know that," said the voice on the other end. "Actually, we think you're kind of cute. We think you might secretly be one of us."

"*What?* You think I might be a Republican?"

"No, sweetie, that's not what I meant."

"I beg your pardon?"

"We think it would be marvelous if a Democrat of your stature could lend his support to the president's efforts against terrorism. You could be very influential with your boss, and be a true patriot in the bargain. It could be our little secret—or one of them."

Burnham told the caller to fuck off and hung up, but he did not sleep that night. There was nothing in his Kansas upbringing to prepare him for the possibility of coming out of the closet. He knew the calls would continue. His ailing mother was in her eighties, and he had to be available if a family member tried to reach him—he was not in a position to ignore the phone.

"If the intelligence is convincing," he told Neponski now, "you may have a very difficult choice. The May Day attacks were less than a month ago, and the public is still traumatized. They're begging for a display of national unity."

"Let's see what he comes up with, and we can gauge public sentiment at that time. That's what we have pollsters for. All I can tell you is, it'd better be good."

CHAPTER 22

EORGE CANE SELDOM GOT ANGRY. His cheerful and self-controlled persona had been forged though dozens of college fraternity parties, countless National Guard weekends, and hundreds of the outdoor barbecues and equestrian events that comprised political fund-raisers in his home state. Those who knew him best recognized that he was repressing his anger when the upper part of his ears flushed bright crimson.

Today, they were deep red.

"What the hell is going on here?" He tossed the piece of paper on the desk with disgust, as Robert Hornsby and Bayard Stevenson sat facing him in the Oval Office. "Someone explain this to me. *Three* countries, for God's sake? My uncle had thirty-two."

"This is what we've got for now, sir," said Hornsby. "Remember that it's a work in progress. More nations will likely join up."

"Although I wouldn't count on them to send troops, Mr. President," said Stevenson. "Expressions of support will probably be the best we can hope for."

"What Bayard means," said Hornsby, shooting the general a sidelong glance, "is that we can probably assemble a substantial list of nations that support the liberation effort in Sumeristan, although they might not be able to send troops because they lack standing armies."

"What kinds of nations?"

"Right off the bat, sir, I'm confident we can get the Solomon Islands, Micronesia, and Palau."

"What the hell are you talking about, Bob? What kinds of countries are those? I've never even heard of the last one. What was it again?"

"Palau, sir. It's an island republic in the Western Pacific."

"You've got to be kidding me." He picked up the memo and stared at it again. "England, Australia, and Poland. *Poland*, for God's sake. Is that it?"

"For the moment, yes. But remember—"

"Where's France?"

"It's a delicate situation for them," said Hornsby. "They have a large Muslim population."

"Wait until some of them fly a plane into the Eiffel Tower. They'll feel differently. What about Italy? No Arabs there, as far as I know."

"Internal politics, sir. The government is just too shaky at the moment, and something like this could topple it."

"I guess that's what we get for saving their asses from Mussolini." The president got up and walked to the window as Hornsby and Stevenson remained silent. "You know, I took everybody's advice and kept Jennifer Caldwell on board. So now I have a secretary of state who looks like a bullfrog *and* is a fire-breathing liberal. She's supposed to be good at making nice with people—that's all those folks are really good for, at the end of the day. Joining hands and singing *kumbaya*. And this is what I get: England, Australia, and Poland."

"Sir." Stevenson cleared his throat. "May I be frank?"

"Go ahead."

"I think many people are confused about our desire to invade Sumeristan and topple Hussein Ghazi from power."

"Why would they be confused about that?"

"Directly after the May Day attacks, you identified the Dua Khamail as a major terrorist threat. You said you believed that they were in league with Husam al-Din, and implied that they had sponsored, or at least sanctioned, the attacks. In your address to the nation, you said they had allowed Husam al-Din to set up training camps in the tribal areas of Kabulistan—and that in order to rid the country and the world of that threat, we had to restore the legitimate government of Selim Hanjuk to power. Now you're saying that you want to invade Sumeristan and topple Hussein Ghazi. There's no evidence that he had anything to do with this. A lot of people just don't get it."

"General, Hussein Ghazi is a bad guy."

"I'm sure he is."

"He tried to assassinate my uncle. Maybe you forgot about that."

"Not at all, sir. I just don't see the evidence that he's linked to Husam al-Din or is a terrorist threat."

"Don't worry about that, General." The president sat down again and looked at the two men. "Bob is working on developing that."

"Developing it, sir?"

"We have people in place," said Hornsby. "It's just a matter of mining the information and assembling it in a form that makes sense."

Cane nodded.

"In any case," said Stevenson, "most of the May Day hijackers were Saudis."

"Don't even think about it," said Hornsby. "Saudi Arabia is our only ally in the region."

"Really? I thought Israel was our only ally in the region."

"You know very well what I mean."

"What he means," chuckled Cane, "is that we don't want everybody here riding around on bicycles for the next two hundred years. Don't forget about the oil reserves in Sumeristan, either. Most of them haven't even been developed."

"Sir?" said Hornsby.

"Yes?"

"It's not wise to mention oil in this context. We don't want the media to get the idea that's what this is about, and then plant that idea in people's heads."

"Whatever." The president came over and put his hand on Stevenson's shoulder. "When we have all the facts, General, it should be more than enough to convince people that Sumeristan is the place to start. Provided, of course, that the evidence is presented clearly, in a manner that the public can understand."

"Well," Stevenson said uneasily, "that's why the two of you were elected."

"Actually, Bayard," said Hornsby, "we were thinking of a different approach. We think it might be best to take politics out of it, so that no one can question our motives in good faith."

"That's right, General," said the president. "When the time comes, we'd like you to make the case for the invasion of Sumeristan to the American people."

"Sir—"

"You're the best person to do it," said Hornsby, "because you're perceived as a moderate on this issue."

"I'm not a moderate." *Shit*, thought Stevenson. *The wrath of Hornsby. Take one step off the reservation and get your foot chopped off.* "My views on the use of military intervention have been well known for a long time. I believe you have to first identify the target, then crush it with overwhelming force."

"Understood and agreed," said Hornsby. "But I believe you stated publicly that you weren't sure that Sumeristan was a terrorist threat."

"I believe I said I hadn't seen the evidence. If it exists, it hasn't been shared with me."

"It will be."

"Well, General?" The president smiled. "Can we count on you?"

"I'm a team player, sir. You know that. If you show me intelligence that links Hussein Ghazi with Husam al-Din and verifies that he's a threat to the United States, I'll be happy to share it with the American people."

"Good, good."

"But even assuming the intelligence holds up, I think it's very important not to take our eye off the ball in Kabulistan. The American people want Salman al-Akbar's head on a platter. Regardless of what happens in Sumeristan, we have to reassure them that we're still committed to hunting him down."

"Absolutely," said Hornsby. "We can send Special Forces to the tribal areas."

"What did you have in mind, sir?" asked Stevenson. "An address to a joint session of Congress?"

"Something grander than that," mused the president. "Maybe a speech to the General Assembly of the U.N."

"With all due respect, wouldn't Jennifer Caldwell be the best person in that context?"

"You're the secretary of defense," said Cane. "You're the hero of Panama. The American people trust you."

"Sir—"

"You're our man."

At least this puts them on the hot seat, thought Stevenson. *They'll either have to give me the intelligence—or make it up.*

CHAPTER 23

A FTER EASTER, AND TOWARD WHITSUNTIDE *in June 1202, the pilgrims began to leave their own country ... So they journeyed through Burgundy and the mountains of Jura, and through Lombardy, and began to assemble at Venice, where they were lodged on an island which is called St. Nicholas in the port.*

At that point started from Flanders a fleet that carried a good number of men-at-arms ... Very fair was this fleet, and rich and great was the reliance that the Count of Flanders and the pilgrims placed on it, because very many of their good sergeants were journeying therein. But ill did these keep the faith they had sworn to the count, because they and others like them became fearful of the great perils that the expedition of Venice had undertaken.

Thus did the Bishop of Autun fail us, and Guignes the Count of Forez, and Peter Bromont, and many people besides, who were greatly blamed therein; and of little worth were the exploits they performed where they did go. And many of the French failed us as well, who avoided the passage to Venice because of the danger; and went instead to Marseilles, whereof they received shame, and were much blamed, and great were the mishaps that afterwards befell them.

Now let us speak of the pilgrims, of whom a great part had already come to Venice. Count Baldwin of Flanders had already arrived there, and many others, and tidings were brought to them that many of the pilgrims were traveling by other ways, and from other ports. This troubled them greatly, because they would thus be unable to fulfill the promise made to the Venetians, and find the moneys that were due.

So they took counsel together and agreed to send envoys to meet the pilgrims, and to meet Count Louis of Blois and Chartres, who had not yet arrived, and beseech them to have pity on the Holy Land beyond the sea, and show them that no other passage, save that from Venice, could be of profit.

They rode until they came to Pavia in Lombardy. There they found Count Louis with a great many knights and men of note and worth; and by encouragements and prayers prevailed on many to proceed to Venice who otherwise would have fared from other ports, and by other ways.

Nevertheless many men of note proceeded by other ways to Apulia ... a great company of knights and sergeants, whose names are not recorded. Thus was the expedition of those who went from Venice greatly weakened; and much evil befell them therefrom, as you shall shortly hear.

Thus did Count Louis and the other barons wend their way to Venice; and they were received there joyfully and with feasting, and took lodging in the island of St. Nicholas with those who had come before. Goodly was the expedition, and worthy were the men. And the Venetians held a market, rich and abundant, of all things needful for horses and men. And the fleet they had readied was so goodly and fine that never did any Christian man see one goodlier or finer. The galleys and transports were sufficient for at least three times as many men as were in the expedition.

Ah! The grievous harm and loss when those who should have come thither sailed instead from other ports! Right well if they had kept their tryst, would Christendom have been exalted, and the land of the Turks abased! The Venetians had fulfilled all their undertakings, and above measure, and they now summoned the barons and counts to fulfill theirs and make payment, since they were ready to start.

The cost of each man's passage was now levied throughout the expedition; and there were people enough who said they could not pay for their passage, and the barons took from them such money as they had. So each man paid what he could. When the barons had thus claimed the cost of the passages, and when the payments had been collected, the monies came to less than the sum due—yea, by more than half.

Then the barons met together and said: "Lords, the Venetians have well fulfilled their undertakings, and above measure. But we cannot fulfill ours in paying for our passages, seeing we are too few in number; and this is the fault of those who have journeyed from other ports. For God's sake therefore let each contribute all that he has, so that we may fulfill our covenant; for better it is that we should give all we have, than lose what we have already paid, and prove false to our covenants; for if this expedition remains here, the rescue of the land overseas comes to naught."

Great then was the dissension among the main part of the barons and the other folk, and they said: "We have paid for our passages, and if they will take us, we will go willingly; but if not, we will inquire and look for other means of passage." And they spoke thus because they wished that the expedition should fall to pieces and each return to his own land. But the other party said, "Much rather would we give all we have and go penniless with the expedition, than that the expedition should fall to pieces and fail; for God will doubtless repay us when it so pleases Him."

Then the Count of Flanders began to give all that he had and all that he could borrow, and so did Count Louis, and the Marquis, and the Count of Saint-Paul, and those who were of their party. Then might you have seen many a fine vessel of gold and silver borne in payment to the palace of the Doge. And when all had been brought together, there was still wanting, of the sum required, 34,000 marks of silver. Then those who had kept back their possessions and not brought them into the common stock, were right glad, for they thought now surely that the expedition must fail and go to pieces. But God, who advises those who have been ill-advised, would not so suffer it.

Then the Doge spoke to his people, and said unto them:

"Signors, these people cannot pay more; and in so far as they have paid at all, we have benefited by an agreement which they cannot now fulfil. But our right to keep this money would not everywhere be acknowledged; and if we so kept it we should be greatly blamed, both us and our land. Let us therefore offer them terms.

"The King of Hungary has taken from us Zara in Sclavonia, which is one of the strongest places in the world; and never shall we recover it with all the power that we possess, save with the help of these people. Let us therefore ask them to help us to reconquer it, and we will remit the payment of the debt of 34,000 marks of silver, until such time as it shall please God to allow us to gain the moneys by conquest, we and they together."

Thus was agreement made. Much was it contested by those who wished that the host should be broken up. Nevertheless the agreement was accepted and ratified.

CHAPTER 24

YOU SEEM ANGRY, ABDUL."
The young man slouched in his chair during his first meeting with Kasim Hamdani, trying to convey to the principal that he was not impressed with him or his academy.

"Right now, I'm angry at many things."

"Such as?"

"I have to wake up before dawn and sit on a bus for nearly one hour to get here. I'm separated from all my friends. And I'm surrounded by students who are parrots for the regime."

"I see. And you feel that all this is unfair?"

"Of course it's unfair. You don't have to take the bus to get here, do you?"

"No, I don't. A car picks me up in the morning and drives me here."

"That proves my point."

"Here's what it proves, young man: You can apply yourself in school and make something of yourself, and someday you can be driven to work in a car. Or you can be angry and take the bus for the rest of your life. Which sounds better?"

The scene at Abdul's house, when his parents informed him that he would be commuting to the new school, was one of the ugliest the family had ever witnessed. Abdul's father was forced to be firmer with him than he had been since the child was born. When Abdul threatened to run away, his father confiscated his transistor radio and his Nike sneakers, ignored his threats, and grounded him until he relented.

"At least," he told the principal now, "I can think my own thoughts on the bus and be my own person."

"Really? What thoughts are those?"

"Not everyone is living like this, even in the Arab world. There are places where the religion of Islam is respected."

"So," said Hamdani. "You are a devout Muslim?"

"I wouldn't say devout, no."

"You pray five times each day?"

"No."

"You read the Koran?"

"No."

"You observe the halal dietary laws?"

"No, I don't."

"You sound like quite a Muslim."

"That is because the religion of Allah is not revered here, as it is in some other places."

"Such as?"

"Persepostan."

"Ah, Persepostan. Do you believe you would be more of a Muslim if you forbade women to work, drive automobiles, or educate themselves?"

"Well—no."

"Do you think you would be more of a Muslim if you stoned adulterers to death?" Hamdani seemed to be enjoying himself now. "If you were able to control the thoughts and actions of others, just as the people you now criticize?"

"I do not believe things are that way in Persepostan."

"Why not? Because they do not advertise it on the radio? Tell me, have you heard of the Chain Murders?"

"No."

"Since 1988, nearly a hundred intellectuals and thinkers have been assassinated in Persepostan. These were writers, poets, philosophers, broadcasters—people who were doing something with their lives other than complaining and worrying about what kind of sneakers they wore. Everyone knows the government is behind the murders, but they are too afraid to say so."

"Is this true?"

"I'll tell you what is true, Abdul. The people who run Persepostan are petty criminals. They may parade around in clerical robes, but they are no different than criminals in military uniforms."

"And this is the reason why I have to support the regime?"

"No. Let me explain to you why you must support the regime. Sumeristan is not a world power. Neither is Persepostan. We will never be like America or Russia. They were the ones who created this situation. Fifty years ago, they divided the region into spheres of influence to suit themselves, much as you might claim one corner of the playground to play football. If this regime is toppled, another one will take its place."

"Some people think that a new caliphate will rise," said Abdul, "and that our region will be restored to its former glory. Then we will not have to take orders from America or Russia."

"That is nonsense. But if it ever did happen, it would be no different from the caliphate of old. Many people would die in the process. You can choose to be one of them. Or you can ride the bus and be an angry young man, thinking secret angry thoughts. Or you can be driven to work in a car."

"Are there no other possible destinies?"

"Perhaps there are, perhaps there are not. But in the short term, Abdul, this is what you will do: You will attend my Wednesday afternoon meetings, and you will learn something about what is really going on in the world. You will begin to put things into a different perspective."

"I suppose I have no choice."

"For the moment, no. But in time, you will realize that it is actually an honor. You will begin to revise some of your misinformed opinions." Hamdani smiled. "In fact, I think someday you may become one of my most valuable assistants."

CHAPTER 25

IN THE DAYS FOLLOWING GEORGE Cane's decision to invade Sumeristan, the last vestiges of the new president's honeymoon with the press dissipated quickly. "Mr. Cane is not to be envied," began a *New York Times* editorial.

After a mere four months in office, he faces a decision that is daunting in its implications and consequences. He must decide exactly how to respond to a terrorist threat that is both global and amorphous. This conspiracy has no discernible face, save for the visage of Salman al-Akbar sneering at us from his headquarters in the tribal area between Kabulistan and Persepostan.

The administration now claims to have intelligence detailing the role Hussein Ghazi played in the events of May 1, along with evidence of his weapons development: chemical, biological, and possibly even nuclear. This intelligence surfaces in the wake of Mr. Cane's initial assertion that the Dua Khamail government of Kabulistan was behind the attacks. The public is confused, and justifiably so. Along with them, we await clarification.

We can only hope that the confusion over the source of our security threat does not extend to the president and his inner circle. We fervently wish that he is receiving accurate information and sage advice. If so, he will be a glorious figure in American history. If not, his excursion into

Sumeristan will be the modern equivalent of the Bay of Pigs invasion, and the consequence will haunt us for decades to come.

The *Washington Post* was considerably less gracious. The paper ran a cartoon depicting Cane as a cowboy decked out in chaps, spurs, and a ten-gallon hat. He had a lasso in his hand and a bewildered look on his face as he squinted at three bulls labelled "Sumeristan," "Kabulistan," and "Persepostan." The caption read: "Which one is easier to rope?"

The *Post* also ran an editorial.

For the ultimate triumph of the neoconservative revolution, George Cane has decided to even the score with Hussein Ghazi. In a scene eerily reminiscent of the ending to the first Godfather *movie, he is determined to settle all the family business. This determination is not so much his, of course, but the sentiment of his uncle's advisors who surround him like gleeful ventriloquists. Very shortly, the secretary of defense will present his case to the American people and the world. The details of his brief will be less important than the reality that will set in after Cane's Sumeristan adventure is finished. The bravado of the exuberant, hard-riding Texan is likely to vanish quickly when he awakens to discover that he is the Mayor of Baghdad.*

Of course, there was support on the other side of the political spectrum. The *Washington Times*, predictably enough, staunchly defended the president in an editorial titled "The Naysayers of the Left":

First they told us that Russia could never acquire an atomic bomb. Then they said that Vietnam couldn't be won, that the Berlin Wall would never come down, and that the Reagan Revolution couldn't possibly succeed. Now they're telling us that George Cane shouldn't invade Sumeristan, and even worse, that the president's desire to rid the world of an evil tyrant, a man who has been hostile the United States for decades, is some sort of personal vendetta.

The professional naysayers who comprise the liberal wing of the Democrat establishment have one thing in common: They weren't elected. They lack a comprehensive view of the intelligence that is convincing the president to invade Sumeristan and topple Hussein Ghazi. The secretary of defense will share some of that information with the public in his upcoming address to the U.N., and more of it will likely be revealed to the opposition leaders in Congress. When they hear it, they will be compelled to search for shreds of their lost patriotism and support the president's plan.

We believe that George Cane was elected for a reason, and that the millions of voters who gave him his resounding victory perceive him as we do: a man of deep faith, who is not ashamed to rely on the guiding hand of God to safeguard this nation.

Robert Hornsby expected the worst as he was ushered into the Oval Office after the morning security briefing. Instead he found a relaxed George Cane sitting behind his desk, playing with his favorite spaniel.

"Morning, sir." Hornsby hesitated. "You look chipper today."

"Sure thing, Bob." Cane grabbed a plastic ring and tossed it across the room for the dog to retrieve. "It's a beautiful day in the neighborhood."

"I gather you haven't read the papers."

"Oh, I skimmed them," said the president. "I wasn't really concerned with the details. I imagine it was predictable enough."

I'll be damned, thought Hornsby. *He's turning out to be a regular Reagan.*

"The key thing, though," said Cane, "is how General Stevenson is doing. I want to make sure he's up to the job."

"He'll be fine, sir. The agency has been briefing him for the past few days. When the speech is ready, he'll rehearse it several times at Langley to make sure it's airtight."

"We need to be careful, of course. He should reveal enough to make the public aware of the gravity of the situation, but not too much that Hussein Ghazi is aware of our plan."

"Absolutely, sir." *Go ahead*, he thought, fighting back a smile. *Tell me how to run the agency.* "It's a balancing act, to be sure. That's why Mike McCardle is going over it so carefully with him."

"Excellent."

"As he said, sir, he's a team player." Hornsby smiled now. "He's a soldier, after all. He'll follow orders."

"Why don't you quit?" asked Beverly Stevenson.

She and her husband were finishing a private dinner at their home in Potomac, Maryland—a rare occurrence, given the demands of the secretary's job and the amount of travel that was frequently required.

"Because I'm not a quitter."

"Bayard—"

"Remember what they said about Bob Dole during the 1996 campaign? After the poor guy left the Senate to focus on trying to beat Hampton?"

"He was a weak candidate to begin with."

"Of course he was. But that didn't stop Hampton's campaign from roasting him to death. Anyway, this is a different situation. If I quit now, it undermines the Sumeristan invasion completely. It sends a message to everyone that the intelligence is spotty. Hell, it undermines Cane's presidency almost at the start."

"Is the intelligence spotty?"

"How am I supposed to know? They haven't shown me everything, and I don't know the sources. Every time I ask, I'm told it was a combination of intercepts, inside informers, and operatives in the field."

"So what's their plan?"

"You know I can't tell you that, Beverly."

"I don't mean his invasion plan." She shook her head. "Invading Sumeristan should be as difficult as driving from here to New York. Even I know that. What about afterward? What do they think they'll do after they remove Hussein Ghazi?"

"Damned if I know. I keep asking, but I don't get a straight answer. This is not like Kabulistan, where would could have gone in, toppled the Dua Khamail and turned the government over to Selim Hanjuk: your country, your problem."

"Isn't there an organized opposition?"

"Organized, maybe, but not out in the open. Hussein Ghazi has systematically tortured and killed anybody who even looked at him the wrong way. The opposition is buried so far underground that we don't know where most of them are. It'll take us months to even find them."

"Do you think this is about oil, Bayard?"

"It might be, partly, but they're not going to admit it. All they're going to talk about is ridding the world of an evil dictator and planting the seeds of democracy in his place."

"This sounds like a no-win situation. Please think about quitting."

"And do what? Become a Democrat? Write a book, similar to the one Jennifer Caldwell is probably typing up right now, telling the world what a bunch of half-baked zealots these guys are?"

"Why not go back to the Empowerment Alliance? You thought that was valuable work."

"It was." Bayard Stevenson pushed himself back from the table. "The problem is that those kids took me seriously. I kept lecturing them about how they had to give the system a chance, to work within it. A lot of them listened to me and joined the army. Now George Cane is going to send them off to get killed in Sumeristan."

"It sounds like he's going to send them either way."

"Let me complete the mission, Beverly." He rose and headed for his office. "Then I can think about quitting."

CHAPTER 26

ENERAL BAYARD STEVENSON STOOD ERECT at the podium of the U.N. General Assembly, calmly delivering his message to a packed hall. "We do know," he recited in a monotone voice, "that Hussein Ghazi had numerous contacts with international brokers of nuclear material, brokers on the level of A.Q. Kahn. One of these go-betweens made five or six trips to Sumeristan within a two-year period, meeting personally with Ghazi in Bagdad. What is unclear to us at this time is the extent of the material that may or may not have been transferred.

"Sumeristan's nuclear centrifuges have not been accessible to international inspectors for more than five years. These centrifuges were rudimentary the last time we saw them, but we have no idea if this is still the case. They are currently buried underground, out of the reach of our intelligence capabilities to photograph them. They may have become more sophisticated, but there is no clear way for us to determine if this is true."

"Damn," muttered William Hampton, former president of the United States. "He cuts a fine figure, doesn't he? Just look at him—is he the guy you want battling the forces of evil, or what?"

"Shitty speaker, though," said his wife, Bethany, Senator from New York. "You'd think they'd at least have sprung for elocution lessons."

The Hamptons watched the speech in the study of their house in upstate New York, which they had purchased in 1998 to establish residency for Bethany's Senate run.

"Naw," said Bill Hampton. "He's the real deal. Just look at him. Even out of uniform, he looks like a superhero."

"How nice for them."

"We tried to get him to join the Democratic Party, you remember, but he wouldn't hear of it. We would have had a better chance with Eisenhower."

"He would have made a good Democrat," said his wife bitterly. "He's a terrific liar."

"What we're far less unclear about," continued Stevenson, "is the extent of his chemical and biological capabilities. We're aware of at least fifteen concealed production sites scattered around the country, with several dozen insulated vans capable of transporting the material throughout the region. We strongly suspect that a great deal of this material has already been weaponized."

"What the hell does he mean, he *suspects* it?" asked Bethany Hampton. "I *suspect* a lot of things, for Christ's sake."

"Why are you so pissed off about this?"

"Because I see where it's going. It's an appeal to patriotic Americans everywhere. Here's the way they'll set it up: If you don't support an invasion, you're an enemy of the state."

"Don't tell me you're seriously considering supporting this?"

"Bill, what choice do I have? If I oppose it and want to run in 2008, they'll paint me as unpatriotic—a typical liberal, weak on defense. This won't be over by then, trust me."

"This will never be over."

"Then I better prepare myself to bite the bullet and support him. Because if I don't, they'll be able to say that their campaign against terrorism was torpedoed by the Democrats."

"We call on Hussein Ghazi," said Bayard Stevenson, "as we have many times in the past, to open his weapons facilities to international inspectors once again and become accountable for his buildup of offensive material. We urge him to do this before a conflagration engulfs the region, a catastrophe that could easily be avoided by a show of cooperation on his part. And if he will not do this, if he resolutely refuses to rejoin the community of peaceful nations, we ask for the support of the Security Council to disarm him against his will."

"Damn," said Bill Hampton again. "You know what I don't get?"

"I imagine you'll tell me."

"How can this guy be so lucky?"

"Stevenson?"

"No, George Cane." He took a sip of his drink. "I was telling the world about Salman al-Akbar for years, and nobody paid the slightest bit of attention to me. Remember when we thought we had him cornered, and we bombed the facility? He got away, they pretended that it was a factory making toys for children, and all the press could talk about was how I engineered the bombing to distract folks from my domestic problems."

"If you hadn't been fucking half the interns on your staff," said Bethany, "maybe they wouldn't have thought that."

"I thought we were done talking about that."

"You brought it up," she said with disgust. "Some people get lucky, others get what they deserve."

"In closing," said Stevenson, "we ask this body to live up to its charter and its mandate. The United States has no desire to act unilaterally, in this case or in any other. But to maintain freedom around the world, we require the cooperation of our security partners. Do not shrink from this responsibility. Join us in assuring that our children and grandchildren may grow up in peace, unfettered by the evil designs of tyrants and dictators."

"Luckiest fucking people on the planet," said Bill Hampton.

"No," replied his wife calmly. "You are the luckiest fucking person on the planet."

CHAPTER 27

WHEN THEY WERE FINALLY PRESENTED to Congress, the two resolutions were predictably vague.

The Resolution for the Use of Force in the Middle East contained few details beyond the responsibility of the president to contain terrorist threats wherever he found them in the region. Andrew Neponski and many others in his party noted that Sumeristan was not specifically mentioned. It was, in effect, a blank check for George Cane and his team to carpet-bomb anyone at any time.

The Resolution for National Security was perhaps more ominous, although few people saw it at that moment. It authorized the creation of a cabinet-level agency to oversee threats to the American homeland, with wide-reaching powers to regulate traffic at border crossings and airports. George Cane had already announced that the agency would be headed initially by retired Admiral Chester Baldwin, who would have authority to spy on U.S. citizens suspected of being in league with the enemy.

"Sir, what do you think of the president's proposals?"

The news outlets swarmed Neponski on the Capitol steps on the day the resolutions were sent to the Hill, as the Speaker attempted to leave for the evening.

"It's the Tonkin Gulf Resolution for the new millennium," spat Neponski.

"Does that mean you won't support it, sir?"

"What it means," he said with visible irritation, "is that we will consult among ourselves, and then engage in a vigorous and transparent public debate, as it is our duty to do. This is still a democracy, despite what the Cane administration might think."

"I have to tell you that you may have overreached a bit, sir," said David Burnham the next morning as they sat in the Speaker's office.

"Forgive me," said his boss. "I was trying to go home and have dinner with my family. Several dozen people shoved microphones in my face. How do you expect me to behave?"

"There's always the rear exit, if you need it."

"Sure. I could put on a disguise—a fake beard and glasses. For the future, we could have a helicopter pick me up when I want to avoid the press. It would make great video on the evening news."

"Sir—"

"And for the record, I have no desire to avoid them. Somebody has to call this as they see it before these bastards get to create the entire reality."

"Sir?"

"Yes?"

"These guys exterminated three thousand of our citizens, and everybody is waiting for our response."

"It won't kill them to wait a few weeks."

"No," said Burnham, "but it might kill us."

Andrew Neponski followed Scott Leventhal into the vice president's inner sanctum at the Executive Office Building.

"Andy!" said Hornsby enthusiastically. "How the hell are you?"

"Just fine, sir."

If you ever talk to Hornsby, an old Democratic congressional hand had told Neponski shortly after he arrived on the Hill, *remember that the friendlier he is toward you, the less he likes you. If he grasps your hand and looks you in the eye, he hates your guts.*

"Come in, come in." Hornsby took the Speaker's hand and held it firmly while he fixed his earnest gaze on him. His look was genial but sincere. "You're looking well."

"So are you, sir. Considering everything that's been going on."

"It's Bob, Andy, just plain Bob. As it's always been." He slapped Neponski on the back. "I used to call my Dad 'Sir' before I figured out he was just a guy like me."

"Thank you."

"Please have a seat." The two men settled in across from each other. "So what's on your mind? What brings you here today from the lofty regions of the Hill?"

"I think you know why I'm here, sir—I mean, Bob."

"It's those resolutions, I bet."

"Correct."

"So are you going to support us on this, Andy? Are we on the same team?"

"I'm not sure. I didn't find General Stevenson's U.N. speech to be particularly convincing."

"You seem to be in the minority, Andy. His speech was one of the most popular TV events since the Super Bowl. And our pollsters tell us that sixty-three percent of the American people thought he was convincing."

"That sixty-three percent wasn't voting in Congress, Bob. Not one of them was the Speaker."

"Okay." Hornsby leaned back in his chair and regarded his adversary. "What's your problem with this?"

"I'm going to give you a hypothetical, Bob."

"Go ahead."

"Say you're wrong. Say the intelligence is somehow faulty. Say the situation on the ground changes between now and then. What are you going to do?"

"Exactly what we said we were going to do: secure a liberated Sumeristan, free of the tyrant Hussein Ghazi."

"What then?"

"Whatever we want—that is to say, whatever the situation on the ground warrants. We go back to the original plan and invade Kabulistan. Destroy the Dua Khamail, restore Selim Hanjuk to power."

"In the meantime, what happens in Sumeristan?"

"Obviously I can't say, because I don't know. We assume that the opposition forces can be invested with the future of the country. It's their country, after all. We'll have to play it by ear."

"By ear."

"Yes."

"And you think that playing it by ear is an appropriate outcome for the invasion of a sovereign country? Has it occurred to you that these people will expect us to do something for them, after we destroy their infrastructure and kill their leader?"

"I believe we'll be greeted as liberators."

"I think so too. But what about the next day, the week after that, the month after that? What do we do then?"

"Andy, Andy." Hornsby paused and gazed out the window. "We may be on different sides of the fence, but I think you're an honorable man. I've always felt that way."

"I appreciate that." *Bad enough he lies*, thought Neponski, *but now he can't even look me in the eye*. "I'm sure you know the feeling is mutual."

"Of course. That's why I know we can work out differences on this. We always have in the past."

"What do you suggest?"

"I'd ask you to remember that emotions are running high right now," said Hornsby patiently. "You probably haven't been home since the attacks, to take the pulse of your constituents, but every poll tells us that the public feels the country is in a state of crisis. We haven't been attacked like this since Pearl Harbor. People want us to take action."

"I know that, but I also know the polls will be different six months or a year from now."

"They probably will. We'll deal with the changes at that time. For the moment, though, we need your support."

"Bob—"

"We need those resolutions to pass, and pass by a significant margin, not just squeak by. This is a situation where we need a show of strength. And that means we need a large chunk of the Democratic caucus to vote yes." He stared at Neponski. "We need you to come through for us on this."

"I'm not totally sure I can do that."

"I'd expect you to make as much noise as you can. That's part of the game. At the end of the day, though, you're in a tough spot. If you don't support the resolutions—enthusiastically—you run the risk of being perceived as unpatriotic."

"There are many forms of patriotism, I thought. I wasn't aware that the only correct one was agreeing with you."

"I need to remind you that we won the election."

"And I need to remind you that we kept Congress. Last time I looked, I controlled those votes."

"All right, Andy. What the hell do you want?"

"I'd like to see us go after the people who actually attacked us on May first, rather than focus on the Cane family nemesis."

"If you're talking about troops in Kabulistan, we're not going to do that, not at this time. Fighting a war on two fronts is extremely unwise. If you had been in the military, you'd know that."

"You were in the military?"

"We intend to send Special Forces," said Hornsby, ignoring him. "Army Rangers. The public will be reassured that we're continuing the hunt for Salman al-Akbar, even as we rid the world of the scourge of Hussein Ghazi."

"How many Rangers?"

"An entire battalion. Between six and seven hundred."

"I doubt that will get the job done. How many Special Forces would you say we have, altogether?"

"I can't tell you that."

"Fifty to sixty thousand? Something like that?"

"Hell, it's not half that much."

"Thought you couldn't tell me. I'd say a total of five or six thousand might be sufficient to hunt this guy down and capture him."

"Can't do it, Andy. It would stretch us too thin, globally speaking."

"You'll do it." Neponski smiled. "If you want my support, that is."

There was a long silence.

"Okay," Hornsby said finally. "Five thousand."

"Six, in an assortment of specialties, deployed throughout the tribal areas. Do you have any idea where he is?"

"We've heard rumors that he might be in Tora Bora, but they're just rumors. We'd deploy forces throughout the region, as you suggest."

"Sounds good."

"Shall we shake on it?"

"I have a better idea." Neponski stood up. "I'd like you to send me the paperwork on the deployment. And I'd like regular dispatches after that on troop movements, intelligence about al-Akbar's whereabouts, whatever. I want to be kept in the loop."

"What's that about, Andy? Sounds like you don't trust me."

"Sure I do." He paused at the door. "Just remember what your buddy Reagan said: 'Trust, but verify.'"

CHAPTER 28

THE BUZZER SOUNDED ON NEPONSKI'S desk in his Capitol Hill office.
"Yes?"

"Bethany Hampton is on the phone for you, sir."

"I'll be damned. How does she sound?"

"Pleasant enough."

"Bethany!" he said, pressing the button on the blinking line. "How are you? How are things in the big house?"

"Boring. It's the elephant graveyard, as usual. Even now."

Neponski chuckled. "I imagine so."

"Andy, I wanted to sound you out on these proposals, since you guys will be voting first. What the hell are we going to do?"

"I talked to Hornsby a few days ago. He won't budge. They're committed to going after Hussein Ghazi first."

"God almighty. Who was it who said that people get the government they deserve?"

"Everybody is telling me that we have to support this." The Speaker paused. "And I can't say for sure that they're wrong. If we torpedo these resolutions and Ghazi gets a nuclear bomb, we might as well hang it up and go home. There won't be another Democrat elected in our lifetimes."

"I'm afraid I agree. The problem is, they have us over a barrel. The public is scared shitless—they wake up every morning with the fear that the Arabs will blow up the school bus carrying their kids to kindergarten."

"Well, I'm not running for president."

"Neither am I."

"Not yet."

"I just want to make sure that we're both able to run for dogcatcher when this is over."

"What does your husband think?"

"I wouldn't refer to his mental processes as thinking."

"Even so."

"He's jealous that George Cane gets to act like a superhero, while he's only remembered for screwing anything that moves."

"Come on, Bethany."

"He thinks Salman al-Akbar is the real threat. He's always believed that, and now he's been proven right. Except this crew is determined to get rid of Ghazi first."

"They'd better hope that Husam al-Din doesn't attack again while they're wasting their time in Sumeristan."

"You've got that right."

"I was able to get some concessions out of Hornsby. He agreed to put Special Forces on the border between Kabulistan and Persepostan, and continue the hunt for al-Akbar while they pursue Hussein Ghazi."

"Well, that's something. You think they'll do it?"

"Oh, they'll send Rangers. How hard they'll look is another question. I hate to say it, but having an enemy like Salman al-Akbar puts them in a position of strength. It's in their best interests to keep him out there. It gives them justification to do anything they want."

"What about the other resolution? How do we know we're not creating another J. Edgar Hoover?"

"Eddie Gambelli isn't J. Edgar Hoover. Neither is Baldwin."

"No, but Hornsby's no slouch. I don't want it to get to the point where people need a security clearance to get a library card."

"We're in the dark here, Bethany. We have no idea what they're planning."

"True." The senator paused. "How does the vote shape up?"

"Half the caucus is on the fence, just as we are—they don't know what the hell to do. If I urge them to vote yes, they'll probably be delighted to have some cover. If things go sour later on, they can always say the Speaker asked them to vote for the resolution."

"It's the same deal over here, I'm afraid."

"Well, keep me posted."

"This is what we get for underestimating these people. I never thought they'd get us into a spot like this."

"It's our own fault, I suppose."

"No," she said. "If you want to know the truth, it's my husband's fault."

"Send him my best," said Neponski cheerfully.

Several minutes later, David Burnham poked his head around the door.

"Have a minute, sir?"

"Of course."

He tiptoed in and sat down across from his boss.

"Without revealing any of your conversation with Senator Hampton, I wanted to get a sense of how you were leaning on the resolutions."

"Well," said the Speaker, "what do you think?"

"We've discussed this before, but not in detail. I have to tell you, I feel strongly you should back the president."

"And why is that?"

"To start with, sir, this is a moment of national unity. The great majority of the population wants to see us take some action against the people who attacked us."

"So do I. I just don't happen to think that Hussein Ghazi was responsible."

"Maybe he wasn't. But the administration has set that as their initial priority. General Stevenson made a very convincing case in his speech to the U.N., at least as far as most citizens are concerned."

"So I understand."

"The situation isn't perfect, but this is a defining moment. How we act now will determine the way voters see Democrats in the future. If we don't back the resolutions and Hussein Ghazi gets out of control, or even becomes more aggressive, we'll be the villains."

"Yes. And if the invasion of Sumeristan turns into a disaster, we'll be vilified along with George Cane and his buddies."

"It's a Hobson's choice, sir. I understand that. And in the end, there's only one course of action that really makes sense."

"I agree." The Speaker leaned back in his chair. "You'll be pleased to know, David, that I've already decided to back the resolutions."

"Really?"

"Hornsby promised to send Army Rangers to hunt for Salman al-Akbar, and I intend to hold him to it. I also plan to introduce an amendment stating that the first priority of the government is to bring Salman al-Akbar and the May Day attackers to justice, and that we will dedicate as many of our resources as possible to that goal."

"Why didn't you tell me this up front, sir?"

"For one thing, I wanted to hear your reasoning on the issue. I also wanted to observe you. To see your body language."

"And what does all that reveal to you?"

"That you might be afraid of something. I've known you a long time, and you seem uncomfortable." He studied his chief of staff. "Anything you're not telling me, David? Anything I should know?"

Burnham's fears had been correct. The phone calls had not stopped, and the voices on the other end of the line had become more demanding.

"Hello, faggot," last night's caller had said.

"Who the hell is this?"

"Wouldn't you love to know. Just think of me as a concerned citizen, someone interested in the workings of government. How are we coming along with your boss supporting the resolutions?"

"Go fuck yourself. You think I can be blackmailed?"

"I think there would be people who would find your lifestyle interesting. For example, people at 314 Walker Avenue in Kansas City," the voice had said, cheerfully reciting the address of Burnham's mother.

"All right." He gripped the phone harder. "All right. Just give me some time. These decisions aren't made overnight."

"They need to be made soon, or we won't just out you. We'll reveal to the world that you've gotten religion."

"Please."

"Faith can be a great consolation, unless you find it in the wrong places."

"I'm going to help you. I promise."

"There's nothing wrong," he told Neponski now. "I'm just a bit stressed out. These have been some long and tough days."

"Well, if you need to talk to me anything, David, you know you can do so. Anything between the two of us always remains confidential."

"I appreciate that, sir." *This would kill my mother*, thought Burnham. *And if he found out the rest of it, he'd fire me in a heartbeat, despite the buddy-buddy act.* "Nothing that a few days off won't cure. After the vote, I'll get out of town for a long weekend."

"If you say so. Just remember that I'm here if you need me."

CHAPTER 29

THE RESOLUTION FOR THE USE of Force in the Middle East, along with the Resolution for National Security, passed both chambers of Congress by a resounding margin. In the House, the Neponski Amendment, along with the Speaker's grudging support for the administration's foreign policy, convinced many of his colleagues that it might be in their best interests to cross party lines in this case. The final vote was 297–133, with three abstentions; 98 Democrats, or nearly forty percent of the majority, voted for the legislation. In the Senate, the situation was reversed; sixty percent of Democrats voted yes, with a margin of 77–23.

There was plenty of grandstanding on both sides, of course. Most of it took place in the middle of the night, when the chambers were empty but the C-SPAN cameras were rolling. Particularly annoying to Bethany Hampton were the antics of Khaleem Atalas, the freshman senator from Pennsylvania, who made several impassioned speeches about protecting the rights of minorities during this troubled period in our nation's history. Born to an Indonesian father and American mother, Atalas had grown up in the Philadelphia suburbs and attended Princeton. While biracial, his appearance was elegant and patrician, and he clearly enjoyed competing for the mantle of champion of the underdog.

"We see them in our cities and towns, on our farms, and in our shops," his voice rang out with dramatic, practiced cadence. "They are the 'Others'—they may be a different color, or practice a different religion, and our first instinct may be to mistrust and even ostracize them. And yet they are Americans, as we are, citizens with the same rights and responsibilities. Let's not allow the fact they are different in appearance lead us to believe that they don't share the same hopes and fears as we do. Let us remember that they harbor the same ambitions for their children."

"Damn," said William Hampton, as he and his wife channel-surfed in upstate New York. "This guy is good."

"Would you like me to get his autograph for you? Or shall I just make some popcorn?"

"Bethany, you better keep your eye on him. He's got something."

"Maybe so."

"Where does he get those clothes? Look at that suit. That didn't come off the rack."

"I can also get his tailor's phone number if you want."

"My point is that this guy has some money behind him. Somebody's bankrolling him."

"Four months in the Senate, and he thinks he can lecture to everybody."

"He's been there as long as you have."

"I was First Lady," she snapped. "I think that counts for something."

"During World War II," continued Atalas, "Japanese-Americans were the Other. We let our fears get the better of us, and we rounded them up and placed them in detention camps. We need to be mindful of that lesson as we navigate through the current crisis. The terrorists who attacked us on May Day may have been Muslims, but they certainly don't represent the majority of people who follow the religion of Islam, both here in America and around the world. The religion of Mohammed is a path of peace and compassion, and we must remember that as we safeguard the rights of our fellow citizens.

"During last year's presidential campaign, George Cane famously advocated a third way. He rejected the views of extremists on both sides of the ideological spectrum. This new approach was an olive branch extended toward those of us who believe in treating minorities with dignity and respect. I call upon the president now to remember that pledge and safeguard the rights of our Muslim brothers and sisters."

"Is this guy a Muslim?" asked the former president.

"How would I know? Want me to check if he's circumcised?"

"He's building a fan base, using this to appeal to blacks, Hispanics, Asians—all of them. Concern for minorities may be a traditional Democratic issue, but it sounds a hell of a lot more convincing when a minority is saying it."

"If the Cane people keep the ball on the court and don't persecute anybody, it doesn't get him very far."

"Don't think so? Be careful, Bethany—this guy's going places."

As the congressional votes were being cast, General Bayard Stevenson was on his way to Turkey to oversee Operation Righteous Liberation. In the weeks that followed, the bulk of America's military might was deployed to the Middle East. The 82nd Airborne Division was stationed on one carrier group in the Persian Gulf, while the 101st Airborne was positioned on another. Slowly and methodically, more than two hundred thousand soldiers were transported to forward bases, along with the logistics and support that would be needed to maintain them in the field.

The Turks made some minor noise when the target of the invasion was changed, but quickly reiterated their support with the promise of more American foreign aid.

In Democrat cloakrooms on the Hill, the gloom was palpable as members realized that they had just participated in a game of Russian roulette, regardless of how they voted. To cheer up his colleagues, Andrew Neponski appeared on *Meet the Press* on the Sunday following Friday evening's vote.

Under close questioning from Tim Russert about his unexpected support for the resolutions, the Speaker stressed the need for national unity in a time of crisis. He emphasized the importance of giving George Cane's policies time to work, while implying that the president wouldn't receive all the time in the world. He reminded viewers that the invasion of Sumeristan would be an easy exercise for the might of the U.S. military, but that the hard part would be transforming the country into a democracy after Hussein Ghazi was toppled. He reviewed the details of the Neponski Amendment, and reiterated that the administration had promised to position Special Forces on the Kabulistan–Persepostan border, "so that the true villains of the May first attacks may be hunted down and brought to justice."

"At a time like this," he said, "we are not Republicans or Democrats. We are Americans, and as Americans we can be counted on to take the patriotic course of action." One journalist counted more than a dozen uses of "patriotic" or "patriotism" in Neponski's ten-minute segment.

By contrast, the upper echelons of the administration were jubilant. Support for George Cane was at a historic high for first-year presidents, and a majority of the population felt the country was on the right track for the first time since the May Day attacks. When Robert Hornsby walked into his office on the Monday morning after the resolutions passed, it occurred to Scott Leventhal that it was one of the rare occasions when he had seen his boss break into a sincere and spontaneous smile.

"Hello, Scott."

"Morning, sir. It's a good day."

"Absolutely. Come on in."

Leventhal followed Hornsby into the inner office and settled into a chair across from the vice president.

"We did better than we hoped."

"Yes. I have to admit that I was a bit surprised at the size of the margins. But we had Neponski and Bethany Hampton on our side, which really helped."

"Neponski was the key."

"I'd like to think I had something to do with that," boasted Hornsby. "I think our little chat was the turning point."

"Actually, sir, it was a bit of a group effort." Leventhal hesitated. "I'm afraid I have good news and bad news for you."

"Go ahead."

"You remember our discussion about David Burnham? About how he might be gay?"

Hornsby grinned. "I believe I told you to get me some naked pictures."

"Well, I couldn't get any pictures, but I did get corroboration from a number of sources. So we applied some pressure."

"I hope you didn't get carried away."

"Not at all. Just some strategically placed calls, reminding him that he was expected to prevail upon his boss to support the resolutions. So his secrets could be kept safe."

"It sounds like you missed your true calling."

"It gets more complicated."

"Yes?"

"It turns out Burnham's having an affair with one of Sanford Bayer's altar boys."

"I don't believe it." Hornsby shook his head. "Sanford Bayer has an office at the White House. George Cane thinks he walks on water. If anything, we'd have to *protect* Burnham now."

"I'm afraid there's more, sir."

"I gather this is the bad news. Go ahead."

"It appears that the altar boy is also carrying on with someone at the agency."

"Jesus Christ." He squinted at Leventhal. "I don't believe this. Which of Bayer's assistants is this?"

"We're not exactly sure. But we suspect that the agent is funneling information to him, which is why Bayer always seems so well informed on administration policy. He's not included in any of the meetings, after all."

"You're not sure. That's great. It's just great."

"I'm out of my depth here, sir. I wouldn't know how to spy on them if I tried."

"Of course. My apologies, Scott." He stood up. "No worries—leave it to me. I'll take care of this."

"I'm sure you will, sir."

When Leventhal left the office, Hornsby picked up the red phone.

"Morning, sir," said McCardle. "And congratulations."

"Mike, we have a problem."

"Go ahead, but I'm just heading out the door for the morning security briefing."

"This will only take a minute. It seems that one of your guys is sleeping with one of Sandy Bayer's altar boys."

"Shit. Which one is it?"

"I have no idea, but there's five of them. I want a tail on each one."

"Will do, sir."

"I know that manpower's an issue, so let's drop the surveillance on the other four as soon as we find out who it is. But I want that one tailed 24/7, so we can discover the identity of the agent."

"I'm on it. But I have to tell you that I find this hard to believe."

"Well, apparently it's true. Somewhere down the line, you'd better tighten up your screening procedures for new hires."

"They're pretty rigorous now, to tell you the truth."

"Not rigorous enough. But let's find this bastard before he gives out all our state secrets in his pillow talk. Understood?"

"I'm on it, sir."

CHAPTER 30

O N THE EVE OF St. Martin, the 10th of November, the expedition came before Zara in Sclavonia, and beheld the city enclosed by high walls and high towers; and vainly would you have sought for a fairer city, or one of greater strength, or richer. And when the pilgrims saw it they marveled greatly, and said one to another, "How could such a city be taken by force, save by the help of God himself?"

The first ships that came before the city cast anchor, and waited for the others; and in the morning the day was very fine and very clear, and all the galleys came up with the transports, and all the other ships which were behind; and they took the port by force, and broke the chain that defended it that was very strong and well-wrought; and they landed in the port that was between them and the town. Then might you have seen many a knight and many a sergeant swarming out of the ships, and taking from the transports many a good war-horse, and many a rich tent and many a pavilion. And thus was Zara besieged on St. Martin's Day.

At this time all the barons had not yet arrived. On the day following the feast of St. Martin, certain of the people of Zara came forth and spoke to the Doge of Venice, who was in his pavilion, and said to him that they would yield up the city and all their goods if their lives were spared to his mercy. And the Doge replied that *he would not accept these conditions, nor any conditions, save by consent of the counts and barons, with whom he would go and confer.*

When he went to confer with the counts and barons, that party who wished to disperse the expedition spoke to the envoys and said, "Why should you surrender your city? The pilgrims will not attack you, have no care of them. If you can defend yourself against the Venetians, you will be safe enough." And they chose one of themselves who went to the walls of the city and spoke the same words. Therefore the envoys returned to the city, and the negotiations were broken off.

The Doge of Venice, when he came to the counts and barons, said to them: "The people therein desire to yield the city to my mercy, on condition only that their lives are spared. But I will enter into no agreement with them—this or any other— without your consent." And the barons answered: "Sire, we advise you to accept these conditions, and we even beg of you to do so." He said he would do so; and they all returned to the pavilion of the Doge to make the agreement, and found that the envoys had gone away by the advice of those who wished to disperse the expedition.

Then rose the Abbot of Vaux, of the order of the Cistercians, and said to them: "Lords, I forbid you, on the part of the Pope of Rome, to attack this city; for those within it are Christians, and you are pilgrims." When the Doge heard this he was much disturbed, and he said to the counts and barons: "I had this city, by my own agreement, at my mercy, and your people have broken that agreement; you have covenanted to help me conquer it, and I summon you to do so."

Whereupon the counts and barons all spoke at once, together with those who were of their party, and said: "Great is the outrage of those who have caused this agreement to be broken, and never a day has passed when they have not tried to break up the expedition. Now we are shamed if we do not help to take the city." And they came to the Doge and said: "Sire, we will help you take the city despite the efforts of those who would hinder us."

Thus was the decision taken. The next morning the expedition encamped before the gates of the city and set up their engines of war, which they had in plenty, and on the side of the sea they raised ladders from the ships. Then they began to throw stones at the walls of the city and at the towers. So did the assault last for about five days. Then were the sappers set to mine one of the towers, and began to sap the wall. When those within the city saw this they proposed an agreement, such as they had before been refused by the advice of those who wished to break up the expedition.

Thus did the city surrender to the mercy of the Doge, on condition only that all lives should be spared. Then came the Doge to the counts and barons, and said to them: "We have taken this city by the grace of God, and your own. It is now winter, and we cannot stir hence until Eastertide, for we should find no market in any other place; and this city is very rich, and well furnished with all supplies. Let us therefore divide it in the midst, and we will take one half, and you the other."

As he had spoken, so was it done. The Venetians took the part of the city near the port, where were the ships, and the Franks took the other part. There were quarters assigned to each, as was right and convenient. And the expedition raised the camp, and went to lodge in the city.

At that time there was an emperor in Constantinople, whose name was Isaac, and he had a brother, [sic] Alexius by name, whom he had ransomed from captivity among the Turks. This Alexius took his brother the emperor, tore the eyes out of his head, and made himself emperor by the aforesaid treachery. He kept Isaac a long time in prison, together with a son whose name was Alexius.

This son escaped from prison, and fled in a ship to a city on the sea, which is called Ancona. Thence he departed to go to King Philip of Germany, who had his sister for wife; and he came to Verona in Lombardy, and lodged in the town, and found there a number of pilgrims and other people who were on their way to join the host.

And those who had helped him to escape, and were with him, said: "Sire, here is an army in Venice, quite near to us, the best and most valiant people and knights that are in the world, and they are going overseas. Cry to them therefore for mercy, that they have pity on thee and on thy father, who have been so wrongfully dispossessed. And if they be willing to help thee, thou shalt be guided by them. Perchance they will take pity on thy estate." And Alexius said he would do this right willingly, and that the advice was good.

A fortnight later came to Zara the Marquis Boniface of Montferrat, who had not yet joined, and Matthew of Montmorency, and Peter of Bracieux, and many other men of note. And after another fortnight came also the envoys from Germany, sent by King Philip and the heir of Constantinople. Then the barons and the Doge of Venice assembled in a palace where the Doge was lodged. And the envoys addressed them and said: "Lords, King Philip sends us to you, as does the brother of the king's wife, the son of the emperor of Constantinople ... because you have fared forth from God, and for right, and for justice, therefore you are bound, in so far as you are able, to restore to their own inheritance those who have been unrighteously despoiled. And my wife's brother will make with you the best terms ever offered to any people, and give you the most puissant help for the recovery of the land overseas.

"And first, if God grant that you restore him to his inheritance, he will place the whole empire of Romania in obedience to Rome, from which it has long been separated. Further, he knows that you have spent of your substance, and that you are poor, and he will give you 200,000 marks of silver, and food for all those of the

expedition, both small and great. And he, of his own person, will go with you into the land of Babylon, or, if you hold that that will be better, send thither 10,000 men, at his own charge. And this service he will perform for one year. And all the days of his life he will maintain, at his own charge, five hundred knights in the land overseas to guard that land."

"Lords, we have full power," said the envoys, "to conclude this agreement, if you are willing to conclude it on your part. And be it known to you that so favorable an agreement has never before been offered to anyone; and that he who would refuse it can have but small desire of glory and conquest."

The barons and the Doge said they would talk this over, and a parliament was called for the morrow.

CHAPTER 31

B Y HIS SIXTEENTH BIRTHDAY, ABDUL'S grades had improved dramatically. After his first semester, he no longer needed the remedial program, and he was once again the honor student he had been. He was well liked by his teachers, who found him alert and inquisitive, if somewhat impulsive in his thinking and too quick at times to jump to conclusions. He had settled into his new school, made friends, and established himself on the playground as high-spirited but not aggressive—someone who would not start fights, but who would not back down once they began.

He was also a regular visitor to a mosque near his home. His father had selected it, taking care to choose a place known to have a moderate imam. Such a mosque wasn't hard to find under the rule of Hussein Ghazi, when most Sumeris were Muslims but the state was distinctly secular. Even so, his father took no chances, and accompanied his son to prayers whenever possible. The two had grown much closer since Abdul's enrollment in Kasim Hamdani's academy.

The young man had not entirely shed his former behaviors, however; he had simply learned not to flaunt them. He still listened to radio broadcasts from Persepostan on his transistor radio, but he did so during the hour-long bus rides to and from school. To him, it was an exciting time in the region. The

Dua Khamail were battling for control of Kabulistan, and the freedom fighters of Husam al-Din were lurking behind them, thumbing their noses at America. They spoke often of the great jihad against the West that would someday come. While Abdul was skeptical of their ability to follow through with their threats and boasts, the talk was definitely more exciting than the Sumeristan of Hussein Ghazi, where everyone seemed to march in lockstep out of fear.

He had learned to be cautious when expressing himself during Dr. Hamdani's weekly meetings. These were gatherings of anywhere from twelve to fifteen acolytes, students that the principal had rescued from unstable home environments. The discussions were animated and freewheeling, with everyone discussing the political events of the day while Hamdani assumed the role of referee. During the summer of 2000, much of the talk revolved around the coming presidential election in America, and what the nomination of George Cane might mean for Sumeristan.

"Mark my words," said a boy named Kareem, "this could be the turning point for Sumeristan. Cane will be influenced by his uncle, and he will invade the country again. He will want to finish off the 1991 war and change the regime."

"Perhaps," said Hamdani, "but he will need pretext. He cannot risk being accused of being warlike. If he does not find a pretext, he will have to invent one."

The boys exploded with laughter.

"Why should the Americans invade again?" asked Mohammed. "Other than oil, they stand to gain nothing."

"Oil isn't nothing," said Kareem, and the group laughed again.

"A great deal depends on how things proceed in Kabulistan," said the principal. "If the Dua Khamail take control of the government, that will destabilize the country from the West's point of view. They will likely give sanctuary to Husam al-Din. More importantly, it will upset the balance of power in the region. America will no longer have a sphere of influence here."

Here it comes, thought Abdul. *The lecture about the end of World War II and the establishment of the three superstates.*

"Remember," said Hamdani, "that we are in this position today because of the actions of Roosevelt, Churchill, and Stalin in 1945. There may not have been an oil crisis back then, but the three men realized how important it was for them to have a foothold in the region. Now things have changed beyond their comprehension: Russia lost Kabulistan, England is no longer a world power, and American interests have been driven out of Persepostan by the mullahs. This was humiliating for them, coming as it did so soon after Vietnam."

He paused. "Kareem may turn out to be correct. America may feel desperate to have a stake in the region, and we could be the likely target. But they will still need a reason to invade. You cannot claim to be a beacon of democracy and occupy countries at your whim."

The group nodded in unison.

"An American invasion might not be a bad thing," said Mohammed. "Life would undoubtedly improve for us."

"In the long run, perhaps," said Hamdani. "But we sit here today after more than two decades of rule by the current regime. This means there are many people, some nearly ten years older than you, who have known no other leader than Hussein Ghazi. Do not think the transition would not be painful. Rebuilding the country could take another two decades."

The boys nodded once again.

"What do you think, Abdul?" asked the principal. "What would life be like under the Americans? You would have access to more sneakers, after all."

"I hope so, sir." Abdul laughed. "But I think I have to agree with you. It is likely that the country will be destabilized, and that we will have to be careful—even more careful than we are right now. The Americans will not stay forever, and there will be many factions warring for control. We must apply the same principles we use now, to have them think they have our support while keeping our own counsel and biding our time."

"You are a wise young man, Abdul," said Hamdani, "You have learned much."

"Thank you, sir."

When someone lacks conviction, thought Abdul, *you can deceive them so easily.*

CHAPTER 32

OPERATION RIGHTEOUS LIBERATION BEGAN ON June 14 with a spectacular, week-long bombing campaign against the city of Baghdad. Robert Hornsby had a ringside seat the for action. He had access to all the CIA data, and because of McCardle's connections at high levels in the Pentagon, Hornsby was also privy to bomb damage assessment, troop movements, and casualty reports, information that would normally be shared only with the president, the secretary of defense, and the commander in the field. Hornsby used this advantage to shape his recommendations to the president, as well as to gauge the effectiveness of his advice afterward.

To avoid excessive civilian casualties, the administration insisted on only evening bombing raids. Starting every day at 5:00 p.m.—or 1:00 a.m. Baghdad time—coalition warplanes lit up the night sky in a scene eerily reminiscent of Fourth of July fireworks. The show of military force was designed to intimidate the population of Sumeristan while simultaneously cheering the American public, and it accomplished both goals with ease.

Theatrics aside, the nightly bombing had little strategic importance. Preparations for the invasion had been closely watched for weeks beforehand on CNN and other news outlets, and the government of Hussein Ghazi had long since been removed to an undisclosed location in the countryside. The destruction of the presidential palace, which occurred on the first evening of the campaign, was largely symbolic.

When the campaign started, the troops landed at the northern and southern ends of Sumeristan and fanned out from there toward the capital in the center. Hornsby was surprised that they encountered little resistance, even from the elite commando and palace guard units that CIA field reports had described as fearless and highly efficient. On June 22, as coalition forces clustered on both tips of the country, he had his customary evening call with Bayard Stevenson.

"Before we advance on the capital," he told the secretary, "I think it would be a good idea to make sure the oil fields are protected."

"Protected, sir?"

"Yes. The last thing anyone wants to see is a replay of 1991, when loyalists blew up the oil rigs and they burned on CNN for months."

"Just so we're clear, sir. Are you telling me to occupy the oil fields?"

"Not occupy them, no—just make sure they're safe. That oil will be a crucial part of the effort to rebuild Sumeristan after the invasion."

"With all due respect, sir, that means we'll have to leave five or ten thousand troops on either end of the country. We may need those forces as we advance on the capital."

"Well, let's not be penny-wise and pound-foolish. I say we protect those rigs and keep all our options open."

Surprisingly, there was no use of chemical weapons on the part of Sumeristan, something the administration had feared. Hornsby was particularly anxious about this as he watched the forces cut their way effortlessly through the countryside, wary that they might be lured into a trap. The nightmare scenario never materialized, and from coalition headquarters the entire operation began to resemble a large-scale war video game. The coalition had been confident of a quick victory—so much so that the troops hadn't even been issued special gear to help them adapt to combat in the brutal Sumeristan summer, when temperatures easily reached 120 degrees Fahrenheit. It looked as though hostilities might be over within one month.

On the morning of day five, after the daily security briefing, Robert Hornsby was ushered into the Oval Office along with FBI Director Edward Gambelli.

"Morning, Bob." The president came out from behind the desk to shake hands. "Eddie, good to see you. How've you been?"

"Just fine, sir, thank you."

"Please, sit." George Cane regarded the two men across from him. "I'm assuming this isn't war-related, since Eddie is primarily domestic. No new terror cells, I hope?"

"No, sir," said Gambelli. "Nothing beyond what you see in the threat assessments."

"Good."

"We're here on another matter," said Hornsby. "Mr. President, I know you're not fond of reading the newspapers."

"Depends," said George Cane, as Hornsby spread the *Washington Post* on the desk. "I assume you're referring to the story about my daughter. Of course I read that."

"Here's what concerns me, sir. 'Courtney Cane professes sympathy with goals of Lavender Menace.' They talk about the developing friendship between Courtney and this Carla Stennings."

"Yep," said the president. "All that stuff sure sounds like something Courtney would like. She's always been an activist without a cause."

"And then there's this," said Hornsby. 'I wouldn't agree with everything she says and does,' said Ms. Cane. 'But I do believe that she has been misunderstood and miscast by the male-dominated media. People in power usually don't yield power gracefully, and sometimes you have to take extreme measures to accomplish your goals.'

"Let's be frank, sir," said the vice president. "This is not good. We're hoping you might have some influence over her."

"What would you like me to do, Bob—cut off her allowance? Tell her if she doesn't stop, she'll be grounded and won't be able to go to the prom?"

"Just reason with her, if you can. Try to explain the distinction between personal feelings and public utterances. Tell her she's embarrassing you."

"She's not embarrassing me. I happen to believe everyone is entitled to their opinion."

"Stennings hasn't been misunderstood," said Hornsby. "At least not by me. I know exactly what she's doing, and for once I actually agree with the *Post*—she's using Courtney for publicity, to advance her agenda."

"This is delicate, sir," said Gambelli. "We all have children."

"She's twenty-eight, Eddie," said the president. "She's not a child. I think she can associate with whomever she wants."

"With all due respect, these people are radicals. They're dangerous. Carla Stennings is a convicted felon."

"Convicted of what?" asked Cane. "Exercising her constitutional right to protest?"

"Blocking the entrance to the Supreme Court," said Hornsby. "Resisting arrest. Battery against a police officer. And a few other things."

"Look guys, I'm sure that no one is going to confuse the Lavender Menace with the Girl Scouts. But at the end of the day, I believe they're harmless."

"Harmless to everyone except *you*, sir," said Hornsby. "Please explain the situation to her. She's the president's daughter."

"Come on, Bob. Amy Carter smoked pot in the White House, for God's sake. The Secret Service agents probably shared a joint with her."

"This is different. She can't join this group and get herself arrested."

"Don't you think we have more important things to worry about? I've sent two hundred thousand of our boys into harm's way. They're risking their lives at this very moment, as you know. Do you really believe it's useful to sit here worrying about a group of radical lesbians?"

"A personal favor, sir." Hornsby folded up the newspaper and looked at the president. "Would you talk to her?"

"I'll have her mother talk to her. That usually does the trick."

"Thank you."

It takes so little to make some people happy, the president thought as the two men left the office.

CHAPTER 33

I N LATE JUNE, MAJOR EDWARD Hawkins sat in his tent on the edge of the
White Mountains in northern Kabulistan. The sun was setting, and the
tent was lit by a Coleman lantern sitting on a makeshift table. Hawkins
read and reread the most recent letter from his wife, and sat staring at the
picture of his infant son as the wind rattled the nearby trees.

"May I, sir?"

Sergeant Phillip Ogden held the tent flap, peering in tentatively.

"Please, come in."

The sergeant entered and stood at attention.

"Sit down, please. Let's stop playing toy soldiers with each other."

Ogden sat down next to Hawkins and removed his cap. His face was
grimy, and his uniform hung on his wiry frame.

"What do we know, Phil?"

"Not a hell of a lot, sir." Ogden's Alabama twang seemed misplaced against
the Kabulistani mountains. "If the CIA boys have any new information, they
ain't sharing it."

"Surprise, surprise."

U.S. intelligence suspected that al-Akbar made his headquarters in a series of
interconnected caves dug into the mountains near the Khyber Pass. While it was

never revealed to the public, the caves had originally been excavated during the administration of Herbert Cane, when the United States funded al-Akbar against the Soviets. The mountain hideouts had been constructed with the aid of the CIA and under the direction of Robert Hornsby. They had been greatly enlarged since then, and were now rumored to be capable of housing stores of ammunition and thousands of operatives in relative comfort. The terrain was mountainous and difficult to penetrate, however. It was also under the control of warlords whose help would be needed to guarantee safe passage through the area. The American government had placed a bounty of five million dollars on al-Akbar's head, but this was probably an insignificant sum compared to the potential cost of buying off the warlords who they suspected were protecting him.

Ogden glanced down at the table. "Letter from home, sir?"

"About a week ago."

"It's rough on them. At least we've got something to do. Or we're supposed to."

"You have family back home, Phil?"

"Just my folks. I guess it's tougher when you're married and have kids."

"Hard to say."

"May I ask you something, sir?"

"Shoot."

"What the hell you doin' here?"

There was a pause, and both men exploded with laughter. Hawkins raised his palm and gave Ogden a high-five.

"Damned if I know. My father was a reserve officer during Vietnam. He convinced me to join up in college."

"But he never went?"

"Never got close." Hawkins yawned. "But he really believed in the idea of a domestic backup force. Vietnam aside, he convinced me to want to serve."

"Well, sir." Ogden grinned. "You got your wish."

"I sure did."

"You from New York, ain't you, sir?"

"Parsippany, New Jersey. I sold insurance."

"Good training to hunt down terrorists."

"You bet. You think there are any actual terrorists in those caves?"

"Sir, I don't know if there's actually *caves*. Haven't seen any yet."

"True enough. What do the Special Ops guys think we're waiting for?"

"I don't know for certain, but it's been two days since the last air strike. Some folks think that Husam al-Din is trying to work out a truce. The theory is, they don't want to fight their fellow Muslims."

"Isn't that nice. And they think Salman al-Akbar is in there?"

"Damned if I know, sir. If they think so, they ain't saying. Me, I wouldn't know him if I ran him over by mistake."

"Nor would I. But you know what I think?"

"What's that, sir?"

"He killed three thousand innocent people back home. So if I have to sit here until I'm old and gray and wait for him, that's what I'll do."

"Right on, sir."

"See you in the morning, Phil."

Ogden saluted and left.

On the evening of July 3, General Bayard Stevenson sat in the White House Situation Room; he had flown back for a day to confer with the administration. The door opened at seven-thirty, and Stevenson stood up as Vice President Hornsby and Admiral McCardle entered the room together.

"Bayard, how are you?" asked Hornsby, as the three men shook hands.

"Just fine, sir."

The Bobbsey Twins, thought Stevenson as he sat back down at the conference table. *There's a marriage made in heaven, if I ever saw one.*

"What's the news from Tora Bora?" asked McCardle.

"More of the same, I'm afraid. The intelligence is muddled, and the situation remains confusing. We can't pinpoint the location of Salman al-Akbar, or even determine for certain if he's in the caves."

"What do the coalition forces tell you?"

"They have no idea, sir. We can't get anybody in there, so there's no way to know what's going on. Things are complicated further by the fact that the Kabulistani fighters loyal to us are leaving the battlefield in the evening to have dinner with their families."

"Great," muttered Hornsby. "They all have to leave at once?"

"It's more or less common in that world, sir. We try to respect their cultural practices if we can."

"There's been no movement since the truce?" asked Hornsby.

"Not that we've been able to detect. But we're starting to think that the truce was a ruse to allow al-Akbar and his top lieutenants to escape."

"How'd we fall for that?" asked the vice president.

"To be honest," said Stevenson, "the CIA operatives on the ground were all for it." He stared at Hornsby. "They insisted we stand down, as a gesture of good faith."

"All right," said McCardle irritably. "How do you think they could have escaped without being noticed?"

"We don't know how extensive the cave complex really is. Our Special Ops guys have studied the plans you gave them, but we have no idea how much the complex was enlarged since you built it."

"We didn't build it," said Hornsby. "It was an administration directive. We contracted it out."

"Regardless," said Stevenson, "there are numerous ways for them to slip away. The situation is muddled, and the intelligence is faulty."

"So you said," replied McCardle. "Can't we do a surgical airstrike?"

"There are too many forces in the area, both from the Kabulistan side and our own. If we retreated to allow a surgical strike, he'd definitely get away. Provided he's there, of course."

"What about Gator mines?" asked McCardle. "We could air-drop those."

"NATO won't allow it," said the general. "They're firm on that."

"And their reasons, once again?"

"The Gator mine system uses dumb bombs. The unexploded bombs stay in the countryside and turn into land mines. There were cases in Yugoslavia where they killed civilians and children years after being dropped. Anyway, they're banned by the land mine treaty."

"We didn't sign that treaty," said Hornsby. "And there are no civilians or children in that area—only people who want to kill Americans."

"True enough, sir. But everyone else in NATO did. And NATO approval is crucial to the success of this campaign, at least in the eyes of the public."

"Fair warning, General," said Hornsby. "I'm going to contact NATO on this. This is bullshit. We need their help here."

"Go for it, sir."

Hornsby scowled at Bayard Stevenson.

"Why not just send a commando unit in there?" asked McCardle. "We've got Rangers in the area, along with the British SDS. Have them go in and clean it out."

"It's likely to be a suicide mission," said Stevenson. "We don't know the layout of the caves, or how many people are down there. All we need is to have them parading around on al-Jazeera, holding the heads of CIA paramilitaries on poles."

There was silence in the room.

"All right," said Hornsby. "We'll brief the president on this in the morning. General, please keep me posted if anything happens overnight."

"Will do, sir."

The three men stood up.

"By the way, sir," asked Stevenson, "where *is* the president?"

"He and the First Lady are attending a Fourth of July reception hosted by the Postmaster General," said Hornsby. "It's part of the strategy—business as usual."

CHAPTER 34

SALMAN AL-AKBAR HAD INDEED ESCAPED, although this nugget of information was not shared with the public. Hornsby reasoned that the American people seemed so overjoyed with the successful prosecution of the war in Sumeristan that there was no point dampening their mood with bad news. Predictable as this outcome of the campaign might have been, it had also gone a long way toward erasing the wave of fear unleashed by the May Day attacks—even though many people seemed to have forgotten that those attacks were orchestrated by al-Akbar himself.

Following their "protection" of the oil fields at both ends of Sumeristan, coalition troops steadily advanced toward Baghdad in the center. As they moved through the country, they left occupying forces behind them: a battalion in medium-sized towns, a brigade in larger provincial cities. On July 9, the coalition arrived on the outskirts of the capital. They entered the city the following day and were greeted as liberators, just as Hornsby had foreseen. Citizens danced in the streets, women and girls presented troops with bouquets, and a mob of young men enlisted the help of American soldiers to pull down the cast-iron statue of Hussein Ghazi that dominated one of Baghdad's central squares. The entire operation had taken twenty-four days.

At Hornsby's urging, the Cane administration organized a celebratory public event to be held at the National Mall on July 14 (Bastille Day—a jab at France, who had refused to join the coalition) that would include as much traditional Americana as possible. There would be a VFW parade, marching bands, hymns sung by children's church choirs, and a surfeit of thankful prayers offered by representatives of every major religion.

The event would culminate with speeches by the president and General Bayard Stevenson, delivered to what the administration hoped would be a record-breaking audience. "It would be nice," Hornsby observed privately, "if we could draw more people than King's March on Washington."

The VIP seating close to the podium would be reserved for the cabinet, members of Congress, and a large contingent of families who had lost members in the May Day attacks. Hornsby personally telephoned Andrew Neponski to offer him a place of honor on the dais, but the conversation didn't take place; the Speaker instructed David Burnham to tell the vice president he had left the office to stock up on energy drinks, but he doubted that the message was ever passed along.

Six days before the National Day of Celebration, David Burnham sat in his Capitol Hill townhouse, channel-surfing as he sipped a glass of white wine. It was Sunday evening, a time he had long ago learned was high tide for reading the psyche of the nation. He usually watched TV for two or three hours, alternating between reruns of the Sunday morning talk shows and the underbelly of cable, accumulating juicy tidbits to pass on to the Speaker in the morning.

"With God's help, our nation has triumphed over the legions of darkness," crooned the Reverend Sanford J. Bayer in his weekly television sermon, broadcast on a Christian cable station. "On May first, the good and God-fearing people of America were attacked by the forces of evil. God called upon us to respond, and with his help our brave troops performed valiantly. Now we must muster our strength, cleanse our souls, and prepare for the battle ahead."

We finally get a faggot in the White House, he thought grimly, *and it turns out he's a Holy Roller.* Burnham figured the administration hated gays almost as much as terrorists, and he found it ironic and amusing that they had chosen Bayer as their spiritual spokesman. As he watched the minister with his purple robe and carefully styled, orange-tinted hair, he marveled at how badly political calculation could come back to bite people on the ass. *They'll live to regret this, and it won't take long. This guy is out of his league—he was hired to encourage people to give more canned goods to the poor, and now he's battling the Antichrist.*

"Our resolve must be firm," said Reverend Bayer, "just as our support for our men and women in uniform must be steadfast. The triumphant campaign we have just concluded in Sumeristan will likely turn out to be the first of many. For the enemy we battle today in this new crusade against the forces of evil in the world is far more formidable than the one faced by our Christian brothers centuries ago, as they journeyed forth to the Holy Land to conquer the infidels. Each and every one of us must be alert to the presence of traitors in our midst, and do our part to identify the enemies amongst us."

We're all infidels now, you asshole. He was amazed that Cane had allowed his spokesmen to refer to the military campaign as a crusade, given the alarm and anger that image must raise in the Muslim world. It had to be Hornsby's doing: the old CIA tactic of throwing the enemy off-balance before the battle even began. *Let the holy wars begin, and may the non-Christians shiver at the sight of us.*

"Remember that the terrorists who attacked us on May Day only succeeded because they had the support of a fifth column of Muslim extremists living among us. Masquerading as ordinary Americans, these agents took their orders from Salman al-Akbar and Husam al-Din. While recognizing that there are many law-abiding Muslims living in America, we must do our civic duty and stay alert for suspicious behavior in our communities."

Shit, why don't we just line all the Muslims up against a wall and shoot them? Then we could take our time and sort out the bad guys, with no resistance from anybody. Disgusted, he switched to *Face the Nation*, where Bob Schieffer was interviewing Admiral Chester Baldwin, head of the newly created Department of National Security. The first days of the new agency had been one misstep after another, and the administration had probably told Baldwin to go on TV and do some damage control.

"Admiral," said Schieffer, "what would you say to those who think that our civil liberties are being sacrificed in the name of national security, who feel that our government is going too far to protect us? For example, the grandmother in Illinois who was detained at an airport by the FBI and questioned for five hours because she was carrying knitting needles?"

"Honestly, Bob, there will always be excesses," said Baldwin. His silver crew cut glinted against the studio lights. "Sure, we've made mistakes, and probably there will be a few more to come. Nobody's perfect. But at the end of the day, we have to think about those three thousand Americans that perished on May Day. Many of them were as innocent as that grandmother in Illinois. Nobody wants to see that happen to us ever again. And I think most Americans understand that it's worth putting up with the occasional inconvenience to make sure we don't ever witness another attack like that."

"Sir," asked Schieffer, "what about the high school students in Louisiana who were questioned because they checked out books on Islam from the public library? At what point do we risk sacrificing the liberty we've trying so hard to protect?"

"Look, Bob, we have sleeper cells in this country. That's a fact. The May Day attacks could not have happened otherwise. Whether someone assembled a suicide belt or helped channel funds into the United States through a suspicious charity, they're equally guilty. Our challenge now is to find these people before they attack us again. Patriotic, loyal Muslims have nothing to fear. We've said this before. We know that most of the Muslim population in this country was as horrified as everyone else on May first. We don't think it's inappropriate to ask Americans to be on the lookout for suspicious behavior. As time goes on, we also think that the Department of National Security will open the channels of communication between the FBI, CIA, and local law enforcement and enable everyone to share information more efficiently. But we also know that the first line of defense is an alert citizenry."

Extremism in the defense of liberty is no vice, thought Burnham in disgust as he turned off the TV. *The dam has burst, and the lunatics have taken over the asylum. It'll take years, maybe decades, to get these people under control. In the meantime, people will be informing on each other, and looking under the bed for the bogeyman. Where's George Orwell when you need him?*

He rose and went to the kitchen, and was pouring another glass of Chardonnay when the phone rang.

"Hello?"

"Hi there, sweetie."

"What the hell do you want now?"

"Just wanted to touch base, in case you missed me."

"Look, I did my part for the war effort. My boss supported the resolutions, and you guys defeated a tin-horn dictator who couldn't win a battle with the Cub Scouts. Why don't you leave me alone?"

"We think it would be nice if your fearless leader showed the flag on celebration day. We'd like to see him on that dais."

"It doesn't look like he wants to do that."

"We think he should. He'd be the only Democrat up there, which would mean something. We think you should persuade him to do it."

"Contrary to what you think, he doesn't do everything I tell him to do. I don't have him hypnotized."

"Well, let's give it your best shot, shall we?"

"I can't promise anything."

"We want him on that dais," said the caller. "Don't make me call Kansas, sweetie-pie."

CHAPTER 35

Inside the VIP tent on the morning of July 14, the atmosphere was jubilant. The crowd had begun flowing onto the National Mall shortly after dawn, and by eleven o'clock hundreds of thousands of citizens filled the space between the Lincoln Memorial and the Capitol, waiting for the festivities to begin at noon. Andrew Neponski spotted Bethany Hampton across the room and came over to give her a peck on the cheek.

"Senator," said the Speaker. "You're looking lovely today."

"Thank you. I was going to wear my Easter bonnet, but thought better of it."

"Where's your husband?"

"He'll be here. He's arriving separately. Surprise, surprise."

"Please give him my best."

"I see they conned you into being the lone Democratic wolf on the dais. How'd that happen?"

"My AA convinced me it was the right thing to do. A display of patriotism, bipartisanship, and God knows what else."

"Better you than me. Your AA? Burnham?"

"That's him. Worth his weight in gold. He balances my antisocial tendencies."

"I would imagine." She smiled sweetly. "Don't look now, but I believe Captain Courageous is coming our way."

Robert Hornsby was in fact moving toward them, but he was intercepted halfway by Mike McCardle.

"Morning, sir. You look chipper."

"If I'm not happy today, Mike, I'm not sure when I will be."

"Sir, can I have a minute? I need a word with you."

They stepped outside the tent. McCardle reached for his key ring and turned on his pocket jammer.

"All clear."

"What have you got for me?"

"We know the identity of the Wooferette. His name is Julian Burroughs. He arrived in town about six months ago from Ohio."

"What's his story?"

"His pastor was a friend of Carlton Post. When word got out that they were organizing the Office of Faith and Reconciliation, the pastor wrote a letter of recommendation to Sanford Bayer. The kid came to town, Bayer interviewed him, and he got the job."

"I'll just bet he interviewed him. Is Burroughs involved with the reverend as well as Burnham?"

"Not that we can tell. He's a real straight arrow." McCardle smiled. "So to speak."

"What about the agent?"

"A low-level analyst by the name of Kevin Furlin. He's been on board a couple of years. Monitors intercepts, things like that—nothing of importance."

"Excellent."

"How do you want to proceed, sir?"

"We have to take Burroughs out of the equation first; that breaks the triangle. I assume you still have a tail on him?"

"Yes, sir."

"So let's assemble all the pictures, to start with. Get shots of him arriving and leaving both houses in the middle of the night. Then we approach Reverend Woofer with the evidence of the affair between Burroughs and Burnham, and we persuade him to send the kid's ass back to Ohio."

"And the agent?"

"That's trickier. We need to make sure this isn't some informal network operating on our dime. But we can't tail him, because he'll pick it up. Just track him electronically for a while, until we know we don't have a sewing circle within the company."

"Consider it done."

"Nice work, Mike. Good job."

"Thank you, sir."

Hornsby walked back toward the tent. The shaded seats were filling up with members of Congress, lobbyists, and the heads of several conservative organizations. Outside, the crowd waved American flags and shielded themselves from the sun. While not quite as massive as the audience for King's March on Washington, as Hornsby had hoped, attendance was still heavy enough to impress the *New York Times*.

"Heavenly and merciful God ..." began the Reverend Sanford Bayer at the stroke of noon, as his orange hair glistened in the sun. "We have assembled here today in our nation's capital to give thanks to you for our blessings. We are deeply grateful for the wisdom and courage of our elected leaders, for the bravery of our men and women in uniform, and most of all for their success on the battlefield. We know full well that their victory could never have been accomplished without your help and guidance. We pray to you for the courage to meet the challenges ahead, and we humbly place ourselves in your hands. We know that as you continue to watch over us and bless those we have chosen to lead our nation, we cannot possibly fail."

"Damn," William Hampton whispered to his wife in the VIP section, "that man needs a new hairdresser."

"Pass me a barf bag, would you? I think I'm going to puke."

"What's Andy doing up on that dais?"

"Somebody talked him into it. He's in a tough spot."

"Let us bow our heads," Bayer intoned, "and engage in a silent prayer for the safety of all those still on the battlefield. May they return to us quickly, after the flame of democracy has been lighted in their wake."

"If anybody knows about flames," Hampton whispered, "it'd be him."

When the silent prayer was finished, Bayard Stevenson rose to address the crowd. His bearing was erect, but he continually fingered the buttons on his uniform as he spoke.

"For well over two centuries," he began, "beginning with the battles of Lexington and Concord, through the agonies of Bull Run, the conflicts of two world wars, and the turmoil of countless other engagements in the four corners of the earth, our soldiers have distinguished themselves on the field of battle. They have never questioned the mission or the wisdom of their commanders, but have given their all to protect the freedoms we hold dear. As your secretary of defense, I am incredibly honored to have the privilege of commanding them. I never doubted for one moment that they would acquit themselves as honorably as the generations that preceded them. I am proud beyond words, and I thank them."

"Poor guy," whispered Bethany Hampton.

"Shucks," said her husband. "He was just followin' orders."

George Cane rose to address the crowd, squinting into the sun, his solemn expression occasionally punctuated by an impish grin.

"My fellow Americans, we assemble here today to commemorate the first in a series of victories over the forces of evil. When we were suddenly and brutally attacked on May first, our national resolve was tested like never before. And true to our traditions and heritage, we rose to the challenge. By triumphing over a ruthless dictator in Sumeristan, we have taken the first steps toward bringing democracy to the region. We have also brought ourselves one step closer to peace."

"What an idiot," Julian Burroughs said to David Burnham. "The worst part of it is that he actually believes it."

The two men watched the president's speech together in bed at Burnham's Capitol Hill townhouse, coffee cups in hand. They had enjoyed a rare evening of leisure the night before—dinner at a small restaurant in Adams-Morgan and dancing at several clubs before retiring to sleep late.

"Well, your boss works for him. What does that make you?"

"He doesn't *work* for him, exactly. He's more of an independent contractor."

"I know all about it. Don't tell me again about funding the outreach programs—"

"A lot of that money went toward AIDS relief, you know."

"I'd pin a medal on you, but you're naked."

"But as your president," Cane continued, "it is my duty to remind you once again that the battle for Sumeristan was only the first step in our crusade against evil. There may be many battles ahead, and they may not all be so easy. Our resolve could be tested as never before. But we must always be steadfast in the rightness of our cause. As Americans, we are a beacon of freedom and democracy to the rest of the world."

"Gag me," said Burnham.

"There are more than six hundred armed snipers in the center of the city," replied Burroughs. "Just wait until they start unloading on our poor guys over there. We'll see what he says then."

Burnham stared at his companion.

"How do you know that?"

"I think I read it in the *Post*."

"Sounds like you might have some sources."

"I do." Burroughs grinned, reaching for Burnham's thigh. "Sources of stimulation."

"Not yet. I want to see the rest of this."

"I want to express my deep appreciation to the members of my national security team, to General Stevenson, and to our brave men and women in uniform who have made this victory possible. But most of all, I want to thank the American people. When I first spoke to you following the horrendous events of May first, I asked for your support and your prayers. You have given generously of both. With your continued support, and with God's help, we cannot possibly fail. God bless you, and God bless the United States of America."

"We should go somewhere," said Julian.

"Absolutely. We're overdue for a long weekend."

"No, I mean somewhere far away, somewhere safe. Sumatra, Thailand, wherever. Somewhere away from politics. Someplace where we can't be harassed."

"You're dreaming," said Burnham. "These bastards would hunt us down and string us up by our thumbs."

CHAPTER 36

I T WAS CHALLENGING FOR SOME people, even those as close to the situation as Robert Hornsby, to pinpoint the precise moment when the wheels came off the situation in Sumeristan.

For many observers, the invasion started to unravel on August 9 with the murder of Sergeant Sam Gravino, just three weeks after the July 14 celebration. The father of three from Arkansas was on patrol with his company when he was shot by a rooftop sniper. His fellow soldiers stormed the building and killed the sniper, but it was too late for Gravino, who died shortly afterward at the base hospital.

This was not the first assassination of an American serviceman. Attacks had begun even as the National Day of Celebration was underway. The administration tried to hide them from the public, but this subterfuge became increasingly difficult as Sumeri snipers stepped up their activity in the weeks following the coalition's occupation. Even before Gravino's death in early August, several soldiers were dying every day.

As details of the soldier's fate filtered back to his family, however, they became outraged as well as bereaved. They hired an attorney and began giving interviews to the press. By Labor Day, the "Gravino Incident," along with rumors of many other Americans being slaughtered on the streets of Baghdad, had gone national. Major news outlets assigned investigative reporters assigned to the story. There were rumors the Gravinos had been booked on *60 Minutes*.

The administration responded by creating a Safe Zone in the central part of the city, an area extending several square miles from the site of Hussein Ghazi's original presidential palace. The edges of the Safe Zone were marked by makeshift concrete barriers and barbed wire, reminiscent of the early days of the Berlin Wall. *Making* it safe, however, was another matter. Clearing the area of Ghazi loyalists and Sumeristani dissidents required weeks of intense, hand-to-hand combat in which every square foot of territory was contested and fought over. "Battle for control of central Baghdad continues," crowed the *New York Times.* "Establishment of Safe Zone creates more casualties than entire invasion to date."

"What the hell's going on here, Bob?" asked George Cane one day in mid-September. The tips of his ears were flushed crimson, and Hornsby knew the president was agitated.

"What exactly are you referring to, sir?"

"Why don't we start with who's killing our troops."

"It's a combination of forces, most likely. Some of them are probably people who were loyal to Hussein Ghazi and want to get even. The rest are probably members of other Muslim sects who are attempting to mark their territory."

"Which Muslim sects?"

"Ghazi actually belonged to a minority sect. An opposing group is asserting their right to run the country going forward."

"If they're all Muslims, what do they care which group controls the country?"

"Well, *we* control it at the moment, and we're not Muslims. They want us out."

"No good deed goes unpunished, I guess." He looked at Hornsby. "This has to stop, Bob."

"That's exactly why we're establishing the Safe Zone, sir."

"Some safe zone. We've lost almost three hundred men since we took Baghdad."

"We're still clearing the area. It's a slow process, almost house by house. When we're done, the troops should be able to stroll down the street eating ice cream cones."

"And when do you think that will be?"

"A matter of a few more weeks, sir. We're almost there."

"All right. Do me a favor and get Bayard Stevenson back here. I'd like to talk to him and get his sense of the situation on the ground."

"Will do, sir, but it may be a few days before we can set it up. He's pretty busy at the moment."

"So are we. Please get him back here."

As-salumu alykum, said Salman al-Akbar. "Peace be unto you."

The leader of Husam al-Din sat in the garden of his compound in central Kabulistan, surrounded by baby goats and the shade of date palms. He watched as his chief lieutenant, Fazil Ahmadi, approached with a smile on his face.

Wa-alaikum salaam, replied his protégé, "And unto you, peace."

"I gather you might have good news for me."

"It seems there is nothing but good news these days, sir."

"Pray, speak."

"The Americans are having problems in Sumeristan, as we suspected they would. Their soldiers are being slaughtered on the streets of Baghdad like sheep in the market. The newspapers at home are becoming agitated."

"Excellent. Do we need to step up our activities in Baghdad?"

"For the moment, no. The city is filled with Ghazi loyalists, splinter groups, and those who seek power. We only need to watch."

"Allah be praised!"

"Yes, sir."

"Are they trying to discover our whereabouts?"

"There is no indication of this. We do not even think they are searching for Hussein Ghazi—only the weapons they believed he had."

"Let us not become complacent. We do not think they will look for us here, in the shadow of the Police Academy. But even so, we must constantly reinforce our ties with the Dua Khamail."

"This is being done. The regional commander is coming here next week for tea."

"You have done well." Al-Akbar stood up and reached for his walking stick. "We will remain vigilant, but we suspect things will only become worse for them as time goes on."

David Burnham hadn't cried since his father died—at least, not the way he was sobbing into the phone now.

"I don't fucking believe this."

"It's not the end of the world, Davey. You can come and visit me in Ohio."

"Sure, once or twice a year."

"Well, it'll be quality time, anyway."

"Why don't you tell them to shove it and stay here?"

"I told you, they have pictures."

"Pictures of us together? We've been out together, but that doesn't mean anything. We could be friends."

"They have pictures of me entering and leaving your place."

"So fight it. You say you were dropping off paperwork."

"Of course—dropping it off at ten in the evening, and leaving at six in the morning. After you thoroughly digested the paperwork. Makes perfect sense."

"So they know about me as well."

"Presumably."

"So they can blackmail me even further."

"What do you mean, *further?*"

"Long story," said Burnham. "Look, this isn't the 1950s. I think we should fight the bastards."

"It's still the 1950s if you're in the closet, which you happen to be."

"It's not fair."

"Davey, don't cry. Just come out. Then they can't do anything to you. It's very simple. Just repeat after me: I'm gay, so fuck you."

"I can't do that. It would kill my mother."

"Okay, listen—"

"Why don't you stay here? *You* tell them to fuck themselves, if it's so easy to do?"

"I can't. Sandy Bayer fired me."

"So go to work at some community action center, passing out Woofer-financed drugs to AIDS patients." Burnham paused. "Unless there's something you're not telling me."

"Davey, it doesn't matter. It's over. You have to accept it."

"Never. I'll get even with them, I promise you."

Julian chuckled. "Well, I have something for you that might help you do that."

"And what might that be?"

"Not over the phone, Davey. I'll give it to you in person. Let's get together before I leave."

"I'd love to."

"After that, I'll see you in Ohio. Or Sumatra, or Thailand. Or somewhere over the rainbow."

CHAPTER 37

I T HAPPENED ONE MORNING TOWARD the end of Abdul's junior year in high school. The May Day attacks and the invasion of Sumeristan were still several months away, but the government of Hussein Ghazi had intensified their campaign against disloyalty. The black cars of the security services were a frequent sight on the streets of Baghdad, and the population had grown more paranoid than usual. It became normal for men and boys suspected of plotting against the regime to be rounded up without warning and never seen again. As frightening as this was, it was eerily reassuring. People loyal to the regime felt that despite the tension and danger, they were still safe walking the streets.

That morning, everything changed when two black cars pulled up to a bus stop on the outskirts of the city shortly after dawn. They had been tipped off that a prominent dissident leader was in the crowd of waiting bus riders. The security agents rolled down their windows and opened fire. Abdul's father was killed instantly. Also among the dead were a construction worker, an elderly man, an eleven-year-old boy, a pregnant woman, and an infant in a stroller.

The dissident leader was not at the bus stop. He had been spotted twenty minutes earlier buying cigarettes at a nearby kiosk, but had then left the area.

The Alghafari family was plunged into the traditional three-day Muslim mourning period. They received many expressions of support from neighbors and fellow worshippers at their mosque, but no acknowledgment from the regime. Abdul was sullen for the first week following his father's death, but after that, his aggressive behavior returned. He fought with classmates, challenged teachers, and stopped attending Kasim Hamdani's Wednesday meetings.

"My heart breaks for you, Abdul," said his mother. She had come into his room one evening after he was suspended for attacking another student after school. "I wish there was something I could do."

"You've done enough," he snapped. "You sent me to Dr. Hamdani's academy so I could learn to be a collaborator with the people who killed my father."

"Please do not think that way. You have made so much progress in the last three years."

"What kind of progress? I've listened to lectures from a pompous idiot who extols the virtues of working within the system, as if the highest honor you could attain would be to pretend to be one of them. And after three years of brainwashing, that same system shoots my father like a dog in the street."

"Abdul—"

"Not for any reason. Not because he was being disloyal, or plotting with the opposition. Because he was *waiting for the bus*. He gets slaughtered along with a half dozen others all as innocent as he. And they give no condolences, make no apologies."

"In time, you will learn to forgive this. I know it seems impossible now."

"Never. What gives them the divine right to kill anyone they want, any time they want? You know who gives them that right? It is people like us, who are so timid that we accept things as they are. And people like Dr. Hamdani, who are so cynical that they profit from the system and teach others to do so. Bad enough that we are sheep, but he has blood on his hands."

"Abdul, I know how upset you are, and I do not blame you. But please do not speak this way."

"Go ahead, tell me it is dangerous. I have heard this my entire life. Shall we all hide under the bed like cowards?"

"It is pointless to think like this. You will not defeat them."

"Perhaps not," said the youth. "But I will get even."

After the May 1 attacks, Abdul's statements became more reckless. While there had been a large amount of anti-American sentiment among the population since the 1991 invasion, Hussein Ghazi's government clearly sensed the danger of the current situation and discouraged people from gloating over the results of May Day. Abdul, however, seemed jubilant. He was becoming more and more of a cheerleader for Husam al-Din, and spoke in public about the new caliphate to come. His mother was forced to pull him out of school, although Kasim Hamdani allowed him to finish the year studying at home with tutors.

"Have you given some thought to what you will do this summer?" she asked one night as the family was finishing dinner.

"Not exactly." He shrugged. "I assumed I would find a job, so I could help with our expenses."

"There is no need for you to do that. Your father left us in a comfortable position."

"I gather you have some suggestions."

"I was thinking it would be nice for you to visit my sister in Anbar province. You could get out of the city and get some fresh air. As you know, she has two boys you have not seen in several years. You could spend time with your cousins, play football with them."

"Football." Abdul laughed. "It sounds like summer camp."

"Life does not always have to be quite so serious, Abdul. I think a change of scenery will do you some good."

"It will not change the way I feel."

"Perhaps not. But at the least, you can spend some time with your family."

"Let me think about it, Mama. I know you mean well."

The next morning, at breakfast, his mother observed that Abdul seemed more relaxed than she had seen him since his father's death.

"Mama, I've been thinking about your offer to visit my aunt and uncle and cousins. It sounds like fun. If we truly don't need the money I would make this summer, I would like to go."

"Abdul, that is wonderful! I will let them know. I think you will come back a different person."

"That could well be." He smiled. "Playing football in Anbar does wonders for the soul."

CHAPTER 38

THUS AROSE MUCH DEBATE AMONG *the expedition concerning the proposal tendered by Prince Alexius of Constantinople. The abbot of Vaux, of the order of the Cistercians, spoke, and that party that wished for the dispersal of the expedition; and they said they would never consent: that it was not to fall on Christians that they had left their homes, and that they would go to Syria.*

And the other party replied: "Fair lords, in Syria you will be able to do nothing; and you might well perceive by considering how those have fared who abandoned us, and sailed from other ports. And be it known to you that it is only by way of Babylon, or of Greece, that the land overseas can be recovered, if so be that it is ever recovered. And if we reject this covenant we shall be shamed to all time."

There was discord in the expedition, as you hear … And only twelve persons took the oaths on the side of the Franks, for more (of sufficient note) could not be found. Thus was the agreement made, and the charters prepared, and a term fixed for the arrival of the heir of Constantinople; and the term so fixed was the fifteenth day after the following Easter.

On the day after Easter… the ships and the transports began to depart; and it was settled that they should take port at Corfu, an island of Roumania, and that the first to arrive should wait for the last. Before the Doge, the Marquis, and the galleys left Zara, Alexius, the son of Emperor Isaac of Constantinople, had arrived together.

He was sent by King Philip of Germany, and received with great joy and great honor; and the Doge gave him as many galleys and ships as he required. So they left the port of Zara ... and came to Corfu. The expedition sojourned thus for three weeks in that island, which was very rich and plenteous. Then did they sail from the port of Corfu on the eve of Pentecost, May 24.

On St. John the Baptist's Eve they came to St. Stephen, an abbey that lay three leagues from Constantinople. Those on board the ships and galleys had full sight of Constantinople, and they took port and anchored their vessels.

Now you may know that those who had never before seen Constantinople looked upon it very earnestly, for they never thought there could be in all the world so rich a city; and they marked the high walls and strong towers that enclosed it round about, and the rich palaces, and the mighty churches of which there were so many that no one would have believed it who had not seen it with his eyes ... And be it known to you, that no man there was of such hardihood that his flesh trembled: and it was no wonder, for never was there so great an enterprise undertaken by any people since the creation of the world.

The barons consulted together and said they would show the young Alexius, the son of the Emperor of Constantinople, to the people of the city. So they assembled all the galleys. The Doge of Venice and the Marquis of Montferrat entered into one, and took with them Alexius, the son of the Emperor Isaac; and into the other galleys entered the knights and barons, as many as could.

They went thus quite close to the walls of Constantinople and showed the youth to the people of the Greeks, and said:

"Behold your natural lord; and be it known to you that we have not come to do you harm, but have come to guard and defend you, if so be that you return to your duty. For he who you now obey as your lord holds rule by wrong and wickedness, against God and reason. And you know full well that he has dealt treasonably with him who is your lord and his brother, that he has blinded his eyes and reft from him his empire by wrong and wickedness. Now behold the rightful heir. If you hold with him, you will be doing as you ought, and we will not do unto you the very worst that we can." But for fear and terror of the Emperor Alexius, not one person on the land or in the city made show as if he held for the prince. So all went back to the expedition, and each sought his quarters.

On the morrow ... the council was held to discuss the order of the battalions, how many they should have, and of what strength. The day was fixed on which the expedition should embark on the ships and transports to take the land by force, and either live or die. And be it known to you that the enterprise to be achieved was one of the most redoubtable ever attempted.

The term fixed was now come, and the knights went on board the transports with their war-horses; and they were fully armed, with their helmets laced, and the horses covered with their housings, and saddled. All the other folk, who were of less consequence in battle, were on the great ships, and the galleys were fully armed and made ready.

The morning was fair a little after the rising of the sun; and the Emperor Alexius stood waiting for them on the other side, with great forces, and everything in order. And the trumpets sound, and every galley takes a transport in tow, so as to reach the other side more readily. None ask who shall go first, but each makes the land as soon as he can. The knights issue from the transports, and leap into the sea up to their waists, fully armed, with helmets laced, and lances in hand; and the good archers, and the good sergeants, and the good crossbowmen, each in his company, land so soon as they touch ground.

The Greeks made a goodly show of resistance; but when it came to the lowering of the lances, they turned their backs, and went away flying, and abandoned the shore. And be it known to you that never was port more proudly taken.

Thus did those of the expedition take council together to decide what they should do, and whether they should attack the city by sea or by land. The Venetians were firmly minded that the scaling ladders ought to be planted on the ships, and all the attack made from the side by the sea. The French, on the other hand, said they did not know as well how to help themselves in sea as on land ... so in the end it was devised that the Venetians should attack by sea, and the barons and those of the expedition by land.

[O]on a Thursday morning (17th July 1203) all things were ready for the assault, and the ladders in trim; the Venetians also had made them ready by sea. The order of the assault was so devised, that of the seven divisions, three were to guard the camp outside the city, and other four to give the assault. ...

Meanwhile the Doge of Venice had not forgotten to do his part, but had ranged his ships and transports and vessels in line ...

Now hear of a strange miracle: those who are within the city fly and abandon the walls, and the Venetians enter in, each as fast and as best he can, and seize twenty-five of the towers, and man them with their people. And the Doge takes a boat, and sends messengers to the barons of the host to tell them that lie has taken twenty-five towers, and that they may know for sooth that such towers cannot be retaken. The barons are so overjoyed that they cannot believe their ears; and the Venetians begin to send to the host in boats the horses and palfreys they have taken.

Then the Emperor Alexius issued from the city, with all his forces, and so many began to issue forth that it seemed as if the whole world were there assembled. The

Emperor marshalled his troops in the plain, and the rode towards the camp, and when our Frenchmen saw them coming they ran to arms from all sides ... It seemed as if the whole plain was covered with troops, and they advanced slowly and in order. And be it known to you, that never did God save any people from such peril as He saved the expedition that day.

That very night the Emperor Alexius of Constantinople took of his treasure as much as he could carry and took with him as many of his people as would go, and so fled and abandoned the city. And those of the city were astonished, and they drew to the prison in which lay the Emperor Isaac, whose eyes had been put out. Him they clothed imperially, and bore him to the great palace, and seated him on a high throne; and there they did to him obeisance as their lord. Then they took messengers, by the advice of the Emperor Isaac, and sent them to the expedition, to apprise the son of the Emperor Isaac, and the barons, that the Emperor Alexius had fled, and that they had again raised up the Emperor Isaac as emperor. And when the expedition heard the news, their joy was such as cannot be uttered, and they said: "Him whom God will help no man can injure."

The barons and counts and the Doge of Venice agreed to send envoys into the city ... to demand of the father that he should ratify the covenants made by the son. The envoys came before the Emperor Isaac, and the emperor and all those about him did them great honor. Geoffrey of Villehardouin said to the emperor: "Sire, thou seest the service we have rendered to thy son, and how we have kept our covenants with him ... And he asks of thee, as thy son, to confirm those covenants in the same form, and in the same manner, that he has done."

"What covenants are they?" asked the emperor. "In the first place to put the whole empire of Roumania in obedience to Rome, from which it has been separated this long while; further to give 200,000 marks of silver to those of the expedition, with food for one year for small and great; to send 100,000 men in his own ships, and at his own charges, to the land of Babylon, and keep them there for a year; and during his lifetime to keep, at his own charges, five hundred knights in the land overseas so that they might guard that land. Such is the covenant your son has made with us, and this covenant we desire you to confirm."

In the end the father confirmed the covenants, as his son had confirmed them, by oath and by charters with gold seals appended. These charters were delivered to the envoys. Then they took their leave of the Emperor Isaac, and went back to the expedition, and told the barons they had fulfilled their mission.

CHAPTER 39

NDREW NEPONSKI SAT AT HIS desk with a pile of newspapers by his side. The papers had been skimmed, sorted, and neatly folded to reveal the day's key stories. Slowly and methodically, he spread them out in front of him in an inverted pyramid, with the most important item closest to him. The ritual was a holdover from his earliest days in the Michigan state legislature, and it was a source of considerable amusement to both his children and staffers ("They have computers to do that now, you know"). As he worked his way up the congressional ladder, he realized that his desks were growing larger as the number of newspapers was continually shrinking.

He eyed the day's top story, a lead piece from the *New York Times*, with grim satisfaction: "Administration still searching for chemical weapons in Sumeristan," ran the headline, with the subhead "Stevenson fails to find stockpiles promised in U.N. speech."

> *Government sources revealed yesterday that U.N. weapons inspectors have thus far failed to discover large reserves of chemical weapons in Sumeristan. The existence of the weapons was detailed by Secretary of Defense Bayard Stevenson in his address to the U.N. prior to the American invasion, and was cited as a key reason for toppling the dictatorship of Hussein Ghazi.*

Stevenson's lengthy presentation to the General Assembly relied heavily on intelligence provided by the CIA. He claimed that Ghazi's weapons program had accelerated in the five years since inspectors were banned from the country, and that the Sumeri ruler had had accumulated stockpiles of deadly nerve gas stored in underground facilities throughout the country. According to his statements at the time, these weapons could be transported in mobile labs and were very close to being weaponized.

"The fact that we haven't found any chemical weapons yet doesn't mean that the weapons don't exist," said Stevenson yesterday. "It's simply proof that Hussein Ghazi was far more cunning in hiding them than we possibly could have thought."

Poor son of a bitch. Neponski shook his head. *And a nice guy, too. I'll bet he's cursing himself for getting involved with these lunatics.*

The rest of the news was not good. Hand-to-hand combat continued in the Safe Zone, as Special Forces cleared out pockets of Sumeri resistance. Outside the perimeter, it was the Wild West. Snipers fired on coalition troops from rooftops and abandoned buildings, and improvised bombs mined the streets. The administration estimated that it was still several months away from declaring the Safe Zone free of hostilities.

There was no mention in any of the stories about the hunt for Salman al-Akbar and Husam al-Din in Kabulistan.

George Cane and Robert Hornsby received a solemn and weary Bayard Stevenson in the Oval Office.

"I asked you to come back here, General," said Cane, "because I wanted to get a firsthand sense of the situation on the ground."

"In a word, sir, it's unstable."

"The *New York Times* quoted administration sources saying that the establishment of the Safe Zone was still several months away. Where'd they get that information?"

"I'm not sure, sir, but I think it's an understatement."

"Really?"

"I'm afraid so."

"Where are these people getting their guns and ammo?"

"The vice president knows more about that than I do, but my guess would be Husam al-Din. I'm told they have a number of cells in the city."

"Bob?" asked the president.

"Three or four to my knowledge, sir," said Hornsby. "Apparently they had quite a bit of hardware stockpiled prior to the invasion."

"Looks like you could say that. General, are you in touch with the weapons inspectors?"

"They send me reports, yes."

"*So where the hell are these weapons?*"

"Nobody knows, sir. One underground facility was nearly empty. Another had a few dozen canisters of gas that were unusable—five years old and out of date." Stevenson took a deep breath. "I suggest you ask the vice president where the weapons are, sir. He's the one who provided the intelligence saying they were there."

"The weapons are there," snapped Hornsby. "It's just a matter of time before they find them. And the intelligence came from the agency, in case you've forgotten."

"All right, gentlemen." George Cane held up his palm. "If Bob says the weapons are there, let's assume they're somewhere. The real question, General, is how long these people are going to be shooting at us."

"Probably as long as we occupy their country, sir."

"We have forty thousand troops in and around Baghdad," said the president. "I think that should be enough to get the place under control."

"With all due respect, Mr. President." Stevenson sat up very straight in his chair. "I'm a military man. You asked me to oversee the invasion, and I delivered the country to you in twenty-four days. The situation now is beyond my expertise."

"That could well be."

"I'm also the secretary of defense. As you know, there are other threats to our security around the world that must be monitored and attended to. I think there should be a limit on how long I sit in Baghdad and police the city."

"Bayard makes a good point," said Hornsby. "I think it may be time to install a military governor there."

"Who do you have in mind?" asked Cane.

If you ask nicely, thought Stevenson, *I'll see if I can bring Douglas MacArthur back from the dead. See how long he'd put up with this.*

"Let's have General Stevenson prepare a short list," said Hornsby. "We can vet the names and make an announcement in a few weeks."

"Sounds good," said the president.

"It should buy us some time with the press. We can tell the public that the campaign in Sumeristan is entering a new phase. We've been victorious, the immediate danger is over, and now it's just a matter of keeping the peace while we nurture the seeds of democracy in the country."

"Thank you," replied Stevenson. "It sounds good to me as well."

The immediate danger is over, he thought, *for those of us sitting here without a sniper pointing a rifle at our heads.*

The phone rang in David Burnham's Capitol Hill townhouse shortly after nine.

"Hello?"

"Evening, sweetie pie. How are you?"

"Fuck off."

"Now, now. Is that any way to talk to a trusted partner?"

"I have news for you: We're no longer partners."

"Oh, really? How do you figure?"

"I'm coming out. You have no more influence over me. I'm gay, so fuck you."

"Nice speech. How do you think the folks in Kansas will react?"

"My mother's fine with it. I already told her. You know what she said?"

"Do tell, sweetie?"

"She said, 'David, I've always told you to be yourself. That's all I could possibly want from you.'"

"Heartwarming, Davey-boy. You know what?"

"What?"

"I think you're lying."

The caller was right, of course, but Burnham figured it couldn't hurt to try and bluff his way out of the situation.

"It no longer matters what you think."

"It matters what your boss thinks. And I suspect he won't be thrilled to find out that your professional advice to him has been tinged with a healthy dose of self-interest over the past few months."

"I've told him as well, and he's also fine with it. He's a politician, he understands self-interest. And for the record, I don't think compromise and bipartisanship are bad things at a time like this. The problem is scumbags like you."

"You give me goosebumps. Nothing like a big, strong he-man fighting for truth, justice and the American way."

"Find somebody else to blackmail," he said as he hung up.

David Burnham was sick to his stomach.

CHAPTER 40

O N SEPTEMBER 27, THE ADMINISTRATION announced that General Charles "Chip" Boudreaux had been appointed as the new military governor of Baghdad. A native of Metairie, Louisiana, Boudreaux's combat experience had been limited to low-intensity campaigns such as Panama, Grenada, and Haiti, but he was known throughout the service for his wry sense of humor and his ability to relate to the common soldier. Hornsby thought he would play well with the press.

"The combat phase of the battle for Sumeristan is over," declared George Cane from the Rose Garden, "and today we enter a new stage in the country's liberation. True to our promise, we begin the task of bringing self-government to a people who suffered for decades under the yoke of a brutal dictator.

"General Boudreaux is uniquely qualified for this assignment. He has a sense of fairness and decency that runs to the very core of his being, and he is committed to nurturing the spirit of self-rule among the Sumeri people.

"I'm deeply grateful to General Bayard Stevenson, our secretary of defense, for his brilliant prosecution of the battle for Sumeristan. In less than one month, coalition troops operating under his direction removed Hussein Ghazi from power and took control of Sumeristan in the name of democracy. It is now time for General Stevenson to pass the torch to his colleagues and focus on the other security threats to the United States around the globe. I'm confident that he will succeed in protecting us from those challenges, just as he safeguarded American interests in vanquishing the evildoers of Sumeristan."

Smiling into the sun, Cane turned away from the podium and walked toward the portico. Reporters shouted questions at him as he retreated.

"Sir, how would you characterize the uptick in violence in Baghdad over the past few weeks?"

"What will General Boudreaux do to restore peace to the city that General Stevenson couldn't?"

"Sir, any updates on the whereabouts of Salman al-Akbar?"

"Sir, what's the latest intelligence on al-Akbar and Husam al-Din?"

The president ignored them and disappeared into the White House.

On September 29, the day after General Boudreaux arrived in Baghdad, a suicide bomber walked into an outdoor market on the edge of the Safe Zone and blew himself to bits. Twelve were killed and dozens more injured, many of them women and children. The carnage was too gruesome to show on the evening news: tropical fruit and heads of lettuce floated in pools of blood, surrounded by body parts and gore. Because the detonation occurred within a hundred yards of the Safe Zone, the media interpreted it as a sign that no one was truly safe.

The following day, a series of IEDs claimed the lives of two American servicemen and maimed four others. The day after that, snipers killed three coalition troops at different points around the city.

And so it went. Instead of improving, things got steadily worse. Although most of the Safe Zone was secure by the end of October, anything outside the perimeter remained extremely treacherous. Experienced combat troops in the coalition had never seen anything like it, and the constant danger frayed the nerves of the occupation forces.

None of these developments seemed to dampen the mood of the unflappable Chip Boudreaux, at least not in public. Hornsby had been correct about the General's appeal to reporters. His press conferences became lovefests. The tone was set at their first meeting on October 1.

"General," began a correspondent from the *New York Times*, "the past few weeks have been marked by some of the worst violence since coalition troops entered the city. What are your projections on how long it will take to bring the situation under control?"

"That's a great question." Boudreaux grinned. "You know, I had a neighbor once who adopted a child, a little boy 'bout five or six years old. I guess today you folks might call him a 'special needs child.' Anyway, this kid was a hell-raiser. He hadn't so much as set foot in that house when he started hootin' and hollerin', breakin' things and terrorizin' the neighborhood. And you know, 'bout an hour after he got there, most of us started askin' those folks how long it was goin' to take them to control him."

The room erupted in laughter.

"General," asked CNN, "one of the main rationales for the invasion was the existence of large stockpiles of chemical weapons Hussein Ghazi had supposedly stored in underground bunkers around the country. Thus far, weapons inspectors have been unable to locate any of these weapons stashes. Without revealing any classified information, could you share with us your sense of where these weapons might be?"

"Damned if I know," said Boudreaux cheerfully. "But if you find 'em, you lemme know right away, hear?"

This bought down the house, and his relationship with the press was smooth from that point on. Even George Cane enjoyed watching the footage of the press conferences and called the General "my kind of guy." Stevenson was mystified at how Boudreaux could get away with any of it.

Despite the general's affability, however, things continued to deteriorate. In the twenty-four days of the Sumeristan campaign, the coalition had suffered 197 fatalities. By the time Boudreaux arrived, the total was 578; it would climb to 1,503 by the end of the year. As 2002 dawned, it was becoming obvious to many members of the electorate that Hussein Ghazi had never possessed any weapons at all—chemical, biological, or nuclear.

Several weeks before Thanksgiving, Bayard Stevenson sat in the Situation Room with Robert Hornsby and Admiral Mike McCardle. The trio had just finished listening to a briefing from a senior CIA staffer on the strength of dissident forces in Baghdad.

Together again, thought Stevenson as the staffer left the room. *One big happy family.* The secretary had just returned the previous day from a conference with NATO commanders.

"What's your assessment of the situation, Bayard?" asked Hornsby. "I know you're in close touch with Chip Boudreaux."

"We talk every day, yes."

"Well?"

"We had a term for it at West Point, sir. We called it a clusterfuck."

Hornsby was startled. He had never heard Stevenson swear before, at least not in the presence of administration officials.

"General, I don't think that's appropriate—"

"There's nothing appropriate about this situation, Mr. Vice President. It's a mess. You haven't been able to infiltrate anyone on the ground, but my guess is that most of the so-called dissidents have been created since we entered Baghdad."

The two men were silent.

"As you both know, the increase in violence has been drastic—and it's not just our troops. The civilian population is being slaughtered indiscriminately. Not a day seems to go by when a suicide bomber doesn't take out a few dozen citizens who were just trying to live their lives. It's become an epidemic. Admiral, be honest with me. How much of this resistance is actually being coordinated by Husam al-Din?"

"It's hard to say for sure," said McCardle.

"There's increased activity from Husam al-Din in the area," said Hornsby. "No doubt about it. That's why we're thinking this might be the right time to step up the operations against them in Kabulistan, renew the hunt for Salman al-Akbar."

"Don't you think we're a bit late?"

"What's that supposed to mean?"

"We let him escape from Tora Bora, didn't we?"

"Listen, General," said McCardle, "we understand this is a frustrating situation for you. It's the same for us. But we're all on the same team here, and what we need now are team players."

"I was in the army all my life, sir. I really don't need the concept of teamwork explained to me."

"All right, Bayard," said Hornsby. "Do you have a solution to offer here? Something constructive?"

"I agree that we should renew the hunt for Salman al-Akbar. Most members of the public now view him as the central villain of the piece, as I do. Can't we put some people on the inside? I assume we must have native speakers."

"Sure, we have native speakers," said McCardle. "Guys whose families came over here in 1958. Kids who grew up in the Midwest and went to Oberlin College. They'd last about ten minutes before they got taken outside and shot."

"Well, gentlemen," said Stevenson evenly, "I'm not the brains of the operation. I just represent the long arm of the law. You tell me where to go, and I send troops in to kill people and break things."

"We know Salman al-Akbar is somewhere in Kabulistan," said Hornsby. "We'll get you some intelligence, see if we can sharpen the focus."

"Intelligence," replied Stevenson. *Somewhere in Kabulistan.* "Sure."

CHAPTER 41

STARING AT THE INVERTED PYRAMID of newsprint on his desk, Andrew Neponski pressed the button to the outer office.

"Yes, sir?" asked Samantha Sperling, David Burnham's assistant and Neponski's number-two person on the staff.

"Sam, ask David to come in here, would you please?"

The Speaker looked up to see her in the doorway.

"Where's David?"

"He's sick, sir."

"Really? Second day in a row. That's not like him. He's never out."

"Is there something wrong?"

"I'm not sure, but he's seemed very upset lately."

"Hmm. You could be right—he hasn't been himself. Any clues?"

"No, but I think I might stop by after work and check on him."

"Excellent idea. Let me know what happens."

He had finished his business in the House chamber and was preparing to go home when the buzzer sounded at seven o'clock.

"Yes?"

"Calvin Dobbs is on the phone for you, sir."

"I'll be damned."

Dobbs was the District of Columbia police chief. The two men had known each other for several decades, back to the time when Neponski was a young congressman and Dobbs was an ambitious detective. He was the prototypical gentle giant: a large black man with a polished bald head, constant glower, and heart of gold.

"Calvin! How are you, buddy? Long time no see."

"I'm fine, sir, but I'm afraid I'm calling on business. Sad business. I need you to come over to David Burnham's place right away."

"What's wrong? Is he okay?"

"No, sir, he's not. Just drop what you're doing and come on over. We can discuss it when you get here."

As Neponski's car approached Burnham's townhouse, he saw the lights flashing on the cruisers. The cop at the door lifted the yellow tape to let him pass.

"Where's Calvin?"

"The chief's upstairs, sir. He's waiting for you."

The Speaker climbed the short flight of stairs to Burnham's study and saw Dobbs on the landing. *Dammit, this is not good*, he thought. *He's got his notification face on.*

"I'm truly sorry to see you again under these circumstances, sir," he said as they shook hands.

"Calvin, come on. It's Andy—always has been. What's going on?"

"I'm afraid he's dead, sir. Andy."

"*What?*"

"I'm really sorry. I know you liked him."

"What the hell happened?"

"Classic suicide. He rigged the rope to the top of an exercise machine near the ceiling. My men cut him down."

"Good God."

"Let's sit down, Andy."

The two men sat facing each other in a pair of overstuffed chairs in Burnham's library.

"I don't believe this. I can't grasp it."

"I'm sorry, but I have to ask you a few questions."

"Of course. Go ahead."

"Was he acting strange recently? Depressed, or anything like that?"

"Someone on my staff thought so, but I didn't see it."

"You know, we checked the bathroom. That's automatic, one of the first things we do in these cases, but there were no prescriptions in there. Nothing for anxiety, no antidepressants."

"How can this be?"

"Look, I have to ask you: Did you know this young man was gay?"

"No. Of course not. How would I know that? I never asked. It was none of my business."

"Well, a lot of other folks seem to think so. They all believe he was in the closet."

"Jesus. It never occurred to me to even think about it. Maybe I should've—"

"No," his friend said. "No guilt. There's nothing you could have done to change things. I can tell you, Andy, that in these situations folks just do what they're destined to do."

"This was his destiny? Swinging from a rope?"

"All I'm saying is that there's nothing you could have done to get a different outcome."

"And you think the fact that he was gay had something to do with this?"

"I don't think anything at all. This is how we do it. We get whatever facts we can and work from there." He paused. "You want me to make the notification to his next of kin?"

"I'll do it. His mother lives in Kansas. She's elderly. I don't want her getting a phone call from someone she doesn't know."

"Whatever you want."

"Did he leave a note?"

"No note, no."

"Nothing at all?"

"I know you're looking for an explanation. Hopefully there'll be one."

"I'd like to see him."

"You know, Andy, I really don't suggest that. It might not be—"

"I want to see him, dammit."

"Right this way, then."

They went into the bedroom, and Dobbs unzipped the body bag on the floor. Burnham's face was a terror mask. His purple tongue protruded from his mouth, and his eyes looked like they were about to pop out of his head. Neponski would remember it the rest of his life.

"All right." He turned away and headed back to the study. "Enough."

The two men sat down once again in the armchairs.

"Can I get you something?"

"Look, I was in combat, but that ... I guess I was hoping that he went peacefully."

Dobbs was silent.

"What's your feeling about this, Calvin? You said he was gay. Can you connect some dots, make any sense of this?"

"People with secrets are unsteady, Andy. They're vulnerable."

"So you think someone was blackmailing him?"

"Not necessarily. But if he was in the closet, he was a walking target for a number of folks. It could've been a jilted lover who threatened to expose him. Could've been any number of things. You said he was from Kansas?"

"Yes."

"Well, that place ain't the gay pride capital of the world, last time I looked. I imagine no one at home knew the truth about him."

"Probably not." He thought about Burnham's mother, a genial elderly widow he had met on her last visit to Washington. "Look, you think you could do me a favor?"

"What's that?"

"Is there any way this doesn't have to go down as a suicide? Can we say he was in a car accident, or something like that?"

"Can't do it, Andy." He shook his head. "For starters, the coroner's going to rule it a suicide. And beyond that, the press will be snooping around. If I say he slipped on a banana peel, I'll get my ass in a sling."

"I'd really like to find out what happened here."

"We'll look into it."

"I know manpower is scarce—"

"I'll help you any way I can," Dobbs said firmly. "Don't you worry about it."

"I appreciate it." Neponski stood up. "So what happens now?"

"The reporters are gathering outside. You'll have to give them some sort of statement."

"Jesus. What the hell am I supposed to tell them?"

"Nothing to it, Andy." He put his hand on the Speaker's shoulder. "Keep it short and sweet. You tell them this was a tragedy, that everyone who knew this young man is suffering tonight. You send your condolences to the family and ask everyone to respect their privacy at this difficult time."

"No one's going to respect their privacy, least of all those guys. Snooping around is their job."

"Well, it's my job too. I'll keep you posted."

"Thank you, Calvin."

Where's that rear exit when you need it? he thought as he descended the stairs toward the waiting gaggle of reporters.

CHAPTER 42

URING HIS DECADES IN WASHINGTON, Robert Hornsby had learned one thing: Phone calls in the dead of night were never good news.

"I'm sorry to wake you, sir," said McCardle.

"Shit." Hornsby yawned and glanced at the clock. It was 2:30. "All right, I'm going downstairs. Call me on the secure line."

He put on his bathrobe and trundled down to the office, waiting for the red phone to ring.

"Yes, Mike?"

"I'm afraid we have a problem."

"Go ahead."

"For starters, there's been a shooting at Carla Stennings's apartment."

"What happened?"

"We're not entirely sure at this point, but we assume it was some sort of lover's quarrel. The woman was a member of the Lavender Menace."

"And she's dead?"

"Yes, sir."

"The cops are there?"

"The street's lit up like a Christmas tree. Neighbors called it in after they heard shots."

"Okay." He yawned again. "What else? You said the shooting was 'for starters.'"

"This is where it gets delicate."

"Spit it out, Mike."

"Courtney Cane was seen leaving the house."

"Oh, Jesus. No."

"I'm afraid so."

"What do you mean, *seen*? Seen by whom?"

"By the agents, of course. They were across the street in a car."

"Did she leave before or after the shooting?"

"Before, as far as we can tell."

"Well, that's something, at least. Where is she now?"

"We don't know, sir."

"What do you mean, you don't know?"

"Your orders were to make the tail unobtrusive. They couldn't very well start the car and follow her."

"Okay, you're right."

"There's another problem …" McCardle hesitated. Hornsby could hear him holding his breath.

"There always is."

"She was seen by someone else. There was another guy on the street."

"That's terrific—absolutely fucking great. Who was this guy?"

"Just a passerby, we think. Somebody who lived in the neighborhood and happened to be coming home. But it gets worse."

"Go ahead."

"It looks like he took a picture of her."

"How the hell could he do that—was he walking around in the middle of the night with a camera?"

"He had a camera on his cell phone of all things, sir. When he first held it up, the agents weren't sure if it was a weapon or not. They were reaching for their guns when they realized it was a phone. He just snapped the picture and walked away."

"God almighty."

"We assume his motivations were innocent. To him, Courtney Cane was probably a celebrity. Like seeing Britney Spears."

"Okay, let me get the chronology straight. She leaves the apartment, the guy sees her, he takes the picture. Then there are the shots, and neighbors call the cops. By the time they get there, she's gone."

"Correct, sir."

"So we've hit the trifecta: a radical lesbian murderer, a dead body, and a picture of the president's daughter leaving the apartment."

"It could have been worse. She might still have been in the apartment when the police got there."

"My lucky day." Hornsby rubbed the bridge of his nose. "All right, let's find this guy. I assume the agents at least saw where he lived?"

"We know the building, yes. We're on it."

"Good. Find out who he is. And let's get that phone."

"What about him, sir?"

"I don't care about the guy," said Hornsby. "I just want that phone."

The Speaker of the House picked up the phone in his office. Normally his staff placed calls for him, but this time he dialed the number himself.

"Chief Dobbs's office," chirped the receptionist.

"This is Andrew Neponski. I'd like to speak with Calvin, please."

"I'll put you through, sir." In a moment the melodious voice came on the line. "Andy! How are you, buddy? Feeling any better?"

"Not really."

"How'd things go in the heartland?"

"It was a horror show."

Neponski had accompanied David Burnham's body back to Kansas on a government plane, and had stayed to attend the funeral. Since Burnham had no siblings and his father was deceased, Neponski had shepherded Mrs. Burnham through the arrangements and the service. Guilt squirmed within him every second of the process—he felt he had been entrusted to protect her son, and his failure to do so ate at him like maggots in his gut.

"Sounds like the mother didn't take it well."

"She's eighty-five, Calvin. The woman is like something out of a Norman Rockwell painting. Five minutes after she meets you she's knitting you a sweater. Then her son goes and hangs himself."

"I feel for you. I truly do."

"What's the news on your end?"

"We pulled his home phone records," said Dobbs. "It was all pretty straightforward. About half of it was work related. There was a string of calls to and from Julian Burroughs."

"Wasn't he the guy who worked for Sanford Bayer?"

"That's him. He was abruptly sent back to Ohio about a month ago. Apparently the two of them had a connection."

"I don't need to know the details."

"There were eight or ten calls from a number we couldn't identify. They were all incoming, and they all occurred between nine and ten in the evening. We're trying to run it down now. It's the closest thing we have to a clue."

"Sounds like you think someone was blackmailing him."

"Andy, no offense," Dobbs said. "The kid had everything going for him—successful, great job, great future. In my experience, guys like that don't suddenly end up hanging from an exercise machine. Something was going on."

"I agree."

"You have any thoughts? Anything that might be helpful to us?"

"No thoughts, no," said Neponski. "Just intuition."

"Let's hear it."

"Intuition doesn't get you bus fare, Calvin."

"Still, everything is useful. Don't make me come up there and beat you with a rubber hose."

"I find it odd that there hasn't been any dirt in the press about this. There haven't been any leaks of any sort. No one on this end would have talked to them, of course, but there hasn't been anything about David leaked from the other side. And you know this administration hates gays worse than they hate Communists."

"True."

"I'm sure you're trying to find out who made those calls. They probably know who it is already, plus what the guy had for breakfast this morning."

"Probably so. But remember that they have to protect Reverend Bayer, particularly if this young man was involved with Burroughs."

"Okay, then think about this: Scott Leventhal called me personally to offer the use of a plane to transport David back to Kansas. I wouldn't have had any trouble getting my hands on a plane, and he knows that."

"How nice."

"Maybe so. But when did we start using 'Leventhal' and 'nice' in the same sentence?"

"Intuition, as you say."

"You asked."

"Look, Andy, we'll get to the bottom of this. And you'll be the first to know." He paused. "And I might be able to help you in some other ways, too. Let's see how it all shakes out."

"I appreciate it. When I find out who was behind this, I'll pursue them to the ends of the earth. That's a promise."

CHAPTER 43

WHILE HE WAITED FOR HIS daughter's voice to come on the line, the president stared at her photograph on his desk. It was a picture of Courtney in her stroller at nine months; she was laughing and waving a rattle.

Two hundred thousand troops in Sumeristan. Our boys are getting killed every day, and I have to worry about the radical lesbians.

"The last thing I need is a lecture, Dad," said Courtney. "Particularly since I talked to Mom last night."

"I'm not going to lecture you, sweetheart, and I doubt if she did either. We're just concerned about your safety."

"I understand that."

"She tells me you were in the apartment. That worries both of us for obvious reasons."

"I left a few minutes before it happened. I saw where things were going, and my instincts told me to get out. So obviously I'm not as helpless as you think."

"No one thinks you're helpless. But honestly, I'm not even sure it's wise to be on the street in a neighborhood like that after dark."

"It's a residential area—there were other people on the street. There was even a guy who waved to me and took my picture."

"Is that so?" asked the president. "He was carrying a camera?"

"He took the picture with his cell phone. The point is, there's nothing wrong with the neighborhood, and I know what I'm doing. I'm not a child, although I understand that you and Mom think of me that way."

"The only thing wrong with the neighborhood is that someone was shot to death there the night before last. Other than that, it's fine." He drummed his fingers on the desk. *People want to know why I keep a baby picture of my daughter on my desk? They should hear this conversation.* "Listen, Courtney, you feel strongly about certain issues. You're involved. You want change. We think that's admirable. I'd just feel more comfortable if you were more careful about your associates."

"And what would you suggest? Because I'm sure you're going to."

"Why don't you try to work within the system? You have a unique opportunity to do that. I've been elected, and the time is right. You could get involved and make a difference."

"Oh, sure. The Republican Party is very progressive on gay issues. I'm sure they'd love to have a lesbian in a position of prominence."

"You could form a group that was the female equivalent of the Log Cabin guys. I'm just talking off the top of my head, you understand."

"Dad, the Log Cabin Republicans are a bunch of patsies. They're faggots who are so desperate for approval that they'll work faithfully for a system that hates their guts."

"Well, they haven't killed anybody recently. Not that I remember."

"Dad, this isn't going anywhere."

"Courtney, just be careful, okay?"

"I don't need to be careful, not with your goons following me everywhere I go. It's not like I can even go out for a carton of milk without being watched."

"So now people are following you? Don't you think that's a bit paranoid?"

"I suggest you have a chat with my Uncle Bob, Dad. Ask him who the Keystone Cops are."

"I will. You just remember that we love you."

He hung up and pushed the buzzer on the console.

"Yes, sir?"

"Get me Hornsby on the phone."

"Right away, Mr. President."

"Bob," said George Cane when the vice president picked up, "are you having my daughter followed?"

"Why would you think that, sir?"

"Because she apparently spotted them a long time ago. Either they're not trying to be invisible, or they're not as slick as you think they are."

"Sir, she refused a Secret Service detail. We had to do something to keep her safe. And as you yourself pointed out when we were discussing the Lavender Menace, she hasn't exactly been attending Girl Scout meetings."

"Well, don't think I don't appreciate it. But they seem to be a bit clumsy."

"Maybe, maybe not. But's not a bad thing if certain people realize she's being protected. It helps keep the wolves at bay."

"More to the point, did you know that someone took her picture the other night in front of the Stennings apartment?"

"We're aware of that, yes. We're running it down."

"I don't want to see that picture on the front page of the *Post*."

"You won't, sir. I'll promise you that."

Later that week, McCardle sat in Hornsby's office at the observatory as the two men wrapped up their meeting. Spread out on the desk in front of them were maps of northern Kabulistan.

"So that's all we think there are?" asked the vice president. "Four installations?"

"Four major ones, yes. I'd say there are about fifty Husam al-Din agents at each, with the same number of trainees at any given time."

"And they're how far from each other?"

"They're pretty close. The two largest ones are about a hundred miles apart, with the two smaller ones in between."

"That's odd," said Hornsby, squinting at the plans. "You'd think they'd scatter them."

"We assume the proximity facilitates communication between them, but your point is well taken. They don't seem to be concerned about detection."

"Works for me." Hornsby smiled. "We can take them out in one airstrike. That's what I'm going to recommend to the president, at any rate."

"We'd really be better off going into the country and cleaning out the Dua Khamail. They're the ones who are harboring these guys and helping to create the situation."

"Well, we can't really do that until we get things in Baghdad under control."

"And you think this will do it, sir?"

"It's a multipurpose gesture. For one thing, it sends a message to these bastards that they can't continue picking off our troops whenever they feel like it. It also lets them know that they're not invincible, that we can hunt them down and find them. And of course it should help in Baghdad. We know that a lot of these so-called dissidents are agitators trained by Husam al-Din. With any luck, we'll be able to point to a downturn in violence almost immediately."

"May I suggest getting General Boudreaux on the same page about that?"

"Don't worry about Boudreaux. I can give him a remedial course in how to follow orders."

"Very good, sir."

"What else, Mike? How are we coming along with this asshole and his cell phone?"

"We know who he is and where he lives. He works in some tech company downtown, keeps regular hours. Commutes by Metro. He's also gay, by the way."

"Jesus. How is it that everybody's *gay* all of a sudden? It's not like they're breeding or anything …"

"I only mention it, sir, because it explains why he thought Courtney Cane was a celebrity."

"When are going to have the phone? That's the main thing."

"We're watching him closely, observing his patterns. Just waiting for the right moment."

"Well, don't wait forever. I want that goddamn phone yesterday."

Shortly before the holidays, Neponski sat in his office watching the evening news with Samantha Sperling, his new administrative assistant and chief of staff. The practice was a holdover from happier times; the Speaker and David Burnham used to end their day this way. Neponski had toyed with the idea of eliminating the newscast and heading directly home, but he found it useful to get feedback on the day's events from someone else's perspective, even if Sam didn't yet possess David's intricate grasp of the political landscape.

"These are sobering days in Baghdad," intoned General Chip Boudreaux. "Nothing saddens a commander more than losing troops on the field of battle. Our brave men and women, the greatest fighting force in the world, are frequently battling an unseen enemy, an adversary that lurks in the shadows and strikes without warning. Rather than engage our troops out in the open, they cower in the doorways of abandoned buildings and wait to take us by surprise."

"Boy," said Samantha, "he's singing a different tune."

"He's just following a script. This isn't even the way he talks normally."

"How can he call the streets of Baghdad the field of battle?"

"They are now."

"In the beginning," Boudreaux continued, "we were told that the ranks of the Sumeri dissidents were filled with those still loyal to Hussein Ghazi; we were also told that the violence was a prelude to a bloody religious war. Recently, though, it has become clear—both to me and to members of our intelligence community—that the dissidents are either agents of Husam al-Din or were trained in their terrorist camps. We know that a number of these installations are located in northern Kabulistan, with the tacit approval of the Dua Khamail, and are feeding a steady stream of belligerents onto the streets of Baghdad. I've asked the CIA to pinpoint the exact location of these camps. When their whereabouts are known, I intend to ask the president to take quick and decisive action against them. Only in this way will we begin to stop the unnecessary and cowardly violence against our coalition forces."

"General Chip Boudreaux," said the news anchor, "addressing reporters at a press conference in Baghdad, and stressing the need for the United States to eliminate the terrorist threat from Husam al-Din training camps in northern Kabulistan."

"What do you think, sir?" asked Samantha.

"I think we'll be bombing Kabulistan within a week."

"It's a strange time of year, don't you think?"

"Not really," said her boss. "Nixon did it on a massive scale in 1972. People will be too distracted with Christmas shopping to pay much attention to it, except in a general way. And the targets aren't Christians, either. There won't be any public outrage over it."

"True."

"Anyway, they have to do something. Our troops are being knocked off faster than we can count. And of course, this is what we should have done in the first place, rather than invade Sumeristan."

"In local news," said the anchor, "the D.C. coroner today entered a finding of accidental death in the case of Colin Berlinger, who died last week after being assaulted outside a Metro station in southeast Washington.

"The case, dubbed the 'Cell Phone Murder' by tabloid reporters, horrified a quiet residential neighborhood that was already traumatized by the fatal shooting at Carla Stennings's apartment several weeks earlier. According to witnesses, Berlinger had been working late at his job in a technology firm on Connecticut Avenue. He was talking on his cell phone as he exited the

Metro station near his home, when he was accosted by three Hispanic males who demanded that he relinquish the phone. Berlinger refused and a scuffle ensued, during which he fell and hit his head on the curb. The injury resulted in blunt force trauma and brain damage. The men escaped with his phone, and Berlinger was rushed to a nearby hospital, where he died during surgery."

"What a world." Neponski shook his head. "People getting killed over a phone. You know, D.C. was really nice when I first came here—you could walk down the street at any hour of the day or night, in almost any neighborhood."

"Sounds like he should just have given them the phone and walked away."

"Obviously so. I'm glad I won't be around here twenty years from now. The way things are going, it won't be much better than Baghdad. From here on out, I think I'd feel better if we had someone escort you to the Metro station at night."

"I really don't think that's necessary, sir."

"Tell that to this Berlinger guy. If I could, I'd have somebody escort you on the other end."

"I live in Arlington, three blocks from the station. It's perfectly safe."

"Sure. Just don't talk on your phone while you're walking." He looked at his watch. "Time for us to go, anyway. Why don't you just humor me, Sam? I don't want to lose anyone else."

CHAPTER 44

THE NEW EMPEROR WENT OFTEN to see the barons in the camp, and did them great honor... and this was but fitting, seeing that they had served him right well. And one day he came to camp and spoke to them, and said: "Lords, I am emperor by God's grace and yours, and you have done me the highest service that ever yet was done by any people to Christian man ... and the Greeks are full of despite because it is by your help that I have entered into my inheritance.

"Now the term of your departure is nigh, and your fellowship with the Venetians is timed only to last until the feast of St. Michael. And within so short a term I cannot fulfill my covenant. If you abandon me, the Greeks hate me because of you; I shall lose my land, and they will kill me. I ask of you to remain here till March, and I will entertain your ships for you one year from the feast of St. Michael, and bear the cost of the Venetians, and will give you such things that you may stand in need of till Easter. And within that term I shall have placed my land in such case that I cannot lose it again, and your covenant will be fulfilled, for I shall have paid such moneys as are due to you; and I shall be ready also with ships either to go with you myself, or to send others, as I have covenanted; and you will have the summer from end to end in which to carry on the war against the Saracens."

The barons thereupon said they would consult together ... and they remained in the camp and assembled a parliament the next day. Then there was much discord *in the expedition, as had been oft times before on the part of those who wished the expedition should break up ... In the end the Venetians made a new covenant to maintain the fleet for a year, reckoning from Michaelmas, the Emperor Alexius paying them for so doing; and the pilgrims, on their side, made a new covenant to remain in the same fellowship, for the same term. Thus were peace and concord established in the expedition.*

Afterwards, by advice of the Greeks and the French, the Emperor Alexius issued from Constantinople, with a very great company, purposing to quiet the empire and subject it to his will. With him went a great part of the barons, and the others remained to guard the camp. The emperor returned to Constantinople on St. Martin's Day. Great was the joy at his homecoming, and the Greeks and the ladies of Constantinople went out to meet their friends in great cavalcades, and the barons returned to the camp.

The emperor, who had managed his affairs right well and now thought he had the upper hand, was filled with arrogance toward the barons and those who had done so much for him, and never came to see them in the camp, as he had done aforetime. And they sent to him and begged him to pay them the moneys due, as he had covenanted. But he led them on from delay to delay, making them, at one time and another, payments small and poor; and in the end the payments ceased and came to naught.

The Marquis Boniface of Montferrat, who had done more for him than any other, went to him oftentimes, and showed him what great services the crusaders had rendered him ... and the emperor still entertained them with delays, and never carried out such things as he had promised, so that at last they saw an knew clearly that his intent was wholly evil.

Then the barons of the expedition held a parliament with the Doge of Venice ... and they decided to send good envoys to demand the fulfillment of their covenant ... and if not, they were to defy him, and right well might he rest assured that the barons would by all means recover their due.

The envoys dismounted at the gate and entered the palace, and found the Emperor Alexius and the Emperor Isaac seated on two thrones, side by side. And there were with them a great company of people of note and rank, so did well the court seem the court of a rich and mighty prince. By desire of the other envoys Conon of Bethune, who was very wise and eloquent of speech, acted as spokesman:

"Sire, we have come to thee on the part of the barons of the expedition and of the Doge of Venice. They would put thee in mind of the great service they have done to thee, a service known to the people and manifest to all men. Thou hast sworn, thou and thy father, to fulfill the proposed covenants, and they have your charters in hand. But you have not fulfilled those covenants well, as you should have done ... Should

you do so, all will be well. If not, be it known to you that from this day forth they will not hold you as lord or friend, but will endeavor to obtain their due by all the means in their power."

Much were the Greeks amazed and greatly outraged by this open defiance; and they said that never had anyone been so hardy as to dare defy the emperor of Constantinople in his own hall. Great was the tumult there within, and the envoys turned about and came to the gate and mounted their horses.

Thus did the war begin; and each side did to the other as much harm as they could, by sea and by land. The Franks and the Greeks fought often; but never did they fight that the Greeks did not lose more than the Franks. So the war lasted a long space, till the heart of the winter... Then the Greeks, being thus embroiled with the Franks, saw that there was no hope of peace, so they privily took counsel together to betray their lord. Now there was a Greek who stood higher in his favor than all others, and had done more to make him embroil himself with the Franks than any other. This Greek was named Mourzuphles. With the advice and consent of the others, one night towards midnight, when the Emperor Alexius was asleep in his chamber, those who ought to have been guarding him—and specially Mourzuphles—took him in his bed and threw him into a dungeon in prison. Then Mourzuphles made himself emperor, with the help and by the counsel of the other Greeks, and was crowned at St. Sophia in January 1204. Now see if ever people were guilty of such horrible treachery!

When the Emperor Isaac heard that his son was taken and Mourzuphles crowned, great fear came upon him, and he fell into a sickness and died. And the Emperor Mourzuphles caused the son, whom he had in prison, to be poisoned two or three times, but it did not please God that he should die. Afterwards the emperor went and strangled him, and when he had strangled him, caused it to be reported everywhere that he had died a natural death, and had him mourned for, and buried honorably and as an emperor, and made a great show of grief.

But murder cannot be hid. Soon was it clearly known, both to the Greeks and to the French, that this murder had been committed, as has just been told to you. . . .

Dire was the war between the Franks and the Greeks, for it abated not, but rather increased and waxed fiercer, so that few were the days on which there was not fighting by sea or land. . . .

And you must know that eighty knights were in this company, and every one was either killed or taken. And well does this book bear witness, that of those who avoided the host of Venice, there was not one but suffered harm or shame. He therefore must be accounted wise who holds to the better course. Then did the barons of the expedition and the Doge of Venice assemble in parliament, and with them met the bishops and the clergy. And all the clergy, including those who had power from the pope, showed to the baron and to the pilgrims that anyone guilty of such a murder had no right to own lands … "Wherefore we tell you," said the clergy, "that this war is lawful and just, and that it you have a right intention to conquer this land, to bring it into Roman obedience, all those who die after confession shall have part in the indulgence granted by the pope." And you must know that by this the barons and the pilgrims were greatly comforted. To speak of the pilgrims who had sailed from ports other than Venice, and of the ships of Flanders that had sojourned during the winter at Marseilles, and had all gone over in the summer to the land of Syria: These were far more in number than the expedition before Constantinople. What a great mischance it was that they had not joined themselves to the expedition, for in that case would Christendom have been forever exalted. But because of their sins, God would not so have it, for some died of the sickness of the land, and some turned back to their own homes. Nor did they perform any great deeds, or achieve aught of good, in the land overseas … Of those who avoided the expedition of Venice, there was not one but suffered harm or shame.

CHAPTER 45

FAZIL AHMADI SAT UNDER AN umbrella and chatted with the training camp commander as he watched the newest batch of recruits run the obstacle course. Even the umbrella offered scant protection from the midday heat of Kabulistan, which approached 100 degrees Fahrenheit in July.

"So," asked the commander, "His Excellency does not think an attack against the Dua Khamail is imminent?"

"The Americans are distracted. Every time they come to believe they are making progress in Baghdad, we intensify the violence." The commander nodded approval. "They look foolish in the eyes of the world," Ahmadi continued, "and this is something they cannot abide."

"The tide is in our favor," agreed the commander. "We now have so many volunteers that we cannot accommodate them all."

"Excellent."

"But I trust you will alert me if you come to believe a move against the Dua Khamail is planned."

"Certainly, but you need not worry. As time goes on, the American casualties will mount, and the public will turn against their government."

Ahmadi watched with interest as a young man sprinted from the start of the course. Despite the heat, he took the obstacles at a dead run, jumping over barriers with his rifle hoisted above his head. As he approached a dummy dressed as an American soldier, the young man unsheathed his bayonet. He attacked the dummy in a surprising burst of hostility, stabbing it repeatedly until the stuffing scattered over the ground.

"Abdul, that's enough," shouted the commander. "Leave some Americans for others to kill."

"Interesting." Ahmadi stroked his carefully trimmed beard. "I would like to meet him."

As the youth jogged toward them, Ahmadi observed that he looked barely old enough to be out of high school.

"Young man," said Ahmadi, "what is your name?"

"Abdul Alghafari, sir."

"I am Fazil Ahmadi. I bring you greetings from His Excellency, Salman al-Akbar."

Abdul bowed deeply.

"I am honored to meet you."

"May I ask what brings you here?"

"I want to do my part in establishing the new caliphate, sir, even if that part is small. Like you, I want to see our land ruled by true believers rather than infidels."

"That is an admirable goal. But you realize that the road to our new caliphate may be long and difficult. It will require much sacrifice."

"I will sacrifice all that I have, sir."

"Excellent. May this passion always burn so brightly inside you."

"Once again, sir, I am truly honored." He bowed again and ran off toward the barracks.

"You have done well," Ahmadi said to the commander.

"I thank you, but quite honestly, we almost rejected him."

"Why on earth would that be?"

"His background. He is from a middle-class family outside of Baghdad. Earlier this year, his father was killed in an attack by Hussein Ghazi's security services. They opened fire on a bus stop where they thought a leading dissident was waiting."

"I see."

"The young man is permanently bitter, but at first we thought he was bitter at the wrong people. After all, anger toward Ghazi and his regime is not useful to us at this point—our focus is creating discord among the Americans."

"This is true."

"But as a few weeks went by, we were impressed by his intensity and his focus. His commitment runs deep. He came to us from Anbar province in Sumeristan, where he was visiting his family. Somehow, he got across the Saudi border and got a flight out of Riyadh. Once he was here, he worked his connections in the jihadi community until he found his way to us."

"Please keep me informed on his progress. He could well turn out to be perfect for a key assignment. If he keeps his current resolve, and if we can point him in the right direction, he could be invaluable to us."

"You think so, sir?"

"Absolutely." Ahmadi smiled. "He wants revenge."

CHAPTER 46

ON DECEMBER 19, AMERICAN STEALTH bombers took off from bases in Turkey and headed for northern Kabulistan. They pinpointed the four Husam al-Din training camps and destroyed them with a handful of bombs. The operation was short and surgical, with no resistance or anti-aircraft fire from the enemy below. In their debriefing, the pilots revealed that the installations were so complacent that no guards even seemed to be posted as lookouts against attack.

The government of Kabulistan filed a complaint with the U.N. Commission on Human Rights, pointing out that they were not formally at war with any of the coalition countries, and that they had never granted permission to use their airspace for the raid. For their part, the Cane administration was jubilant to finally have some good news to share with the public, particularly at holiday time.

Five days before Christmas, George Cane addressed the nation from the East Room of the White House. "Yesterday, the expert pilots of our valiant air force eliminated four terrorist training camps in northern Kabulistan. These camps were operated by Husam al-Din, with the complicity of the Dua Khamail government. Over the past few months, they have trained hundreds of recruits, producing terrorist agents who were then transferred to Baghdad, where they were responsible for attacks both on our peacekeeping troops and on innocent civilians.

"No civilians were injured in yesterday's raid. Unlike our cowardly adversaries, we targeted only the evildoers who were intent on doing us harm, and quickly eliminated them from the field of battle. I applaud all those who participated in this operation, whether they were part of the air crews or members of support teams on the ground.

"I have spoken to General Boudreaux and assured him that as a result of this action, our brave men and women in uniform will be safer in Baghdad in the days and weeks to come. This is a victory for the forces of democracy, as well as a warning to our adversaries in Kabulistan and elsewhere: You may think you can hide, but we will hunt you down and bring you to justice."

"Sam," said Andrew Neponski, watching the president's address from his Capitol Hill office. "Turn it off, please. Before I throw up."

"Sure." She clicked off the set with the remote. "You don't think this will help, obviously."

"I don't know what will help at this point, but I seriously doubt that these guys know the answer either. It's a good formula, though. When in doubt, bomb."

"Haven't other presidents done the same thing?"

"Hopefully you're not referring to Bill Hampton," said Neponski patiently. "He bombed a building that was a Husam al-Din headquarters—not a toy factory, as some people claimed. Salman al-Akbar was in that building until the day before, when he was tipped off. Nobody wanted to hear about him back then, though. All they cared about were Hampton's personal difficulties."

Personal difficulties. She smiled. "What a tactful way to put it."

Neponski laughed. "Why don't you go and find something to do? Give the taxpayers their money's worth."

The buzzer sounded as he was preparing to leave for the evening.

"Calvin Dobbs is on the phone for you, sir."

"Calvin," said Neponski, lifting the phone to his ear. "How are you?"

"I'm just fine. But you sound tired, my friend."

"Probably so. I'm tired of a number of things, to be honest."

"Well, just remember that you're defending upstanding citizens like me against the forces of evil—'the evildoers,' as our president would say."

"I'll be damned if this isn't Vietnam all over again. All those years, we sat around thinking that the only consolation we had was that we had learned our lesson, that we'd never have to go through something similar again. And now, bingo—it's the instant replay."

"True enough."

"I assume you're calling because you have some news for me."

"Not much," said Dobbs. "The evening phone calls to David Burnham's place came from a guy by the name of Frank Rosetti."

"What's his story?"

"No ties to the administration, as far as I can tell. He's a freelancer—worked for a long string of wacko right-wing groups. Sometimes in an official capacity, mostly not. Basically, he's your equal-opportunity hatemonger."

"Why would he be targeting David? If he was at all?"

"You got me there, buddy. I can't connect the dots for you."

"What do his phone records show?"

There was a silence.

"Well, now. Why do you think I'd pull his phone records?"

"Because I know you, Calvin. You're a bulldog—you have to find out where the bodies are buried."

"Andy, we're speaking confidentially?"

"Of course."

"For real? This didn't come from me?"

"Cross my heart and hope to die."

"His phone records show a bunch of calls back and forth to Scott Leventhal."

"Son of a bitch. And you think *that's* no connection to the administration? Give me a break."

"It proves nothing, Andy. You put me on the witness stand, under oath, and ask me what those calls mean—you know what I tell you?"

"What?"

"I have to say they don't mean shit. I'd be legally obligated to testify that the fact he spoke to Leventhal any number of times had no connection to any wrongdoing."

"Of course. Just a coincidence."

"Maybe they were friends. They went out for beers from time to time. They were in the same bowling league. Whatever."

"But we know differently, don't we?"

"Not really. Look, Andy—"

"At least I know now why David kept pressuring me to support the administration's war resolutions. It didn't make much sense at the time."

"I'm sorry about this, buddy. I truly am."

"I know. I do appreciate all your efforts, though."

"I'm not sure what you can do about it. Short of detonating a suicide bomb in the West Wing, that is."

"I'll think of something."

"Well, you remember when I told you I thought I could help you? I do believe I can. I have something I'll be sending your way shortly."

"Do tell?"

"No can do. But you'll know it when you see it."

"I love it. The man of mystery. The supercop with the secret agenda."

"That's me."

"Remember what I told you. I'll pursue these people to the ends of the earth, if I have to."

"Hopefully, I can give you a shortcut."

"You think so?"

"God, I hope so." Dobbs paused. "If what I've got doesn't do it, I'm afraid nothing will."

CHAPTER 47

PETER SCHOENFELD HAD BEEN A newspaperman his entire life, but he had never seen anyone run through a newsroom, except in the movies. In fact, the only person he ever remembered doing it was himself, as a young copy boy racing toward the desk the day Jack Kennedy was shot. Nearly forty years later, as the *Post*'s top national correspondent, Schoenfeld was sensitive to traffic patterns and clusters in his workplace that revealed the formation of important stories.

Little wonder, then, that he was amazed to see Kenneth Jablonski—his boss, the national editor—barreling toward him, particularly since he tipped the scales at nearly three hundred pounds. Jablonski stopped short in front of him, sweating profusely and clutching a Manila envelope.

"Kenny, take it easy. You could have a heart attack."

"Come into the office, right now. I have something to show you."

When they entered Jablonski's glassed-in office, the editor closed the door behind him. Still breathing heavily, he opened the envelope and spread pictures on his desk.

"Take a look. This is huge—absolutely fucking huge."

Schoenfeld recognized the lunar landscape of Kabulistan in the background of the photos. There were clusters of makeshift buildings, many of which had been destroyed and lay in pieces on the ground. And scattered throughout all the pictures were figures that looked like tailor's dummies, except that they were far more lifelike.

"Don't tell me—?"

"You better fucking believe it. These are the so-called terrorist training camps we bombed a week or so ago."

"How on earth did you get these?"

"Good old-fashioned flimflam." Jablonski grinned. "These areas are guarded by Special Forces guys that have the sites sewn up tighter than a prom queen's twat. So our guy on the ground bribed some native women to walk around on the perimeter—you know, heavily-veiled broads with goats and little kids following them around. He gave them miniature cameras, they concealed them underneath their burqas, and—bingo."

"I'll be damned." He picked up a picture and examined it more closely. The dummies were convincing; someone had actually gone to the trouble of painting faces on them. "Well, I have to agree with your assessment. This is absolutely fucking huge, all right."

"Better believe it. We only got pictures of two out of the four so-called camps, but that'll be more than enough."

"And there were no people there?"

"Not a soul."

"So how are you going to proceed?"

"We're running with it, baby. Top of page one, tomorrow morning."

"You think that's wise? We're not going to put them in the loop?"

This was standard procedure. Major dailies generally checked with the administration before they ran military-related stories, particularly those that referenced troop locations or future operations.

"No fucking way. This isn't national security, not by a long shot. This is nothing but bumbling idiocy."

Schoenfeld smiled. "Well, to Bob Hornsby, they might be one and the same. He'll be furious."

"Ask me if I care. What's the worst that can happen? I don't get invited over to his house for meatloaf?"

"The worst that can happen is that he gets on your case."

"Do I look scared? Remember, we report on government harassment too—not just incompetence."

"I love it. Go get 'em, tiger."

"Yeah." Jablonski grinned again. "Sometimes, life is good."

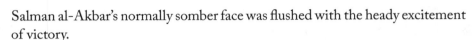

Salman al-Akbar's normally somber face was flushed with the heady excitement of victory.

"Shall I pour you some tea, sir?" asked Fazil Ahmadi.

"Yes, please."

"In the West," said al-Akbar's chief lieutenant, "if they had our success, they would be drinking Champagne right now."

"All the Champagne in the West could not sparkle any brighter than our good fortune at a moment such as this."

He's positively giddy, thought Ahmadi; in nine years, he had never seen his boss in so joyous a mood. The two men sat in the garden of al-Akbar's central Kabulistan compound, surrounded by tall concrete walls topped with barbed wire.

"Our good fortune is beyond my comprehension," the leader continued. "Allah be praised! Who would have thought such a thing possible?"

"I was afraid we had placed the fake camps too close together, and that would make the Americans suspicious. But apparently, their laziness trumped their curiosity."

"I still cannot understand how they were so easily fooled." Al-Akbar shook his head. "If you go back in history, you'll see this was originally their idea."

"How so?"

"They did the same thing themselves, on a much larger scale, before the invasion of Normandy. The Germans were expecting a landing on the Normandy beaches, and had their forces concentrated there. The Americans sent General Patton nearby, to Pas-de-Calais, and told him to build a fake invasion force. Patton replicated everything down to the last detail: aircraft, tanks, landing craft … except that it was all papier-mâché. The Germans responded by diverting their troops to Pas-de-Calais, and were unprepared when the Americans landed at Normandy."

"Interesting, sir."

"That was where I got the idea. But all we did was build some dummies and paint faces on them. It should never have fooled them so easily."

"Perhaps they are becoming complacent."

"Well, let us not become so. We are no match for the Americans. On paper, at least." He laughed hollowly. "I would not want to be at their White House today, but I would give anything to see the face of Robert Hornsby."

"Indeed, sir."

"In any case, we must remain vigilant. All is well at the real camps?"

"They are filled to capacity. And this event will only aid in our ability to recruit new operatives."

"Excellent. If we keep up pressure on the Americans, their invasion will become unpopular at home. And then they will turn and run, as they did in Vietnam. As surely as I am sitting here, Sumeristan will someday be part of the new caliphate."

"I believe you are correct."

"Hopefully, I will live to see it. In the meantime, let us enjoy our tea."

Walking through the West Wing on the morning the story broke, Robert Hornsby was undecided as to which was worse: the way he felt, or the looks he was receiving from senior staffers. Even the secretaries regarded him with the same mixture of pity and morbid curiosity usually reserved for convicts taking their last walk toward the gas chamber.

"Come in, Bob, come in," said George Cane as the vice president was ushered into the Oval Office. "Have a seat."

The two men faced each other. Hornsby noted with surprise that the tips of the president's ears weren't red.

"All I can say, sir, is that I'm terribly sorry."

"I'm sure of that."

"I'm prepared to give you my resignation."

"I don't want your resignation, for God's sake. Don't be childish. What I'd like, for starters, is some reliable intelligence."

"Sir, they looked like terrorist camps. They had all the earmarks. They just pulled the wool over our eyes."

"I'd say so. You're telling me that our spy planes don't have heat sensors to tell the difference between human beings and full-sized G.I. Joes?"

"The surveillance planes operate at nearly 60,000 feet. Heat sensors don't work at that altitude."

"Okay." Cane picked up the front page of the *Washington Post* and looked at the paper with disgust.

"Administration bombs fake terrorist camps," screamed the headline. "Coalition warplanes mistake dummies for Husam al-Din."

Exclusive photos secretly obtained by our correspondent in Kabulistan reveal that the training camps struck in last week's bombing raid were actually fake sites constructed and staged by Husam al-Din.

The photographs depict lifelike dummies scattered around the sites in different positions, designed to give the appearance that the outpost was being used to train terrorist recruits. The dummies were accurate down to the last detail, including beards, Muslim attire, and various jihadi uniforms.

"This is a victory for the forces of democracy," announced President Cane in his address to the nation last week, "as well as a warning to our adversaries in Kabulistan and elsewhere: You may think you can hide, but we will hunt you down and bring you to justice."

"You have to say this is one of the most monumental failures in American military history," said retired General Keith Kent, former commander of NATO forces, "not to mention one of the most embarrassing. It's beyond me why the administration didn't at least inspect the sites before they started crowing about it."

"I guess we can cross Keith Kent off the state dinner guest list," said Cane.

"He's under the delusion that he's going to run for president someday, sir. As you know."

"Other than reliable intelligence, if I can ever get any, you know what I'd like? I'd like to understand what the hell is going on in Baghdad, and what we can do to get the situation under control. Before the invasion, you told me that Hussein Ghazi's inner circle was filled with ties to Husam al-Din."

"And we believe it was, sir. Many of those former officials are still in the city, directing the resistance. Except now they have the luxury of operating in a vacuum."

"We have forty thousand troops in and around Baghdad, Bob. I wouldn't call that a vacuum."

"They know we can't stay there forever, sir. They're positioning themselves for the moment we leave."

"Well, we're not leaving anytime soon, I can tell you that—not when things are as bad as they are right now. It'll look like we're being driven out."

"I'll see what we can find out."

"Please do. And make sure that anything you tell me this time has been verified ten ways from Sunday."

"I understand." Hornsby pointed to the newspaper. "How are you going to proceed with that, sir?"

"Well, I don't want any retaliation against these guys. They'll scream bloody murder, and that'll only make things worse."

"Agreed, absolutely."

"Beyond that, I guess I'll have to go out and do an 'aw shucks' interview on some network or other. I'll take full responsibility, but at the same time I'll say the intelligence was faulty. I'll have to hang McCardle out to dry, and then he'll have to set up some poor staffer and burn him at the stake."

"I'll let him know, sir."

"I'm not concerned with looking like a jackass," said Cane. "Half the voting population already thinks of me that way. I just want to hold on to the other half."

CHAPTER 48

THE VIDEO WAS RELEASED ON the morning of Christmas Eve. It depicted a glowing Salman al-Akbar sitting on a large rock in the midst of what appeared to be the plains of central Kabulistan. A dummy sat next to him. The dummy wore a knitted Muslim skullcap, sported a scraggly beard, and was missing his right arm.

"To my courageous and worthy adversaries in the West," began al-Akbar, "I bring you greetings on the eve of your holiday, an occasion celebrated throughout the Christian world as a day of peace.

"Several days ago, as you are aware, United States warplanes bombed four of our training camps in northern Kabulistan. These installations were destroyed, and many of our brave warriors were killed or maimed. This young man to my right, for example, suffered grievous injuries. He lost a limb in the attack, which will require many long months of rehabilitation for him.

"We did not seek this conflict with the United States or any other Western nation. Our coordinated operation on May first was merely a response to decades of aggressive treatment from what President Cane refers to as 'the forces of democracy.' But just as we have not sought war with you, neither do we wish to avoid it. For every injured warrior such as the young man on my right, we have hundreds more waiting to take his place.

"Be assured that so long as you make war with us, you and your families will not be safe. Not in your schools or churches, nor in your libraries and shopping centers, nor in any of the other places where you congregate to enjoy the fruits of democracy. For we will not rest until the ancient caliphate is restored throughout this region, and the banner of Allah waves above our land.

"May I conclude by wishing you a joyous holiday. As you go in peace, so may peace come to you."

Then came the moment that went viral around the world: Salman al-Akbar put down his walking stick and raised his right palm, as he simultaneously grasped the left hand of the dummy and raised it into the air. Smiling into the camera, he waved both hands at the audience as the scene went black.

The video was repeated on al-Jazeera almost continuously throughout Christmas week. The U.S. networks also had a field day with it, regardless of political orientation, especially since it was the only unexpected story to emerge during a traditionally slow news cycle.

The secretary of state's limousine snaked slowly through the holiday traffic toward the Old Executive Office Building.

"Ma'am," said Mandy Parisi, "any hints on what I should or shouldn't say to Hornsby?"

"I'm sure you won't speak to him beyond pleasantries, at most. I imagine I'll see him alone."

"May I ask, then, why you wanted me to come along?"

"Moral support." Jennifer Caldwell shrugged. "And you can always play patty-cake with Scott Leventhal in the outer office."

"Can't wait."

"He's not a bad-looking guy, Mandy, if you can get past the ideology. You might consider giving him a break."

"Gag me with a spoon, ma'am."

"You know, you won't always have this exciting life in the public arena. Sooner or later you'll want to settle down and bake cookies."

"Just like you."

Caldwell laughed. "That's right. Just like me."

"I'm really curious about something. If you have a chance, maybe you can ask him."

"What's that?"

"Why didn't they at least verify the damage to the sites? Before the president went on TV and looked like an idiot?"

"That's easy. They desperately needed some good news to share with the public on the terror front."

"They couldn't have inspected them?"

"Given their location, no. Not personally."

"I assume we must have aerial surveillance."

"Of course. But if the surveillance planes couldn't tell the difference between a terrorist and a tailor's dummy before the raid, we can assume they couldn't do it afterward."

"What about the stealth bombers? Those things come in really close to the ground."

"When you're on a bombing raid, Mandy, you're focused on killing people. You're not evaluating the authenticity of their uniform or their hairdo."

Scott Leventhal was waiting for them outside the vice president's office.

"Madam Secretary, you're looking well. Happy holidays."

"Same to you, Scott—whatever holiday you're celebrating these days."

"Miss Parisi," he said graciously, ignoring her. "Welcome."

"Thank you."

"Please come in. The vice president will see you privately, Madam Secretary."

"I told Mandy you'd be delighted to keep her entertained."

"Any time."

Leventhal escorted her to the door of the inner office. As the door opened, Caldwell had a glimpse of the vice president rising from his chair and smiling glowingly. *Bad news*, she thought. *They say he's always at his most dangerous when he's smiling.*

"Jennifer!" said Robert Hornsby. "How the hell are you?"

"Very well, thanks."

"Please, take a seat."

"I imagine you've had a difficult time," she offered as she settled in across from him.

"Well, I've had better weeks. No doubt about it."

"How's the president holding up?"

"Surprisingly well. He seems to have the knack of letting things roll off. Someday I'll master it."

"To what do I owe the privilege of this private conversation?"

"The situation in Sumeristan remains difficult."

"So I see."

"It's likely to be challenging for some time to come, I'm afraid."

"Have you considered declaring victory and pulling out?"

"The president refuses to take that course. For one thing, it would be perceived as defeat in many quarters. For another, it would be abandonment. He doesn't want to leave Baghdad until the Sumeri people have a stable government."

"Then it looks like you have your work cut out for you."

"That's what I wanted to discuss with you. As you know, there wasn't much in the way of a formal opposition to Hussein Ghazi. For many years—decades, actually—he simply killed anyone who showed signs of disloyalty to the regime. So it's been difficult for us to identify someone who might be capable of taking over."

"If the goal is to have them govern themselves, may I suggest it might be better to allow their new leader to emerge of his own accord? Rather than having us identify him?"

"We're not interested in spending the rest of our lives in Baghdad," said Hornsby firmly. "Much less the rest of this administration. And we need to be honest with ourselves. These people will require some help in forming a government. Any vestige of democracy in that culture has been repressed for many years."

"I assume there's some way I can help you."

"Yes, there is." Hornsby removed his glasses and thumbed through a file on his desk. "We've zeroed in on someone we think would be a good candidate to form a provisional government. With the right amount of support, we think he has the potential to take the country in the right direction."

"And who might this be?"

"His name is Kasim Hamdani. He seems to have the temperament for it, along with a good base of popularity among the population."

"What did he do during the Hussein Ghazi era?"

"For a long period, he supervised an academy in central Baghdad. Equivalent to one of our large high schools."

"A high school principal." She stared at Hornsby. "You can't be serious."

"Jennifer, we don't have much to work with. Everyone who publicly opposed Hussein Ghazi is dead. This is a person of some intellectual attainment. He seems to know how to work with people. He's well respected. He may not be George Washington, but he's the best of the bunch."

When did intellectual attainment become a qualification for leading a country? she thought. *Look at us, for God's sake.*

"What exactly do you want me to do?"

"We need you to go over there and meet with him. Spend a day or two, have high-level talks. Get a sense of how ready he really is. Give him some insights. Prepare the ground."

"Is there some reason General Boudreaux can't do this?"

"Yes. *You're* the secretary of state. That strikes me as a good reason."

"So by meeting with him, I legitimize him in the eyes of the world."

"Precisely. It raises his profile. And hopefully brings us closer to the day when he can form a government and we can get the hell out of there."

"And I imagine it also helps erase the image of Salman al-Akbar and his dummy waving to everybody."

"Propaganda is part of war, Jennifer. It's not just reserved for them."

"Do I have some assurance that I won't have snipers shooting at me from the rooftops? I'll be the best target they've had to date."

"You'll be staying at General Boudreaux's residence in the Safe Zone. It doesn't get any more secure than that."

"Very well. When is this supposed to take place?"

"We'd like you to leave as soon as possible. Tomorrow, if you can."

"I can do that, yes."

"We appreciate it, Jennifer." Hornsby handed her the file on Kasim Hamdani. "I'm grateful, and so is the president."

"Well, Mandy," she said as the limo inched its way back toward Foggy Bottom. "Looks like you'd better pack an overnight bag."

"Where are we headed, ma'am?"

"Sumeristan. Baghdad, to be precise."

"No kidding. Is it safe?"

"To get to us, they'd have to kill Chip Boudreaux first."

"And what will we be doing there?"

"Talking to a high school principal," she smiled. "Preparing him to run a country where everyone is pissed off at him. Generating footage to bump Salman al-Akbar off the evening news."

"I'm not sure I get it."

"Stage-managed PR, Mandy. That's the business we're in."

The president had initially objected to giving Barbara Walters his first in-depth interview following the training camp raid.

"Why does it always have to be her? You know I don't like her."

"I'm sure she doesn't like you much either, sir," said Hornsby. "But better her than some aggressive young anchor trying to make his or her bones, and who'll pepper you with a lot of embarrassing questions."

The interview aired on a Sunday evening following an NFL playoff game, and it attracted a record viewership.

"Mr. President, I'm sure you know I hate to bring up uncomfortable matters with you."

"Hey, Barbara." George Cane grinned. "That's why I'm here."

"But you do know that in the aftermath of the training camp fiasco, there are some Americans who question your ability as commander in chief. Can you share your perspective on that experience, and perhaps give us some insights into what you learned from it?"

"First, Barbara, I think the people who question my abilities are the same folks that questioned them before the raid. Sooner or later, you have to realize that you can't please everybody."

"Of course not, sir. But there are some people who are comparing the raid to Jimmy Carter's failed attempt to rescue the Persepostan hostages in 1979."

"I think the better analogy, Barbara, is to the Bay of Pigs. What JFK discovered in the aftermath of that disaster was that intelligence isn't always accurate, and that you can't always trust the recommendations of your military commanders. I believe most presidents come to that conclusion sooner or later.

"But you asked me what I learned from it, and that's a great question. It was a mistake, obviously—not my first, certainly, maybe not my last. But there were no civilians injured in the raid, and no collateral damage. The only thing that was injured was my pride. So one thing that I learned, or relearned, actually, was the importance of owning up to your mistakes and going forward. The other thing I learned is that you've got to have a thick skin to be sitting where I sit. I think most folks out there—not the professional political class, mind you, but average Americans—realize that they've made mistakes themselves, and that others usually forgave them for it. As you know, Jesus said that only those without sin could cast the first stone. I would make the analogy that the folks criticizing me must think they're perfect. If so, I could use them in my administration."

Some in the professional political class noted the president's reference to "inaccurate intelligence," since there was still no trace of the chemical weapons Hussein Ghazi was supposed to have stockpiled. Other than that, the interview was considered a tour de force. A typical reaction came from Jonathan Goldsmith, ombudsman for the *New York Times*, in an interview with CNN.

"Jonathan," said the anchor, "most political pundits seem dumbfounded by the spike in the president's poll numbers following his recent one-on-one conversation with Barbara Walters. As a longtime observer of these situations, how would you explain his surge in popularity?"

"Well," replied Goldsmith, "on one level, it was a classic double reverse: honesty. That's the last thing anyone expects nowadays from anyone who holds national office. I'm sure right now there are people sitting around thinking that they underestimated him, but they shouldn't be surprised. He's used this strategy before.

"On a more basic level, George Cane simply seems to have the ability to connect with a large segment of the American people. They view him as a guy very similar to themselves, someone who's not a genius, who makes mistakes, and has the capacity to own up to them. I'll bet there were a lot of people who watched that interview and thought, 'You know, this reminds me of the time I called my mother-in-law as a fat loudmouth, and it turned out that she was standing right behind me.' These situations happen to everybody, and many of us tend to be tolerant of them.

"During the campaign, we used to say that George Cane would win because he was the kind of guy you wanted to have a beer with." Goldsmith laughed. "Now it turns out that he'll succeed in the presidency even as he spills beer on the electorate."

CHAPTER 49

HE PLANE CARRYING JENNIFER CALDWELL and Mandy Parisi landed at an airstrip outside Baghdad in the middle of the night. The two women had stopped at an air force base in Turkey, where they were transferred from the secretary's plane to an unmarked military transport. As the transport came to a stop near an armored Humvee, it was immediately surrounded by a heavily armed platoon of Army Rangers. The soldiers pointed them toward the Humvee.

"This seems a bit theatrical," said Mandy Parisi to no one in particular.

"Get in the vehicle, ma'am," said the commander of the platoon. "And keep your head down."

The ladies rode into the city in the back seat, sandwiched between Rangers holding Mk 48s.

The next morning, Jennifer Caldwell had a private breakfast meeting with Chip Boudreaux.

"A pleasure to meet you, ma'am," said Boudreaux cheerfully. "I've always appreciated the frankness of your public statements. Very refreshing for a politician."

"I'm not a politician." She smiled. "There's the difference. And I must say that I've enjoyed your press conferences as well. I'm not sure which I like more—your candor or your sense of humor."

"Well, the situation ain't gettin' any better, so we might as well have some fun with it."

"I've also spent many happy days in New Orleans. It's a great city."

"Actually, ma'am, I'm from Metairie. Different kettle of crawfish."

"Sorry about that."

"No worries. Sometimes Yanks have trouble distinguishing folks from my part of the country."

"I have an idea, General." Her voice was cool and pleasant. "Why don't we focus on the war in Sumeristan, rather than the War between the States?"

"That's a deal." Boudreaux grinned. "This is your party, after all. How can I help you?"

"The president would like to see most of our efforts concentrated on building up the Sumeri peacekeeping ability, specifically police and military. Can you give me an idea of how we're doing with that?"

"Their military's a sorry bunch. A lot of 'em are the same guys who shed their uniforms and ran away from the field of battle during the invasion. It took us a good six months to sort out the good guys from the bad guys. Now that we've separated the Hussein Ghazi loyalists out of the picture, we're left with a whole mess of troops that don't care much for riskin' their lives."

"How long do you think it will take to mold them into a respectable fighting force?"

"Shoot. It might take between six to eighteen months to get 'em to *look* like honest-to-God soldiers. What they do after we leave is another story."

"What about the police?"

"We've brought in specialists to train them. It's basically the same deal as the army, though. They'll run the other way at any sign of trouble. At best, they're just gonna be reactive."

"What about community policing? I imagine most of these residential neighborhoods must be tightly knit."

"That'll work up to a point. Problem is, when you go around arresting anybody who looks suspicious, you don't seem much different than Hussein Ghazi."

"We're particularly concerned about suicide bombers. Isn't there any way to filter them out, on a preventive basis?"

"We don't know who's who, ma'am. As you can see, it's chilly outside. Everybody's wearin' jackets or winter coats. So if you're one of these guys and you're walkin' around all wired up, there's no way to tell. In the hot weather, things might be different."

"True."

"As you know, most of these bombers are coming from the Husam al-Din training camps in Kabulistan." He hesitated. "I don't want to offend you, but we haven't exactly been doin' a bang-up job of eliminatin' those camps."

"No offense taken. I'm not the brains of the operation."

Boudreaux grinned. "Just the good looks."

"Precisely. Do we know where these people are coming from? How they're being recruited?"

"It ain't hard. The Husam al-Din agents look for angry young men, and there's plenty of them. They're all pissed off about somethin'. The ones from good families grew up in fear of the regime—they were afraid to open their mouths 'cause they'd be tortured and shot. Half of them had that happen to a friend or someone in their family. And with the poor kids, it's the same story you see with poor kids anywhere. They have no skills, no job possibilities, no future. They're easy pickin's. And it's a shame, 'cause most of 'em are no older than my own teenagers."

"Are they all religiously motivated?"

"Some are. They promise them they'll be welcomed by Allah at the gates of heaven, with trumpets blaring. And of course, they'll have their seventy-two virgins up there."

"I thought it was seventy-six virgins."

"Whatever. You ask me, it sounds like a lot of heavy liftin'."

"Okay." She smiled. "Now, the administration feels that Kasim Hamdani is the best choice for someone to form a provisional government. Do you agree with that?"

"Hard to say. I'm not sure if there's a good choice at this point."

"Well, do you feel that he can keep a lid on things?"

"I don't rightly know, ma'am. He seems like a nice enough guy—very well educated, obviously, expresses himself well, gets along with folks. He looks like a bit of a wuss, though."

"I appreciate your perspective, General."

"Wish I could be more upbeat for you, ma'am."

"You've been informative. And I realize you don't get to choose your assignments."

"Yep." He grinned again. "If I had any brains myself, I wouldn't be here."

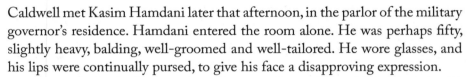

Caldwell met Kasim Hamdani later that afternoon, in the parlor of the military governor's residence. Hamdani entered the room alone. He was perhaps fifty, slightly heavy, balding, well-groomed and well-tailored. He wore glasses, and his lips were continually pursed, to give his face a disapproving expression.

I guess high school principals are the same all over the world, she thought. *He looks like he's about to punish me for skipping calculus.*

"It's a pleasure to meet you, Madam Secretary," he said as he extended his hand. "You came a long way to see me, and you have my gratitude."

"A pleasure to meet you as well. I'm delighted that we won't need an interpreter."

"No, I spent three years in England as a young man. Hopefully I can make myself understood."

"Your English is very good."

"Shall we sit?"

They settled into two leather armchairs; between them, a small table held a pot of tea and a tray of candied dates.

"One of the reasons I'm glad we're meeting face to face is to discuss the timetable for the turnover." Hamdani spoke slowly, appearing to choose his words with caution. "Many of my associates are apprehensive that we might be moving too quickly."

"I understand."

"We will need some time to develop the structure of government, not to mention provide for the security of our citizens."

"President Cane would like to see a formal handover ceremony in six months' time."

"With all due respect, Madam Secretary, we cannot possibly put all the necessary mechanisms in place in that amount of time."

"I can assure you the United States will not leave you high and dry. We will have troops here for quite some time."

"May I ask how many troops?"

"We have two hundred thousand in the country right now. Within one year, the president would like to see that reduced by half. We will continue to provide training support for your police and armed forces. But at some point, those forces have to be able to provide the necessary security for your population."

"This is a delicate matter." Hamdani shifted uncomfortably in his seat. "May I be frank?"

"It's just the two of us. All we have to do is be smiling when we let the photographers in."

"The United States invaded Sumeristan without invitation. No one here asked them to do so. They deposed Hussein Ghazi, but they also created a set of circumstances totally unforeseen by them."

"And now you believe it's our responsibility to straighten everything out for you?"

"On a humanitarian level, we feel that you are in debt to us."

"Is that so? Were you better off with Hussein Ghazi?"

"With Hussein Ghazi, at least we knew what to expect. If you spoke out against the regime, you were imprisoned, and unlikely to come out. Now Baghdad is in chaos, and the violence is totally random. Rather than being killed for opposing Hussein Ghazi, you may be killed for no reason at all. Perhaps it is not as bad as Detroit or East Los Angeles, but it is an untenable situation."

"Well, Mr. Hamdani, I can get you a humanitarian visa. You can come to Detroit or East Los Angeles, and get a job as a taxi driver or hospital orderly. Eventually, you can become a citizen. And then, if you are unhappy with the level of urban violence, you can write a letter to your congressman."

"Madam Secretary—"

"If you're going to stay here and be the provisional head of government, you're going to have to come up with a solution that will make Baghdad a safer place."

"I'm not blaming the Americans for the situation."

"I'm afraid it sounded that way."

"Perhaps I am not communicating clearly. At its root, what we're seeing now is sectarian religious violence, although sometimes it may not appear to be so. And it will not stop. The people who are creating this unrest are committed to establishing a fundamentalist Muslim state in Sumeristan. They don't care if it takes a thousand years. You've heard Salman al-Akbar talk about the caliphate. Please remember what happened in Persepostan."

"Don't remind me."

"I really do not believe that you want to see another Persepostan here, any more than I do."

"Of course not."

"If that is the case, I have to suggest that at some point you address the true cause of the current violence. We both know that the problem is emanating from the Husam al-Din strongholds in Kabulistan. We also know that Husam al-Din is operating freely there, with the approval of the Dua Khamail government."

"So you think we should have invaded Kabulistan rather than Sumeristan?"

"It is not my place to tell the United States how to conduct its foreign policy."

"Nor is it mine. I don't make policy. I implement it."

"So I understand. And perhaps we are more in agreement than we think. But the new government here cannot fight off an endless supply of agitators and suicide bombers from Kabulistan. Sooner or later the population will become frightened and demoralized, and they will embrace a fundamentalist government with a sense of relief."

"Mr. Hamdani, I can tell you that the administration is focused on taking a more active role in Kabulistan, and will do what it can to fight Husam al-Din and stem the violence. And I can also assure that that I will use my influence, such as it is, to make sure that remains a priority."

"I am happy to hear that."

"However, much as I hate to lecture a high school principal, I have to stress once again the importance of taking control of the situation with a firm hand. Please remember that law enforcement in a democracy has different goals than it does in a police state, but there are times when the methods might seem similar."

"I think we understand each other."

"Shall we let the reporters in?"

"Certainly. What do we have to do?"

"Just look like we're setting off on our honeymoon."

CHAPTER 50

I N THE SIX YEARS SHE had been working for him, Andrew Neponski had never seen Samantha Sperling quite so excited.

"He's in the office, sir," she said as she met him at the building entrance. "I've already apologized to him for keeping him waiting."

"I'm not concerned about that. He kept me waiting any number of times."

"Still, it's not polite."

"Sam, please. We'll get you his autograph."

"I already have it. I also called the photographer in to get a picture of us together."

Good thing you're not an intern, he thought. *We'll send a copy of the picture to your mother, and label it "The one that got away."*

"Sam, take it easy," he said as they rode up in the elevator. "We're not going to nullify the 22nd Amendment anytime soon, so he's still an ex-president."

"Well, it's exciting for me, sir."

"Evidently." Neponski nodded to the Secret Service agents in his outer office and opened the door to greet William Hampton. He was sitting in the chair across from the Speaker's desk, flanked by a huge stuffed bear.

"Mr. President, you're looking well," said Cane. "Thank you for coming by."

"Hell, it's Bill now, Andy."

"Sorry to keep you waiting, but I didn't know you were coming."

"Well, what else do I have to do these days?"

"You really are looking remarkably well. Did I hear a rumor that you had stopped eating meat?"

"Damn right. I decided I wanted to live to see another Democratic president."

"I have to ask you, sir—what's with the bear?"

"Oh." Hampton chuckled. "This is a gift for your granddaughter."

"Thank you. I didn't realize the two of you had met."

"We haven't, actually. What's the child's name?"

"Karli."

"Charming name. And how old is she?"

"Four." Neponski leaned back in his chair with an amused expression on his face. "All right, sir. I haven't seen you in nearly a year, and you show up here with an enormous stuffed bear for my granddaughter, whom you've never met. What's up?"

Hampton laughed. "Well, I needed to see you. And I had to have one of those conversations that technically never took place."

"Aha."

"But I figured you kept a visitor's log, which could always be subpoenaed. So I brought you this bear, which is the pretext for my visit."

"Well, I'm sure she'll love it. Thank you."

"So those are the ground rules. It was a social call, and we never had any conversation beyond small talk."

"Understood."

"I have something for you."

"Really."

"But first, I want to express my sympathies over the death of David Burnham. I'm sure it was a shock."

"It was horrendous, yes."

"I imagine so. You know, Andy, in spite of everything, Washington remains a small town."

"That's quite true."

"And of course we have friends in common. For example, Calvin Dobbs."

"He's a good man.'"

"Hell, he's solid as a rock. They don't come any better."

"We've been friends for more than twenty years."

"You know, when I was going through all that impeachment bullshit, he stood up for me. They asked him for help a couple of times, and he told them to shove it."

"That's the kind of guy he is."

"Absolutely." Hampton pulled reflectively at his chin. "So let's go back to that awful night when he called you over to David Burnham's place."

"Yes."

"I believe you asked him if the young man had left a note."

"Yes. Yes, I did."

"Well, he didn't leave a note—old Calvin was telling you the truth. But he did leave something else."

"Is that so?"

"Now, you gotta remember that Calvin's a cop. He was out of his depth on this. That's why he called me." Hampton reached into his suit pocket, unfolded a piece of paper, and handed it to the Speaker. "Here you go, Andy."

Neponski stared at the sheet of paper in disbelief.

Presidential Daily Brief for April 21, 2001

"My God."

"Take your time and read it."

"Is this real?"

"It's as real as it gets." Hampton chuckled. "I had to look at these fuckin' things every morning for eight years, so I can vouch for its authenticity. It's a copy, of course."

"I'm a little disoriented, sir."

"Okay. Then scroll down to item number four."

Salman al-Akbar Determined to Strike Within the U.S.

Anecdotal intelligence from various sources (government, civilian, and media) points to the likelihood that al-Akbar's highest priority is to carry out a terrorist strike within the continental United States, as it has been since at least 1997 or 1998.

Recently, increased chatter on jihadi websites indicates that an attack may be in the planning stages, although nothing concrete has yet surfaced to back this up. Both the NSA and CIA recommend a high state of security alert around the country, with focus on bus and train stations, airports, national monuments, and other targets with potential symbolic significance. Close attention should be paid in particular to airports, as al-Akbar has previously shown great interest in hijacking commercial airliners to carry out terrorist strikes.

Over the past decade, we know that Husam al-Din has established groups of sympathizers within the United States. While we know about some of these cells and are monitoring their activities, we are probably not aware of them all. Suspicious individuals or groups should be watched

with the utmost caution, since their presence could only help to facilitate
an attack if and when it occurs.

"Holy shit. These bastards knew about the May Day attacks ten days ahead of time."

"Yep," said Hampton. "That about sums it up."

"Are you showing this to me, sir, or giving it to me?"

"It's yours. It was found on David, so it would have come to you in the course of things if he had lived."

"How the hell did he get something like this?"

"Did you know that David was involved with someone who worked for Sandy Bayer? A guy by the name of Julian Burroughs?"

"Yes."

"Well, Burroughs was also carrying on with a CIA staffer named Kevin Furlin."

"I wasn't aware of that."

"This guy was a low-level analyst, a desk jockey, but he obviously had some access. He was channeling information to Burroughs, who used it to get brownie points with his boss—no pun intended. After Bayer fired Burroughs and broke up the love triangle, I assume Furlin was angry enough to dig up the PDB and pass it to Burroughs, who must have given it to David before he left town. Calvin didn't have a clue what to do when he found it—it's still classified, so he realized it was way above his pay grade. That's when he called me."

"Son of a bitch. These bastards have no conscience."

"I gather you think somebody was blackmailing David?"

"That's what I believed from the beginning, and this convinces me. Where I come from, you don't want to get even with someone unless they've harmed you."

"Sounds 'bout right to me. But here's the thing, Andy—this one's for all the marbles. It's like finding the eighteen-minute gap on the Nixon tapes. You have to be very careful as to how you proceed."

"Well, lay it out for me. I'll do whatever you suggest."

"I think you should leak it to the *Post*."

"Wouldn't the *Times* carry more weight?"

"Maybe, but the *Post* is hungrier. They'll get more mileage out of the story."

"Okay. Where do I say this document came from?"

"I think your best bet is 'confidential sources within the CIA.' That'll drive Hornsby and McCardle up the wall."

"I'm sure they'll be able to figure out who he is."

"Hell." Hampton chuckled. "Furlin will probably talk to the *Post*."

"I doubt that."

"Oh, I imagine he will. He's probably madder than a wet hen right now. Remember, he was fired. You can't even get fired from the government if you chop up a dozen people with an axe, so I'm sure his résumé isn't making much of an impression on his future employers. I'll bet he's steamin'."

"You could be right."

"Let's just coordinate on the timing. If I were you, I'd let this business with the dummies die down a bit. After the public has digested that, I'd hit 'em again."

"I won't do anything without checking with you first."

"Sounds good." Hampton stood up. "That's all I got for today, Andy."

"Thank you, and please send my best to Bethany. How's she doing?"

"Hell, she's a force of nature. You know how it is."

"Sir, I'm really grateful for this. I owe you."

"Nothin' to it." He grinned. "You just tell little Karli to enjoy her bear."

CHAPTER 51

J ENNIFER CALDWELL AND MANDY PARISI landed at Andrews Air Force Base shortly after 8:00 p.m. on New Year's Day. With lights flashing and sirens wailing, escort cars led their limousine across the District of Columbia line and down Pennsylvania Avenue toward the White House.

"Quite impressive," said Mandy. "We never get treated this way when we're driving around town."

"That's because nobody's interested in getting any footage of us when we're racing around returning overdue library books."

"Explain to me again why we have to go over there the instant we land."

"I've told you before—it shows the president's in charge. He wants to debrief us as soon as we arrive. He's dynamic, informed, on top of things."

"We'd all be better off getting some sleep. Kasim Hamdani won't be any more or less qualified to rule Sumeristan in the morning."

"The eleven o'clock news won't wait that long, Mandy."

Scott Leventhal was waiting in the outer office when they arrived.

"Madam Secretary, welcome back. Miss Parisi, a pleasure to see you again."

"Likewise."

"Jennifer!" Robert Hornsby opened the door of the Oval Office and came over to give her a peck on the cheek. "Good to see you. Come on in." He looked at Leventhal. "You two behave yourselves out here, okay?"

"Don't worry about a thing," said Mandy.

George Cane rose from his desk to greet her. "Jennifer, thanks for coming over. I'm sure you're tired, so we won't keep you long."

"No problem, sir. I'm at your disposal."

"Great job over there," gushed the president. "It couldn't have gone better if we had scripted it ourselves."

Didn't you? she thought. In fact, Caldwell's visit to Sumeristan had been a public relations victory for the administration. There were the pictures of her and Kasim Hamdani, both of them beaming. There was the triumphant tour of the Safe Zone with the prospective leader, punctuated by lectures on the glorious history of Sumeristan, which he would soon have the privilege of restoring. There was the press conference that followed her one-on-one talk with Hamdani, in which she offered her assessment of the country's rosy future. "He's thoughtful, measured, and competent," she had said carefully. "Just what Sumeristan needs to recover from the excesses of the past and lay the groundwork for an open society."

"Since you had some face time with Hamdani," said Cane, "we wanted to get your sense of what he was like. We need to make sure we're betting on the right horse."

"It's hard to say, sir. He's smart enough, of course, but not exactly what I would call an inspirational leader. He comes across like a guy processing driver's licenses at the DMV."

"Do you think he can do it?" asked Hornsby.

"Depends on what you're referring to. I'm sure he can manage a bureaucracy."

"Well," said the president, "I think the last thing those people need now is charisma. They really need somebody who can make the trains run on time. So to speak."

"I wouldn't exactly call him a cheerleader for the United States."

"Is that right?" said Hornsby.

"He feels that we owe them a large amount of support while the country gets glued back together. I got the feeling he would be pressing for elevated troop levels over a long period of time. He also made quite a point of saying that the dissidents were being created by Husam al-Din in Kabulistan, and he urged us to go after them more aggressively."

"Of course that's where they're coming from," replied Hornsby. "But we can only divert troops to Kabulistan as we withdraw them from his country."

"Bob's right," said Cane. "There's no way we can send half a million troops to the region. The public won't stand for it. I assume you stressed to him the need for the Sumeris to take control of their own security."

"In no uncertain terms, sir. But for the record, General Boudreaux indicated to me that the police and the army still had a long way to go."

"No doubt."

"And Hamdani expects quite a bit of help."

"He'll get help, although we may disagree on the numbers as we go along. Regardless, Jennifer, I want to see some sort of official handover within six months, something that makes it clear, to the public at least, that these folks are now responsible for their own country."

"He understands that, sir, although I wouldn't say he's happy about it."

"His happiness isn't our concern. I'm not going to spend the rest of my presidency occupying Sumeristan. When things go wrong, when they have problems, which they will, people need to start blaming them, not us. All we did was liberate them from the clutches of a dictator."

In the outer office, Mandy Parisi did her best to project an aura of amused tolerance toward Scott Leventhal. *It's nice of my boss to be concerned about my social life*, she thought with an inward scowl, *but I wouldn't go out with Hornsby's chief of staff if he looked like Brad Pitt.*

"So," Leventhal asked cheerfully. "How was Sumeristan?"

"Horrid," she said. "It was like something out of the Twilight Zone. Baghdad is filled with bombed-out buildings, even in the Safe Zone. The people walk around like whipped dogs. Of course, every day somebody goes out to buy a loaf of bread and gets blown to pieces by an IED or a suicide bomber, so I'm not sure how cheerful I'd expect them to be."

"Sounds like a vacation paradise. What about Hamdani? Did he impress you?"

"You'd have to ask the secretary—I didn't speak with him."

"What's he look like?"

"Your average high school principal, not surprisingly. A leader of boys. I'm not too sure about men."

"I heard something about him that I thought was touching."

"Do tell?"

"I understand he has a bunch of his former students on his staff. Young men that he rescued from difficult family situations."

"He has a bunch of young people around him, yes."

Parisi flashed back to the most uncomfortable moment of her visit. It occurred during the photo session following Hamdani's private meeting with Jennifer Caldwell. The secretary and prospective leader were shaking hands and smiling beatifically, cameras flashing nonstop. As expected, everyone had their eyes trained on the two key actors.

By chance, Mandy looked back at the crowd gathered around the two leaders. There was a group of students clustered on Hamdani's left, and they, too, were smiling ecstatically at the show of unity between the United States and Sumeristan—with one exception. A young man of about twenty glared at his former principal with a look that bordered on hatred. He was tall and slim, with an olive complexion and short, wiry black hair; his face was contorted into an expression that she could only describe as murderous rage.

The image had stayed with her.

"Well, I think that's quite something. Even if it's a publicity stunt, it's still a remarkable thing to do."

"Remarkable," said Mandy. "Yes. I suppose so."

"I have to admit that you've aroused my curiosity," said Peter Schoenfeld as he settled in across the desk from Andrew Neponski.

"How so?"

"It's not every day that we have the chance to talk privately. Nor is it every day that the Speaker tells you he wants to discuss a matter of national urgency."

"I thought that would get your attention."

"Although I have to tell you, sir, it'll be hard to maintain that this conversation never took place."

"Oh, you can say it took place. If anyone asks, tell them I wanted to give you an exclusive on my plans to pull funding for the war in Sumeristan."

"Is that something you actually plan on doing?"

"Not at the present time, no." Neponski smiled. "It's not a bad idea, though."

"Indeed."

"So here are the ground rules. This story cannot be traced back to me, even by implication."

"Agreed, but I can't vouch for what others might do."

"When you have the scope of it, I think you'll realize the wisdom of keeping me out of it."

"I'm all ears."

"I have something I think you'll be interested in," said the Speaker, extracting the sheet of paper from his breast pocket and handing it to Schoenfeld. "This just might be your next Pulitzer."

The reporter glanced at the title.

"I'm not sure I understand."

"Read item number four."

Schoenfeld studied the document, then stared at Neponski with a quizzical look on his face.

"Sir, this is classified information. May I ask where you got this?"

"No, you may not. If you want the story, you'll say it came from a confidential CIA source."

"If this is real, it could bring them down."

"Possibly, although I think that's too much too hope for. At the very least, it'll be another monumental embarrassment. At some point it will all add up in the public mind, but I suspect we're not at that point yet."

"And how do I know this is real?"

"You'll have it verified, I'm sure."

"No offense, but you do realize that just about any ten-year-old kid in America could go online and produce a document like this in less than half an hour."

"I'll give you a list of retired high-ranking CIA officers. They can verify it for you."

"But you can't tell me how it came into your possession?"

"I'm afraid I can't, no."

"I have to know the identity of the source, or I can't use it."

"His name is Kevin Furlin. He was released by the agency about six months ago. I think he'd be willing to talk to you."

"Why would he do that?"

"I believe he's somewhat embittered. My guess is that he feels he was treated unfairly."

"I assume he was pretty high up in the chain of command."

"Actually, no. He was a desk analyst. He broke protocol to get his hands on the PDB."

"Mr. Speaker, with all due respect—you hand me a classified document that anybody could have cooked up. Then you tell me it was leaked by a recently fired CIA grunt. This guy was supposedly so pissed off that he poached a copy of the PDB, which mysteriously found its way to you."

"That's pretty much what happened, yes."

"So you realize that if your guy doesn't talk to me, we don't have a story."

"From what I've heard, I'm pretty sure he will. And if he does, the ball is in your court from there on out. I'm going to say I never saw this until I read it in the paper."

"This won't happen overnight, sir. If it checks out, I'm pretty sure the legal team will get involved at that point."

"I understand you have to cover your bases. Does a week sound reasonable?"

"I think so, yes."

"Fine. Just come back then and give me your decision."

"And what if I say no?"

"Well." Neponski smiled. "There's always the *New York Times*."

CHAPTER 52

I AM DELIGHTED TO WELCOME YOU back, Abdul."

"Thank you, sir."

The school year was starting, and violence was unravelling daily life in Baghdad. As the youth sat across from Kasim Hamdani in his office, he noticed that his principal's suit seemed new and expensive. The man also seemed more pompous and self-assured, something that Abdul would not have thought possible.

"I sense that it did you a great deal of good to get away for a while."

"It helped to see my family, yes. And it allowed me to do a lot of thinking."

"You know, everything you were feeling at the end of last year was perfectly natural. I can relate to what you were going through, because I also lost my father as a teenager."

"Really? Was your father also killed by Hussein Ghazi's security forces?"

"Abdul …" The principal paused. "This is the start of a new era for our country. There is every reason to be optimistic."

"Perhaps, but things don't look very different to me. People are still being slaughtered every day. Except now, instead of the regime doing it, our own people are killing each other."

"This is a time of transition, an awkward time. There will be some growing pains in the months and years ahead."

"I believe you are absolutely correct."

"I want you to rejoin our weekly discussion group. It is more important now than ever." Hamdani smiled. "What would you say if I told you that I have been appointed to a special advisory panel by the Americans, to give them advice during the transition to democracy?"

"I'd say, sir, that I now understand where your new suit came from."

"Very good," he laughed. "But remember that to be a person of importance, you must look the part. Sometimes words and deeds are just part of the picture."

"And you think you will be such a person in the new regime, sir?"

"The Americans need a great deal of help at the moment. They may have the strongest military in the world, but they lack a fundamental understanding of our culture. They need local authorities to guide them. Also, if I may say so, they are not interested in occupying Sumeristan for the long term. They would like to hand off authority as soon as this is feasible."

"Sir, are you familiar with an English rock group called the Who?"

"I have heard of them, but I don't know their music."

"One of their songs is called '*Won't Get Fooled Again.*' And the last line of the song goes 'Meet the new boss, same as the old boss.'"

"Abdul," he said patiently, "you must realize that nothing is perfect. Just as people are not perfect, neither are their governments. Someday you will accept this. For the moment, I find it difficult to believe that things are no better now than they were under the regime."

"If you think back to some of our meetings in the discussion group, sir, I think you will remember that many of us said an American invasion would destabilize Sumeristan. This is exactly what has occurred. The country has been plunged into chaos, and it will only become worse. The only thing I know for sure is this: The Americans may hand over the government, but they will not surrender control of the oil fields. They will have an economic stake here for a long time to come."

"Probably so. But that will be the price we pay for getting rid of the regime." He leaned over and patted Abdul on the shoulder. "Welcome back. This conversation resembles our discussion group already. I trust I will see you there."

"Certainly. Just as long as I wait at the right bus stop in the morning."

CHAPTER 53

A CONFIDENT GEORGE CANE STEPPED TO the microphone in the East Room of the White House.

"My fellow Americans, I come before you tonight to report on our efforts to restore human rights and foster democracy in Sumeristan."

"There's never a reporter in sight when he makes these speeches," said Mandy Parisi, watching the broadcast with her boss in the secretary's office.

"He hasn't talked to a reporter in over three months, with the exception of Barbara Walters," said Jennifer Caldwell. "Obviously, they've concluded that there's nothing to be gained by it. I thought Reagan was insulated from the press, but this is remarkable."

"How does he get away with it?"

"Sooner or later, most of them realize that talking to the press is a losing proposition. The exception was Bill Hampton. He craved so much attention that he practically invited reporters in to watch him shave in the morning. But this strategy works, Mandy. The press gets so desperate that they devour any scraps the administration tosses their way."

"Six months ago," continued the president, "coalition forces invaded Sumeristan and delivered the population from the clutches of an evil dictator. We made it clear from the start that the operation was not an exercise in empire building, but a sincere effort to bring self-government to a country that desired it.

"Recently, we have been working with a number of individuals and groups to help define the best way forward for the Sumeri people. The process has not been an easy one. The removal of Hussein Ghazi's dictatorship created a power vacuum that allowed people with many different agendas to call attention to themselves. Some have been Hussein Ghazi loyalists who would like to see the dictator restored or who wish to rule the country in his place. Others are extremists who sympathize with an assortment of radical Islamic groups, including Husam al-Din. Some of these have used tactics such as suicide bombings, snipers, and improvised explosive devices to strike terror into the hearts of the population. They wish to demoralize the people of Sumeristan so it becomes easy to accomplish their nefarious objectives.

"Fortunately, the Sumeri people have proved more resourceful and resilient than their enemies could have anticipated. They have resisted the dangers of daily life in Baghdad and focused on the hard work of creating a government that will respect the rights of all its citizens."

"Too bad they don't have to buy TV time," said Mandy. "If they did, he'd make his point a lot quicker."

"In our work with the citizens of Sumeristan," said Cane, "over time, one man stood out as a potential leader of this newly freed people. His name is Kasim Hamdani. He has been deeply involved with the fabric of daily life in Baghdad for decades, serving as superintendent of one of the city's academies of higher education. He is a person who combines both intellectual attainment and real-world knowledge. He is respected by his people and has the ability to listen to others before arriving at his own conclusions. Prominent civil and military leaders feel that he would be the right person to form a provisional government, and we agree with them.

"Recently Secretary of State Jennifer Caldwell travelled to Sumeristan to meet with Mr. Hamdani. After their in-depth talks, she came away as impressed as everyone else who has made his acquaintance. She said, and I quote, 'He's thoughtful, measured, and competent—just what Sumeristan needs to recover from the excesses of the past and lay the groundwork for an open society.'"

"You better be careful, ma'am," said Mandy. "It sounds like they're setting you up."

"Don't worry about me. I'm the fox in the hen house. I know enough about these people to bury them deeper than Blackbeard's treasure."

"Over the next few months," droned Cane, "we'll work with Kasim Hamdani and other responsible, moderate officials to sketch out the framework of their provisional government. We will be available for help and support, but ultimately the decision of how to govern Sumeristan rests with the Sumeri people themselves. Based on the progress they have made thus far, we anticipate being able to turn over the symbolic reins of power to the Hamdani government sometime this summer.

"We look forward to this new and exciting chapter in the history of Sumeristan, which will hopefully serve as a beacon of democracy for oppressed peoples everywhere."

"Ever read *The Peter Principle?*" asked Caldwell.

"No," said Parisi, "but I think I'm familiar with the concept—that everyone gets promoted to their level of incompetence."

"I think it's called the 'Hamdani Principle' now—no pun intended."

"Thanks for coming back, Peter," said Neponski as he closed the door of his office. "When you've been in this town as long as I have, you learn not to trust telephones."

"Thanks for your patience, sir. I know you gave me a week, and it's been eleven days."

"That's fine."

"As I told you, the legal guys held us up—checking the precedents, that kind of thing."

"Nothing like being surrounded by lawyers," said the Speaker. "God knows where we'd be if we didn't have them telling us what to have for breakfast in the morning. Do you plan to tip off the administration?"

"No, we don't. The executive editor will call Hornsby the night before as a courtesy. But it's not going to happen until the first edition is put to bed."

"That's a gutsy move. Hornsby will go berserk."

"Well, when we went back and examined the Pentagon Papers case, we realized this was classic example of prior restraint. At least, that's how it would play out if it went to court. But we don't believe they're going to litigate."

"Why not?"

"You were correct about Kevin Furlin." Schoenfeld smiled. "He was quite forthcoming. I had the impression that he doesn't have much to lose at this point. He gave us a lot of dirt about major players, particularly Sanford Bayer. You and I might be jaded about this kind of stuff, but it would strike the average voter out in Peoria as pretty sordid."

"That's what I figured. I've never actually talked to him, but he was described to me as a potential gold mine."

"So with all the ammunition we have, I think the administration will just decide to hunker down and make the best of it. There'll be payback down the road, but we'll deal with it then."

"What about the timing?"

"We wanted to wait until Secretary Caldwell returned from Sumeristan. We're thinking about next Monday."

"Sounds good to me."

"I think you'll also be pleased to know that after the initial story runs, we're not going to keep this to ourselves. The intention is to share the information with any news outlet that wants to pursue it."

"Outstanding."

"I suspect a lot of them will want to jump on the bandwagon. In the meantime, we're grateful that you approached us first."

"Well, you guys have been out front on things from the beginning. That story about the dummies was a thing of beauty."

"Thank you."

The Speaker smiled. "And after all, loyalty begins at home."

CHAPTER 54

NEPONSKI WASN'T ENTIRELY CORRECT. ROBERT Hornsby didn't go berserk when the story broke in the *Post* about the presidential daily brief of April 21, 2001. He didn't have time. When Philip Gladstone, the paper's executive editor, called him at 8:00 p.m. on Sunday evening, he did his best to channel his anger into persuasiveness.

"I'm asking you to pull the story, in the national interest."

"Can't do it, Mr. Vice President. We have it locked in, and the first edition is already in production. And we wouldn't pull it in any case. I'm just calling as a courtesy."

"I appreciate that, but stop and think about what you're doing. You're giving aid and comfort to the enemy."

"Hell, I don't think so, unless you define the enemy as the public's right to know."

"Cut the high-horse crap, Phil. You and I have known each other a long time. That information is both classified and extremely sensitive."

"One of your guys leaked it to us. Or shall I say one of your former guys. He didn't have any trouble getting his hands on it, so apparently it wasn't quite so sensitive."

"May I ask who the source was?"

"You can ask, but obviously I'm not going to tell you. And we both know you won't have any trouble figuring out who it was, so let's not kid ourselves."

"I have a pretty good idea. Look, Phil, you know you're not going to get away with this. There are people in the administration who are getting tired of being embarrassed by you guys, and this time they'll take you to court. Don't think they don't have a case, either."

"I doubt that they do, but here's the thing—we have a lot of information that we're not using, exactly because we don't want to embarrass people unnecessarily. Information that might come out in the course of a long court case."

"Now you're threatening me?"

"Hell, we're just having a conversation."

"What kind of information are you referring to?"

"It seems there's some sort of homosexual cabal going on over at the White House. The Office of Faith and Reconciliation is more like the Office of Threesomes and Foursomes."

"Goddammit—"

"You and I might not care about any of this, and people on both coasts may believe its normal, but they think differently in the heartland. Enough said."

"I don't believe this."

"This guy is monumentally pissed off, Mr. Vice President. So much so that he doesn't care anymore. If he gets pushed, he'll go public."

"The world is round, Phil. We'll talk again."

He slammed down the receiver and called McCardle at home.

"I hope you're sitting down."

"Yes, sir?"

"The *Post* got their hands on the PDB for April 21—the one with the item about Husam al-Din's interest in hijacking commercial airliners and using them to attack us. They're running it in tomorrow's paper."

"Holy shit. How'd they get hold of that?"

"Obviously, Mike, it was that goddamn faggot that we fired. That guy Furlin, the one who was leaking information to Reverend Bayer."

"I'm really sorry, sir. Looks like you'll have a rough time for a while."

"*You're* sorry? We boot this guy for leaking classified information, and he grabs a PDB on his way out the door? What's that about?"

"I can't be everywhere at once, sir."

That's what we pay you for, thought Hornsby, counting to ten.

"What do you want me to do about this?"

"Absolutely nothing. This fucking guy has been singing to the *Post* like the lead tenor at the Met. If you lean on him, it'll get much worse. We're trying to get the situation in Sumeristan under control so we can get the hell out of there. The last thing we need is a string of stories over the next few months detailing how Sandy Bayer is cavorting with his assistants on the government's dime."

"Are you going to tell the president now?"

"He can find out in the morning. Let him be aggravated then, rather than all night long."

"All right, sir. Keep me posted."

"You bet your ass I will."

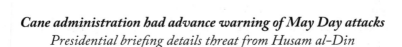

Cane administration had advance warning of May Day attacks
Presidential briefing details threat from Husam al-Din

Special to the Washington Post—The Post has obtained exclusive access to the presidential daily brief for April 21, 2001, which contains information on plans by Husam al-Din to attack the United States.

The PDB is a compilation of the day's most urgent security-related topics, delivered personally to the president each morning by a high-ranking official from the intelligence community.

In the April 21 document, one of the item headings declares: "Salman al-Akbar determined to strike within the United States." The brief goes on to state that al-Akbar's "highest priority" seems to be coordinating a terrorist attack inside this country. It recommends an elevated state of security alert around the nation, "particularly airports, as al-Akbar has previously shown great interest in hijacking commercial airliners to carry out terrorist strikes." The report also refers to the existence of sleeper cells, groups formed to assist Husam al-Din in carrying out an attack.

The PDB was obtained by the Post from a source within the Central Intelligence Agency. This anonymous source, who was involuntarily separated from government service this year, indicated that he came across the document in the course of his work and was profoundly disturbed by it. Even though the contents of the PDB were both sensitive and classified, he decided to share it with the public after a long struggle with his conscience...

Hornsby was waiting outside the Oval Office when the president arrived from the residence the next morning. Although the tips of George Cane's ears were bright red, he seemed remarkably composed.

"Come in, Bob. Ladies, please hold my appointments and calls until you hear from me."

They settled in across from each other, and Cane tossed the newspaper on his desk.

"How the hell did this happen?"

"The source was a low-level analyst. We fired him earlier in the year because he was funneling information to Sanford Bayer."

"Why would he do that?"

"He was involved with one of Bayer's assistants."

"Involved? As in, having a relationship?"

"That's it, sir."

"Explain to me how he got his hands on the PDB. I thought that kind of stuff was locked up so tight nobody could get to it."

"The policy is that analysts can request documents to help them in their research. This guy apparently made a copy."

"With the intention of giving it to the *Post?* I still don't get the chronology here. He couldn't possibly have done this after he found out he was fired. Wasn't he escorted from the building?"

"I believe he was angry because we convinced Bayer to get rid of his lover."

"You convinced him?"

"We were trying to stop the leaks, sir."

"Well, you did a hell of a job." Cane shook his head. "I want this guy strung up by his thumbs. You have my permission to take the gloves off."

"I'm afraid that wouldn't be wise."

"And why not?"

"Well, I've been told—or rather, it has been implied to me—that this individual has very damaging information about Reverend Bayer's lifestyle and associations."

"Does this mean what I think it means?"

"I'm afraid so."

"What the hell is going on over there? It sounds like some version of the Roman baths."

"Sir, I hate to say this, but I did warn you about Reverend Bayer. If you think back to our conversation right after the election—"

"Still, I had no idea it would be this bad. I assume you didn't, either."

"That's correct."

"It sounds like it's time to kiss the Reverend goodbye. Let's thank him for his meritorious service and send him on his way."

"That really wouldn't be wise, either—not at all. We're pretty close to handing off Sumeristan to Kasim Hamdani. The last thing we need is to have the next few months consumed with front-page stories about homosexual rings in the White House."

"God almighty."

"Let's get Sumeristan off our plate, make it somebody else's problem. Then we can say goodbye to Reverend Bayer and put our attention on Kabulistan."

"And what happens then?"

"With Bayer? I'm not sure, but it will give us some time to figure out a strategy."

"No, no—with Kabulistan."

"I think our best bet is to shift some troops into the country, topple the Dua Khamail, and sharpen the hunt for Salman al-Akbar."

"How many troops?"

"Maybe half, hopefully less. We send the reservists home and move the regular guys over there. They signed up for it."

"Sounds good. In the meantime, we'll need you to get out there and do some damage control."

"I'm on it. We're working on *Meet the Press* for next Sunday. To be honest, I think I'll have the pick of the talk shows."

"I hate to ask, but what else do you have to tell me? What other skeletons do we have hiding in the closet?"

"That's it, sir. Nothing else you need to know at this time."

"Really? Where's that sign that Harry Truman used to have, saying that the buck stopped here? I'm starting to think I'd be better off knowing it all."

"Not really. Remember, you can't be blamed for something you didn't know."

"You don't think so? Anything happens that I don't know about, the press will say that I was out of the loop."

"No, I'll get the blame. I withheld information from you, after all. Remember that you're still extremely popular with a large segment of the American people. You're a wartime president, so you get the benefit of the doubt."

"I hope so."

"And things may get nasty in the next few months. Let's try to keep you above the fray."

"Think so?"

"You know what they always say up on the Hill? That passing legislation is like making sausage, and that the public doesn't want to look too closely?"

"That's what they say."

"Well, the guys up on the Hill don't have to kill and gut their own animals before they make sausage out of them."

CHAPTER 55

GOOD MORNING. I'M TIM RUSSERT, and welcome to *Meet the Press*. My guest this morning is the vice president of the United States, Robert Barton Hornsby."

"This should be good," said Mandy Parisi, settling on a couch in Jennifer Caldwell's office.

"This should be better than good," said the secretary.

"Mr. Vice President, welcome back."

"Thank you, Tim." Hornsby squinted into the camera. "Good to be here."

"You've had quite a week, sir. Both Washington and the nation have been buzzing since last Monday, when the *Washington Post* released the contents of the presidential daily brief for April 21. Exactly how damaging do you think this has been for your administration, sir?"

"Not damaging at all, Tim—very far from it. Everyone in the intelligence community, and most of us in government, understand that there are dozens of threats that come in on a daily basis. If we responded to them all, we wouldn't have any national resources left. Every army and police officer, every reservist and national guardsman would be looking over his or her shoulder. So what we do, of course, is prioritize these threats. We need to stay vigilant, but not at the cost of keeping the population in a continuous state of panic."

"With all due respect, sir," Russert interjected, "the entry in the April 21 PDB about Husam al-Din is pretty specific. It talks about the possibility of hijacking airplanes to create a terrorist attack, and advises putting the country on high alert."

"Actually, Tim, if you read it carefully, you'll see that it is quite speculative. We both know that hindsight is 20/20, but this item is one of a multitude of warnings that we've had about terrorist threats of all sorts. If I was free to reveal them to you, which I'm not, you'd see that they'd be overwhelming if they were added up."

"Still—"

"What the April 21st PDB *said* is that an attack was *possible*. It gave no timetable, no definitive intelligence, no clues as to where to look. This is a dangerous world, Tim. We're under the threat of attack every day from many different directions. Yes, we have to be vigilant, but we also have to be prudent in the way we react."

"Sir, a number of congressmen on the Hill have been calling for the president's impeachment. Are you concerned about this coming to pass?"

"By 'congressmen' I assume you mean 'liberal Democrats.'" Hornsby smiled. "No, we're not concerned at all, Tim. George Cane enjoys the support of a wide majority of the American people. They understand that he's a wartime president, very much against his will, and they're behind him one hundred percent. I'm sure you've seen the polls, just as they have. I work closely with the president every day, and I can assure you that he'd much rather be healing domestic problems in this country than being at war with an amorphous terrorist enemy. But that's the way things have worked out."

"I'm surprised that Andrew Neponski isn't pursuing the impeachment angle," said Mandy Parisi.

"It's a nonstarter," said Caldwell. "He doesn't have the votes."

"Even so, it could give him a bargaining chip."

"No, Hornsby's right. People like this guy, for some reason."

"There are also people," continued Russert, "capital insiders, who feel that the PDB scandal has given new momentum to the president's potential opposition in 2004. There are many Democrats, notably Bethany Hampton, who seem to be positioning themselves for a White House run. Do you think this makes the president vulnerable in that regard?"

"Don't take this the wrong way, Tim, but we couldn't care less. We're totally focused on keeping this country safe and making sure that our children and grandchildren inherit a better world. I can tell you with complete honesty that no one in the administration has given so much as a thought to 2004.

The global situation that we're presented with right now is dangerous, and it's something that requires our complete attention. And I can also tell you, without exaggerating the dangers we face, that you and I might not be sitting here right now if George Cane hadn't moved decisively to squash dozens of threats to our security."

"Our savior," said Jennifer Caldwell. "This is heartwarming."

"A lot of people are rooting for Bethany," said Mandy. "They're energized, because they think this PDB scandal has given her the platform to mount a successful campaign."

"She won't run."

"Why do you say that, ma'am?"

"Because she can't win. She knows how hard it is to defeat a sitting president. George Cane gets reelected in 2004, unless someone unmasks him as a secret Husam al-Din agent. It's another nonstarter."

"Sir," said Russert, "the *Post* identified the source of the leak as a former CIA staffer who had been, and I quote, 'involuntarily separated from government service.' I take that to mean fired. Can you comment on this source? Do you know who he is?"

"We're not concerning ourselves with the source, Tim. We accept that he is an honorable person, who leaked the document to satisfy his conscience—at least, this is what we were told. I can only point out that his perception of the contents was likely just as skewed as those of Democrats on the Hill."

"Given that this information was classified, and given that the source released it without authorization, are you contemplating any legal action against him?"

"Not at all. As I said, we accept the assertion that this was a matter of conscience for him. In response, we can only say that our defense of America is a matter of conscience for *us*, and we stand by our actions."

"Sir, turning to the situation in Sumeristan, how would you evaluate the progress that Kasim Hamdani is making toward forming a provisional government? Do you feel that he's likely to meet your timetable for a summer handover of authority?"

"We feel he's making great progress, Tim. Remember that this is a country without political infrastructure in place—for several decades, the political landscape was totally dominated by Hussein Ghazi. It's certainly not like our country, where you have tens of thousands of qualified candidates to choose from if you want to form a government. Taking that situation into account, we think he's making terrific progress."

"What—"

"I also need to point out that the choice of a summer transition wasn't our timetable, as I believe you said. It was a timeframe that was agreed upon by all the parties involved. Mr. Hamdani told us that he could probably have all the groundwork laid to form a government by that date, and we endorsed that. If it doesn't work out, we're certainly flexible. It's their country, after all."

"Damn," said Mandy. "He's good."

"Better believe it. He's not where he is by accident."

"How would you respond to critics," asked Russert, "who point out that we have yet to locate the stockpiles of chemical weapons that Secretary Stevenson described in his speech to the U.N. General Assembly? These weapons, after all, were one of the main reasons why we invaded Sumeristan rather than intensify our search for Salman al-Akbar in Kabulistan."

"I'm confident that we'll find the weapons in due time," said Hornsby. "Remember, Tim, that it's been slightly more than six months since we invaded Sumeristan. Quite honestly, finding the weapons hasn't been our first priority. Our initial focus was to rid the country of a brutal dictator. After that, we've been concentrating on helping the Sumeri people achieve self-government—which, of course, was our objective from the beginning."

"And what about Salman al-Akbar and Kabulistan, sir?"

"Salman al-Akbar is continually on our radar. We are committed to apprehending him and destroying the terrorist network of Husam al-Din. And after we transfer governing authority for Sumeristan to the provisional government of Kasim Hamdani, we'll have the resources to intensify our efforts in Kabulistan. I'm sure that al-Akbar is watching this broadcast right now. And assuming that's the case, I'll echo the president's words and send him this message: You can run, but you can't hide. We will bring you to justice."

CHAPTER 56

SALMAN AL-AKBAR AND FAZIL AHMADI relaxed in the garden of al-Akbar's central Kabulistan compound.

"So tell me," asked the leader of Husam al-Din, "how are preparations coming along for the American transfer of authority in Baghdad?"

"It will be quite a spectacle, sir: parades and many stirring speeches. A high American official will be in attendance, but we do not yet know the person's identity."

"Excellent. And you are developing some strategies?"

"We are working on a few possibilities, yes. I will present them to you shortly."

"Very good."

"Sir," asked Ahmadi, "do you believe it may be time to shift some of our recruits to the coming conflict here between the Americans and the Dua Khamail?"

"No, no." Al-Akbar shook his head. "Absolutely not. We must keep our focus on Sumeristan. Why do you ask this?"

"Because at some point, if the Americans are successful in stabilizing Sumeristan, they will turn their attention to us."

"This is precisely why we must concentrate on disrupting them there. Let us always remember what happened in Vietnam. It is not enough to make them appear foolish in the eyes of the world. If we keep up the pressure, the population will turn against the American president. They do not have the stamina for a prolonged conflict, particularly after Vietnam."

"This is true."

"And at the same time, they are stubborn." He smiled. "It is a beautiful combination. If we focus our resources on Sumeristan, we will slowly wear them down."

Ahmadi nodded.

"I do not believe they will squander ten years there, as they did in Southeast Asia. But this is a situation where time works to our advantage, particularly here in Kabulistan. If enough time passes, we will see a generation rise who only knew the Dua Khamail as their leaders."

"You are wise, sir."

"Thank you. In the meantime, I will await your plans for the ceremony in Baghdad."

"You will have them shortly, and we can decide the best way to deal with the Americans and their high school principal."

Like many other political junkies, Andrew Neponski inevitably spent part of his day watching C-SPAN. Although his own speeches had become more pointed and compressed in recent years, he was fascinated by the oratory styles of his colleagues, particularly those who were gifted enough to retain the public's interest during a lengthy, strident address.

The Speaker had been paying more and more attention to Khaleem Atalas since the invasion of Sumeristan. He was not alone. The freshman senator from Pennsylvania was turning up frequently on the radar of many Capitol insiders. By now, his background was familiar: The son of a black Indonesian father and a white American mother, the young man had grown up outside Philadelphia and attended Princeton. After graduation, he gained a reputation as a community activist and rose quickly through the ranks of the local political machine. He was bright, personable, and dynamic, but more importantly, he bridged the gap between many different constituencies—a multiracial wonder child with the street smarts to appeal to the disadvantaged, yet elegant and polished enough to put wealthy donors at ease.

"First, the administration told us that Hussein Ghazi was a brutal dictator," Atalas recited in his crisp, practiced cadence. "He was a tyrant who tortured and executed his population at will, and it would be an act of supreme kindness to remove him from power. Now that we have done so, the daily death toll in Sumeristan far exceeds anything that Ghazi's goons ever produced. The population of that country once faced the danger of an oppressive dictator; now that they have been liberated, they are afraid to walk down the street."

Atalas was one of a handful of Democratic senators who had voted against the resolutions to use force in the Middle East. It seemed like political suicide at the time, a violation of the age-old rule that politics stops at the water's edge. As the months passed, however, his opposition was looking more like genius.

"Then, the Cane administration told us that Hussein Ghazi possessed stockpiles of chemical and biological weapons," Atalas continued, "and that he was even working toward a possible nuclear capability. We were presented with a pair of resolutions that gave the government sweeping powers to wage war in the Middle East. As the day approached for us to vote on those resolutions, the perceived danger of Ghazi's weapons seemed to grow larger and larger. Many of my colleagues in this chamber voted to give the administration those broad war powers, and I'm certain their intentions were motivated by patriotism and concern for national security.

"We have not found any weapons, however. And the likely reason we have not found them is that they do not exist. As the days and weeks pass, it becomes clearer and clearer that we have made a mistake of monumental proportions. We have dismantled the government of a sovereign nation, and we paid a large price in American blood and treasure. And the reality is that we will not find those weapons until the Tigris River freezes over."

Poor Bethany Hampton, thought the Speaker. *She screwed up big time over this. I'll bet she's sharpening her fangs and fantasizing about executing the advisers who told her to vote yes. But this guy isn't going to go away. Things are going to get worse, and by 2008, he'll look like a hero.*

"Of course we are concerned for the welfare of the people of Sumeristan. No one thinks for one moment that Hussein Ghazi was a prince of peace, and any well-meaning person would have helped his people if possible. But our real concern should be for the people of the United States. We should care more for our own citizens—those who are hungry, who are disenfranchised, who lack the skills to find a decent job, and who cannot afford health insurance. When we live up to our responsibility to help those among us who are in need, who suffer from oppression and lack the ability to fully participate in our society, then the United States of America will be the beacon of democracy the Cane administration wants it to be."

I don't have the heart to tell Bethany, thought the Speaker, *but six years from now, this guy is going to be unbeatable.*

CHAPTER 57

I N JUST A FEW MOMENTS," the CNN anchor said, "we'll be going to the White House, where George Cane is scheduled to give his first press conference in nearly six months. Let's check in with our correspondent on the scene, Rebecca Hagerty, and get a sense of the atmosphere as the press corps waits for the president to arrive. Rebecca, what's it like inside?"

"Good afternoon, Larry. I think it's safe to say that the press is champing at the bit. George Cane hasn't faced reporters since shortly after the invasion of Sumeristan, and many critics have accused him of being in a bubble. I think he'll face a number of tough questions today, and we can expect that he'll try to control the situation by calling on individual reporters."

"What's the press corps likely to focus on?"

"It's going to be Sumeristan, Larry, and all about Sumeristan. Cane is likely to try to deflect the focus in his prepared remarks by touting the administration's progress on jobs and the economy, but at the end of the day, the war is really what the American public wants to hear about."

"You know, Rebecca, the polls seem to indicate that the majority of the public still supports and approves of the job the president is doing."

"That's true, Larry, although there's been some slippage over the past few months. I think people are still giving him the benefit of the doubt, realizing that he has faced unprecedented challenges in his first year in office. But at the same time, the public seems to be growing weary of the continued violence, and many people are worried that the war in Sumeristan could turn into another long-term American commitment."

"Rebecca—"

"I have to break off now, because the president is entering the room."

George Cane strode to the podium, a confident smile on his face.

"Please be seated, folks," he said with a downward motion of his palms. His cheerful demeanor seemed to fade into defiance as he stared at the gaggle of reporters, who were poised like jungle cats ready to strike at their prey.

"Over the past two or three months, my administration has witnessed dramatic progress on the economic front. All the indicators are pointing in the right direction. GDP is up, unemployment is down, and the climate for American entrepreneurship has never been stronger. We are continuing our efforts to work with the private sector to encourage the growth of small businesses.

"At the same time, crime in most of our major urban areas has declined dramatically. I want to take a moment to thank our dedicated men and women of law enforcement, who are out there on the front lines every day. As a matter of course, they risk their lives every day to ensure the safety of all Americans.

"Last and most importantly, I want to thank our brave troops who are defending our security interests all over the world, particularly those who are helping spread democracy to troubled nations. I'm proud to be their commander in chief, and all Americans should be proud of them as well.

"I'll take your questions now, but we'll do this on an orderly basis. No jumping to your feet or shouting, please, or I won't recognize you. Catherine, let's start with you," he said, indicating the *Christian Science Monitor.*

"Sir, many Americans are alarmed at the ongoing wave of violence in Sumeristan, and particularly in Baghdad. Not a day seems to pass when we don't hear about the death or injury of at least half a dozen servicemen, not to mention dozens of innocent Sumeris. You mentioned that the country is making progress toward a democratic government, but I think most people are wondering why this violence is happening, and how long it will continue."

"Excellent question, Catherine," Cane replied. "I'm as appalled as anyone else by the continuing domestic problems in Sumeristan, but remember that they were only recently liberated from the clutches of a brutal dictator. I have to remind you that the path to democracy is frequently a long and painful process. If you look back at history, you'll see that the American Revolution began in 1775 and ended in 1783, and it took several years before a national government was established.

"No one grieves more than I do for the fallen servicemen and women that I have put in harm's way. And like most Americans, I have deep empathy for the people of Sumeristan. But I think we need to be mindful that these processes do not occur overnight."

"David," he said, indicating the correspondent from Fox News.

"Sir, one of the main reasons given for the invasion of Sumeristan was the stockpiles of chemical and biological weapons supposedly owned by Hussein Ghazi. Secretary Stevenson detailed these stockpiles in his address to the U.N. General Assembly, and portrayed Ghazi as a threat to Western civilization. Thus far, U.N. weapons inspectors have failed to find them. Can you give us an update on the search for these weapons?"

"According to all the intelligence we received, David, the existence of those weapons was very real. I have no doubt that they were concealed carefully by Hussein Ghazi, particularly in the days leading up to the invasion. At the same time, I'll admit that I'm baffled by the fact that they haven't yet turned up. I've asked Admiral McCardle to conduct an independent review of the sources and information that contributed to the intelligence about those weapons.

"But regardless of what that review ultimately reveals, I take full responsibility for the invasion. I felt at the time that it was the right thing to do, and I'm still convinced of that. Hussein Ghazi was an evil man—a man who slaughtered nearly a million of his own people, and who had dreams of conquest and world domination similar to those of Hitler sixty years ago. Removing him from power was the right thing for Sumeristan, the right thing for the United States, and the right thing for the world."

"The gentleman from al-Jazeera," said the president.

"Sir, many in the Muslim community here in America are disturbed over the increasing incidents of discrimination against them. We see Muslims being pulled off airplanes simply because they are carrying prayer beads. Attacks against Muslims are becoming more common in our communities, and just last week, as you're aware, a mosque in Michigan was defaced."

"Ahmed, I've said many times that Islam is one of the world's great religions, a path of peace and understanding for billions of people. I've also said that what happened last May was not just the hijacking of airliners, but also the hijacking of this great faith by people with evil and destructive goals. We condemn this, but we also are mindful that it happened. I'm committed to safeguarding the rights of all Americans, but I'm committed to safeguarding their security as well."

"Jeffrey from the *Weekly Standard*."

"Mr. President, we were attacked last May by agents of Husam al-Din. In your statements to the American people immediately following the attacks, you indicated that the Dua Khamail government of Kabulistan had given aid and comfort to Husam al-Din, and that they would be our most appropriate target for retaliation. Shortly afterward, our military focus shifted to Hussein Ghazi and Sumeristan. So my question has two parts. First, are you still convinced that Hussein Ghazi had links to Husam al-Din? And second, is Kabulistan next?"

"Thank you, Jeffrey. Yes, I'm absolutely convinced that Hussein Ghazi had connections to the folks who attacked us on May first. Unfortunately, I can't share all the classified information with you. But I can say that if you were sitting where I'm sitting, you would share the conviction that Hussein Ghazi was part of a global terrorist conspiracy that threatened our safety. As far as Kabulistan goes, I obviously can't identify the focus of any future attacks. But you and most others are aware, as I am, that the evildoers who masterminded the May first attacks are still out there, plotting to do us harm. And I can assure you that I will bring them to justice."

"Barbara from the *National Review*," he said.

"Sir, some of your critics are charging that Dr. Kasim Hamdani is perhaps not the best person to head up Sumeristan's provisional government. They point to his complete lack of experience in both politics and statesmanship. How would you respond to that, and can you explain your choice of an inexperienced outsider to take the reins of a troubled nation?"

"Well, first of all, Barbara, it wasn't my choice. Mr. Hamdani was chosen after lengthy consultation with prominent sectors of the Sumeri community. What emerged in those discussions was that he possessed the right temperament for the job, even if he lacked experience. It's important to remember that there's no one in Sumeristan with government experience, other than the people who aided and abetted Hussein Ghazi.

"No one knows if Mr. Hamdani will be the leader of Sumeristan five years from now, but we're grateful to him for stepping up and assuming the responsibility for his nation's future during this troubled period. Regardless of who leads the country, there will be ups and downs in the years to come, but it will be the Sumeris themselves who will deal with them. When we officially hand off authority to Mr. Hamdani a few months from now, it will represent one of the fastest transitions in history on the part of occupying forces.

"As I said before, the path to democracy is sometimes a long and troubled one. Very similar to true love, at times." The president smiled. "Speaking of true love, where's Peter Schoenfeld?"

Laughter rippled across the room. "Right here, sir."

"Peter, do you have a question?"

"I do, Mr. President, and thank you." He rose to his feet. "There are many observers, at least those old enough to remember, who are drawing a parallel between the war in Sumeristan and our involvement in Vietnam. They feel that regardless of who surfaces to lead the Sumeri government, the United States is bound to be involved for a decade or more with troops, advisors, support staff, and financial aid. How do you feel about that?"

"I think it's nonsense," said Cane amiably. "Of course, it's certainly true that we'll have a military presence in Sumeristan for some time, but the number of those troops will gradually be drawn down. A few years from now, I anticipate that it would be nothing more than a peacekeeping force. And we'll be providing them with aid to rebuild their country, although we project that their oil revenues will largely accomplish that goal. But I'll say it again, Peter. Sumeristan is not Vietnam. When we hand over authority to the provisional government of Kasim Hamdani in June, Sumeristan will belong to the Sumeris for the first time since Hussein Ghazi seized power more than two decades ago."

As the press conference ended, CNN cut away to correspondent Rebecca Hagerty, standing on the White House lawn and holding a microphone.

"So there you have it, Larry—the president chose to end the event with Peter Schoenfeld, which I assume was intentional, since it allowed him the last word in his exchange with his nemesis."

"That's certainly the way it looks, Rebecca," said the anchor. "It also allowed him to finish with that ringing statement about Sumeristan belonging to the Sumeris. One thing isn't certain, though—whether Sumeristan will in fact turn out to be Vietnam."

CHAPTER 58

EVER SINCE SHE WAS A girl, Jennifer Caldwell had loved cherry blossoms. She was fascinated by their color and fragrance, their cloudlike appearance, and suggestion of impermanence. One of the highlights of her childhood was a class trip to the Cherry Blossom Festival in Washington, D.C., when she had been able to see oceans of them in April bloom.

Now, as April morphed into May, she sat in her Foggy Bottom office and watched the cherry trees shed the last of their plumage. The blossoms covered the lawns and parks like newly fallen pink snow, a contrast to the rapidly approaching summer heat of the capital.

"Ma'am?"

She pushed a button on the office console to respond to the buzzer.

"Yes, Mandy."

"Dr. Hamdani is on CNN, if you want to see it."

"Not really. Why don't you watch it and tell me what he says."

She forced her attention away from the window and shuffled through the pile of reports in front of her. The French president continued to snipe at the United States for imperialism and warmongering, and the British prime minister was getting roasted twice a week in the House of Commons for his support of the Sumeristan invasion. There were insurgent movements in Azerbaijan, Myanmar, Indonesia, and Laos; torrential rains and deadly mudslides in India; drug murders in Mexico, mass graves uncovered in Yemen, and rumors of nuclear research in Persepostan.

What a world, she thought. *Thank God I never had children.*

There was a knock on the door.

"Come in."

Mandy Parisi sat down across from the secretary's desk.

"So tell me," asked Caldwell, "what's the news from sunny Sumeristan?"

"Dr. Hamdani says he's making significant progress toward forming his government."

"I would hope so. The keys to the kingdom will be handed to him in less than six weeks. Who are the lucky individuals?"

"Mostly intellectuals who left the country one step ahead of Hussein Ghazi's security services. The foreign minister has been summoned back from exile in Geneva. The interior secretary has been in Africa on a U.N. grant, working on land reclamation. That sort of thing."

"In other words, they're all exactly like him, guys who have spent their time expounding theory, not acting."

"Pretty much. Hamdani seems level-headed, though. He's not charismatic, but he sounds practical. For all we know, he could turn out to be exactly what Sumeristan needs right now."

"Who knows what the country needs at this moment." She laughed. "Other than Robert Hornsby, of course. I'm sure he knows."

"You seem tired, ma'am. Pardon me for saying so."

"I'm disgusted, Mandy. And I'm tired of constantly sticking my fingers into holes in the dike, trying to plug the leaks. Lately, the leaks seem to be more numerous than my fingers." She shook her head. "You know, when Bill Hampton bombed the Husam al-Din headquarters a few years back, trying to kill Salman al-Akbar, all we got was criticism. The talking heads said that he was just trying to cover up his indiscretions."

"I remember that. Didn't everybody say it was a toy factory?"

"The only toys they were hand-held rocket launchers. But nobody cared at the time."

"The indiscretions were real, weren't they?"

"So was Husam al-Din, as it turned out. But the press didn't want to hear it."

"You know, after our conversation a few months ago, I did some reading about the Fourth Crusade. You were right—the parallels here are uncanny."

"Just wait and see what happens. Only a small fraction of the crusaders ever made it to the Holy Land—about the same percentage of our troops who will reach Kabulistan to hunt down our real enemies. Most of them wasted their resources fighting over the spoils and riches of Constantinople, just as everyone will compete for a share of the oil revenues when this thing is over. And the pope, who condemned the crusaders for their greed in sacking Constantinople, was more than happy to accept the stolen riches when they were offered to him."

"Well, I guess you can put all this in the memoir everybody thinks you're writing."

"Sure. In my spare time, I suppose."

"Don't tell me you're not even taking notes, ma'am."

"Oh, of course." She smiled. "I keep a journal. But who wouldn't?"

"I know we've been through this before, Bob," said the president, "but I want you to run it down for me again. I want to make sure we're on the same page."

"Of course, sir." In fact, the two men had reviewed the arrangements at least three times. "What are your concerns?"

"There's too much that can go wrong. I'm concerned about the structure of the event, about how folks will perceive it. We want to make it clear that we're closing this chapter and moving on. Most of all, I'm worried about security."

"The event itself will last about two hours," said Hornsby patiently. "It's been choreographed very carefully. We'll open with the student orchestra from Dr. Hamdani's academy, who will play the Sumeri national anthem. They'll continue to play during the parade, which will last about twenty-five or thirty minutes. Our community liaisons have rounded up as many wholesome groups as they could, the local equivalents of the Boy Scouts, young girls from orphanages, whatever."

"Very good."

"Then the speeches will start. Jennifer will say something, of course. We've tried to include the top two or three guys from Hamdani's new government, to showcase them a bit."

"I still think it would be more appropriate if we had someone else there representing us."

"Well, you and I can't go, sir. The Secret Service won't allow it."

"What about Bayard Stevenson? He's the guy that liberated the country."

"It's a delicate situation. We really don't want to stress the militaristic aspect of this. If we can, we want to try to hit a note of optimism, focus on the emerging democracy, that sort of thing. Having Bayard there would just remind everybody of the invasion. Jennifer's the secretary of state, and she already has a relationship with Hamdani. The more we emphasize that relationship, the more responsible she becomes for his success—in the public mind, that is."

"Okay." Cane smiled. "I like it."

"As to security, it's going to be handled primarily by the Sumeri national police, with our people supervising."

"This is what bothers me. I'd feel a lot more comfortable if we were in charge of security."

"It just wouldn't look good, sir. The whole point of this is that we're turning over authority to the Sumeris. It's supposed to be their country. In these situations, everything is symbolic. We can't give the impression that we're putting them in charge, but we don't trust them with the security arrangements."

"I still don't like it."

"We'll have our Special Forces stationed at the gates alongside the Sumeri national police. There will be two entrances. Everyone attending will go through metal detectors and be screened by hand. No exceptions. Our guys will be watching closely, but the Sumeris will be doing the screening."

"Well, I suppose that's okay."

"We're still working out the seating arrangements, but the thinking is to put some physical distance between the U.S. contingent and Hamdani's new government. They'll be reasonably close to each other, of course, but there has to be some space. Again, it's symbolic. The goal is to reinforce the impression that Sumeristan is a sovereign nation. So we'll have Dr. Hamdani sitting with the key figures of his new government. He'll be surrounded by his little honor guard of high school students, those kids that follow him around wherever he goes. The public seems to like that stuff, for some reason. It projects Hamdani as a nurturing figure."

"I suppose."

"One thing I need to clarify, though. I believe you said something about us closing this chapter, and of course we're not doing that, at least not yet. We'll still have two hundred thousand troops in country for the initial phase of the Hamdani government, at least until we're sure that he can control the situation. After that, we can start the drawdown. But the likelihood is that we'll still have a hundred thousand troops there by 2004."

"I'd like it to be less than that."

"Sumeristan is a big country, sir. We'll certainly have Baghdad under control by then, but the border regions are a source of concern. It's important that we leave enough troops in place to cover any insurgent movements. My best guess is one hundred thousand, but coming up on the election we can reassure the public with a carefully crafted timetable for further drawdowns."

Hornsby grinned. "Voters love timetables."

"I am very proud of you, Abdul."

With dinner finished, they sat across the table sipping a final cup of tea. Abdul's mother had noted in recent weeks that the young man seemed more open and communicative, increasingly able to have a discussion and listen to opposing points of view without becoming angry.

"Thank you."

"I know you've had much heartbreak in the past year, but you have conducted yourself very well. You have truly triumphed over adversity. Not only am I proud of you, but your father would be as well."

"I appreciate that, Mama."

"Looking back, I think it did you good to reconnect with your aunt over the summer, since she was your father's only sister. It seems that you were able to regain your sense of family during that visit."

"Yes." He smiled. "That was the turning point."

"And who ever would have thought that Dr. Hamdani would have risen so high? Certainly not I, when I went to see him three years ago and begged him to enroll you. He turned out not only to be your savior, but a mentor for the entire country as well."

"Yes, Dr. Hamdani is a wise man. He has taught me much. Without him, I might not have come to the place I am in now."

"Watch him and learn, Abdul. You will have an exceptional view of the new government during this country's transition. You will not be involved in policy now, of course, but someday you may be a leader yourself. Whatever path you choose, your connection to Dr. Hamdani will turn out to be a golden opportunity."

"I agree, Mama."

"Have you given any thought to what you want to do in the fall? You will attend university, I hope."

"I will enroll over the summer, yes, but right now I am unclear on a course of action. I cannot see the future."

"You have time." His mother reached out and patted his hand. "There is no need to rush. Just bide your time, continue to watch and observe, and you will learn much."

"It's interesting that you say so, because that is exactly what I have been doing. Sometimes when you study a situation closely, you learn much more than people think they are teaching you."

"Very true."

"Sometimes you even learn things they don't want you to know."

"What do you mean, Abdul?"

"I don't know." He shrugged. "People are transparent. They reveal themselves to you by their words and actions."

"You are wise beyond your years. Someday you will accomplish great things."

"I hope so, mama. This is my goal—to bring honor to you and our family."

CHAPTER 59

L ATER, WHEN THEY RECALLED THE events of that day, survivors fell back
on the human tendency to use clichés when describing things that
were impossible to understand.
Everything seemed to happen in slow motion.
There was a sudden flash of light.
After the deafening roar, the backdraft almost knocked them off their
seats and up into the air.

One thing was certain: It was a beautiful day. The morning was bright
and sunny, clear and free of humidity, the type of weather rarely encountered
toward the end of a Baghdad spring. Looking back, the atmosphere was so
exhilarating that those prone to clichés might have said that the air contained
the promise of hope.

Both governments had agreed to hold the festivities at a soccer field in
the city's Safe Zone. The centerpiece of the seating area was a huge Sumeri flag,
occupying two rows in the center of the bleachers. Seating began on either side of
the flag, about fifteen feet off the ground. The old-style bleachers had open backs
and lots of room between the benches, something that would prove lucky later on.

The dignitaries began to arrive shortly after eleven. According to Robert
Hornsby's seating plan, the Sumeri delegation was placed on one side of the

flag. Dr. Kasim Hamdani occupied the center of the group, flanked by his cabinet and his coterie of students. On the other side, General Boudreaux was accompanied by his top military aides; next to them were Jennifer Caldwell, Mandy Parisi, and a contingent of consular officers. They were late getting started. At ten minutes past noon, Mandy Parisi saw Abdul Alghafari mount the bleachers. He made his way to his place next to the new minister of defense, several seats away from Kasim Hamdani. The youth was wearing a loose-fitting linen jacket, and he was sweating profusely.

She knew.

"Ma'am, let's get out of here," she told the secretary. "Right now."

"What are you talking about? We're almost ready to start."

"You're in danger. We're leaving right this second. I'll explain later."

"We can't even get down from these bleachers. Their flag is in the way, and the band is tuning up beneath us."

"All right, follow me."

She turned around and eased herself down, until she held on to the wooden bench with both hands.

"Mandy, are you crazy? I can't do that."

"Right now—right this second! I'll explain later."

Both women were now dangling from the bench, seemingly suspended in midair.

"I can't do this," panted the secretary. "I can't hold on."

"Just let yourself go," said Mandy. She released her grip on the bench and fell to the ground, where she tucked and rolled in one smooth gymnastic move, rising to her feet. Caldwell was not as fortunate. She landed in a heap with her feet beneath her, and immediately grabbed her right ankle in pain. She was breathing heavily, and her makeup was running.

"Okay, let's get the hell out of here."

"I don't think I can go anywhere," she wheezed. "I can't put any weight on my ankle."

Mandy helped the secretary to her feet and draped her right arm over her shoulder.

"Just hop," she said. "As fast as you can. We need to get as far away from here as possible."

They had traveled about ten yards and cleared the bleachers when Abdul Alghafari detonated his suicide belt. The wooden structure imploded, collapsing the Sumeri flag and sending the audience down on top of it; had the blast gone outward, they likely would have been killed by flying shards of wood. The agonized screams of the spectators echoed in Mandy's ears; she would remember that sound for the rest of her life. As she dragged her boss away from the carnage, she allowed herself a backward glance. The once-festive site of the handover ceremony had disintegrated into a war zone. There was a pile of wooden planks where the bleachers once stood, with a fire blazing in the center and black smoke spiraling toward the clouds. Members of the Sumeri honor guard were pulling bodies from the rubble; their tan uniforms were bright red with spattered blood.

The last thing Jennifer Caldwell saw was the crystal blue sky.

When she woke up in the hospital, Mandy Parisi was sitting in a chair beside her bed.

"Where am I?"

"You're at the infirmary at the military base outside of Baghdad, ma'am."

Caldwell looked down at the cast on her right leg.

"What's wrong with me?"

"Not much, fortunately. Your ankle is broken from the fall, but you're a very lucky woman."

"All I can remember is dangling from the bleachers."

"You did very well."

"I hope no one got a picture of a two-hundred-pound woman hanging on to a bleacher bench. The secretary of state, no less."

"I imagine someone probably did."

She chuckled. "Well, better to be a live jackass than a dead one, I suppose."

"Tomorrow we're going to fly you out to the main military hospital in Germany. If everything checks out, we'll be on our way home after that."

"So what happened, Mandy?"

"One of Dr. Hamdani's students turned out to be a suicide bomber."

"How the hell did he get through security?"

"The ceremony was supposed to start at noon. The Sumeris abandoned the security stations and moved closer to watch the event. The kid just strolled right in, all wired up. God knows how he got past our personnel."

"Sounds like great work."

"I'm afraid so."

"How did everyone make out?"

"General Boudreaux is dead, unfortunately."

"Damn." She shook her head. "He was a good man."

"Absolutely right, ma'am. Hamdani is also dead, along with most of his cabinet."

"Well, no great loss there. I'm sure Hornsby will come up with someone just as qualified. Maybe the former head of the sanitation department, or the director of animal control."

"I'm glad you haven't lost your sense of humor."

"How did you know, Mandy? What was it that tipped you off?"

"I've had my eye on this kid for a while. There was something about him. My mother always said I was a witch."

"Good thing you were alert, or we'd both be dead."

"No need to pat me on the back, ma'am. I should have said something earlier. This whole thing could have been avoided if I had only listened to my gut."

"You had no proof, so don't feel guilty. Governments don't operate on intuition."

"Maybe they should."

EPILOGUE:
TEN YEARS LATER

PRESIDENT KHALEEM ATALAS LEANED BACK in his chair, closed his eyes and rubbed his forehead. He allowed himself this gesture of fatigue because he was alone in the Oval Office with Joel Gottbaum, his closest political advisor. The chair had been a birthday gift from his wife many years before, and it had travelled with him from his home outside Philadelphia to his Senate office and down Pennsylvania Avenue to the White House—a journey almost as remarkable as that of Atalas himself. At the time he received it, he had been an unknown community organizer and the chair seemed like an extravagance. By now, the leather was worn and fraying in spots, and the contraption resembled something from a garage sale. His insistence on using it had less to do with humoring Korinne than reclining in one of the few places he felt truly comfortable.

Gottbaum waited patiently.

"You'll have to make a statement about the troop levels," he said when the president opened his eyes. "And I'm afraid you'll have to do it soon. Both Fox and CNN are pressing me on it."

"They'll have to wait a couple of weeks."

"That gives them a couple of weeks to continue comparing you to Cane. We can't afford it. The election is eight months away."

"I'm waiting for the CIA to cough up some information on al-Akbar. They thought they had a lead on his whereabouts. If we can catch the son of a bitch, people will forget about the troop levels."

"They don't much care about them now, to be honest. We're talking about containing the network noise. And you've reduced the force in Sumeristan by thirty percent since you took office."

"And we've put a hundred thousand troops in Kabulistan with nothing to show for it."

"Here's the deal," Gottbaum said earnestly. "You inherited a mess from George Cane. People understand that. It doesn't hurt to keep reminding them of it, regardless of what Saturday Night Live says. Sooner or later someone will give up Salman al-Akbar and voters will forget how many troops we have in Kabulistan."

"Maybe so, but that's not going to stop the insurgency in Sumeristan."

"So you do a George Cane and propose another surge. It worked for him."

"Look, Joel. As a political operative, you're the best in the business. I wouldn't be sitting here if it weren't for you. But this goes beyond politics. People are sick and tired of being at war, and I don't blame them. It's sucking our economy down the tubes. We're making no progress. It's one thing to tell them that we're engaged in an ongoing battle against the forces of terror, but this has been going on for nearly a decade."

"And it's been a decade with no domestic terror attacks inside the United States. You need to keep reminding them of that as well."

"Is that what I tell working mothers in the ghettos? That we can't expand social programs for their kids because we're funding a hundred thousand troops in Kabulistan?"

"You could tell them that because of your efforts, no suicide bombers have committed mass murder in their neighborhoods."

"Every single one of those attacks that we've foiled was scripted to take place in rich, white areas—gated communities, luxury condos. These guys know they won't get any mileage out of bombing the 'hood." He drummed his fingers on the desk. "Cane and Hornsby had it easy. All they had to worry about was the Dua Khamail and Husam al-Din. I'd like to see them take on the New Caliphate for a week."

It was difficult for anyone to believe that less than two years had passed since Husam al-Din had spawned their latest mutation, the New Caliphate. Dismissed at first by the CIA as a radical but harmless fringe group, the organization had swelled to nearly fifty thousand members dedicated to establishing an Islamic state in Sumeristan. The first beheading had occurred six months earlier when the group executed a captive from Doctors without Borders. Since then, brutal decapitation videos had become a staple of the nightly news.

New Caliphate troops were organized into military brigades and wielded weapons supplied by Russia and China and filtered through allies in Persepostan. Even worse, they fought with a fearlessness totally absent in the Sumeri army units that opposed them, and they were starting to accumulate territorial gains in the provinces.

"If we play our cards right," said Gottbaum, "maybe we can get them to start beheading the Republican primary field. One every few weeks ought to do it."

The president grinned. "Well, at least you can still cheer me up."

"Just trying to earn my salary."

"If you want to earn it, you can worry about what happens if these people start capturing provincial capitals before the election. If they're marching on Baghdad by the middle of the campaign, the Republican nominee can stroll in here with his head in his hands and a higher approval rating than I have at the moment."

"With all due respect, you're starting to get tunnel vision. You're at forty-eight percent—within the margin of error and trending upward. We've locked down all the key Democratic constituencies, even the ones that were wobbly last time, particularly gays and Hispanics. The economy has moved out of recession, and real estate prices have rebounded. But you need to tell people all of this."

"I do."

"I mean, on a regular basis. Like weekly."

"You're right." Atalas rubbed his forehead again. "Who's worried about a few dozen beheadings when the stock market is doing better?"

"People vote their checkbooks. The video of yesterday's beheading is ultimately not as scary as the increase in food prices or the decline in the value of retirement accounts."

"Shit." The president grinned again. "You're pretty slick for a white guy."

"That's because I play basketball. I can dance, too, by the way."

Atlas rose, walked to the window, and stared at the manicured grounds.

"The one thing I don't want to do, Joel, is kick the can down the road. If we don't figure out a way to contain and defeat the New Caliphate, we're no better than Cane. I don't want somebody else sitting here ten years from now, bitching about my mistakes."

"First, let's focus on having you sit here next year. Then you can do the rest. But we need every possible edge we can get. The word on the street is that the Haft brothers are prepared to spend hundreds of millions to defeat you."

"All right. What do you suggest?"

"Stay on message. Repeat the catechism: We're in this mess because of George Cane's invasion of Sumeristan. You're doing everything you can. You've reduced the troop levels by thirty percent, you've strengthened our forces in Kabulistan. Your motivations for this were ousting the Dua Khamail and restoring the legitimate government, which you've done, and catching Salman al-Akbar, which you're going to do at any moment. You're on the verge of a breakthrough. In the meantime, those troops are holding the New Caliphate at bay."

"Sounds encouraging."

"It's all true."

"And how long before we start bringing those troops home?"

"With any luck, you'll catch a break and find al-Akbar before the election. In the meantime, we'll issue a projected timetable for withdrawal."

Gottbaum smiled. "The public loves timetables."

THE END

———— ✹ ————

ABOUT THE AUTHOR

Mark Spivak is an award-winning writer and political junkie who loves turning his fascination with the seamy underbelly of the American political system into taut, page-turning thrillers. Spivak is the author of two nonfiction books (2012's *Iconic Spirits: An Intoxicating History* and 2014's *Moonshine Nation: The Art of Creating Cornbread in a Bottle*) and one novel (2016's *Friend of the Devil*). He is currently writing a sequel to The American Crusade, tentatively titled *Impeachment*. Spivak lives in Florida with his wife and his imaginary friends.

CONNECT WITH MARK

Sign up for Mark's newsletter at

www.markspivakbooks.com/free

To find out more information visit his website:

www.markspivakbooks.com

Facebook Page:

www.facebook.com/groups/376161459459968

Twitter:

@eatdrinkjourney

OTHER BOOKS
BY MARK

Iconic Spirits: An Intoxicating History

Moonshine Nation: The Art of Creating Cornbread in a Bottle

Friend of the Devil

GET BOOK DISCOUNTS AND DEALS

Get discounts and special deals on our bestselling books at

www.TCKpublishing.com/bookdeals

ONE LAST THING ...

Thank you for reading! If you enjoyed this book, I'd be very grateful if you'd post a short review on Amazon. I read every comment personally and am always learning how to make this book even better. Your support really does make a difference.

Search for *The American Crusade* by Mark Spivak to leave your review.

Thanks again for your support!

CPSIA information can be obtained
at www.ICGtesting.com
Printed in the USA
BVHW081227010419
544230BV00028B/1486/P